THE SEASONS THAT CONQUER

SEASONS DUOLOGY
BOOK TWO

H.E. SHOWS

READHEAD

to everyone fighting the battle of their life
you'll get through it, I just know it

AUTUMN
LAND
SE

SUMMER

OF
ON
LEGEND
TERRITORY LINES
TREE OF SEASON
CONFORMITY CASTLE
STABLES
CABIN/BUILDINGS
CATHEDRAL
MANOR
GAZEBO
WALL
HILLS
MOUNTAINS
STREAM
TREES
SHRUBS
FIRE PIT
TOWER
CLIFF
WINTER
SPRING

I

In the Land of Season

The Tree of Season quivered in the freezing wind. Snow fell on its branches, coating the golden-hued bark in white. Everything was cast in gold. Everything but the blackened patch of earth where a human head had burned to nothing.

The large tree pulsed with energy. Four roots snaked through the earth, veering away from the trunk, separating the land into four sections. They pulled at four sources of power. The frigid water of Winter, the unbearable heat of Summer, the comforting breeze of Autumn, the new life of Spring.

A girl was at the end of each thread of power. Sisters. And the Tree of Season would make one of them its queen.

2

Eira Brown waited on the steps of the manor for her mother to return to Winter. She tapped her foot against the wooden floorboards of the manor's porch, crossed her arms over her chest, and tried to keep her eyes focused on the road before her. Finally, a horse appeared.

Queen Quinn slid off her horse, feet pounding on Winter's frozen ground.

"Well," Eira said, going to Quinn's side quickly, eager for an update. She had been waiting for days for her return. Days with no communication. If there was one thing she disliked about Season, it was the fact they didn't have technology. They didn't have cell phones. All they had were messengers who were hardly any faster than the army.

"We found her," Quinn said, slipping into the manor and ridding herself of her heavy coat.

Eira peeked back outside to see the soldiers dismounting, leading the horses to the barn, going home. "Then where is Aviva?"

"Aviva is strong. Stronger than I had thought," Quinn said,

a faint smile on her lips. "It seems that all my daughters are very gifted."

"Now is not the time to dote on the daughters you abandoned," Eira said, seething. She turned her back on Quinn, walked to the big window of the foyer, and looked outside at the disorganized mess of Winter. "We're not ready," she whispered, gripping the windowsill so tightly it crumbled in her frozen hands. "The Trial of Winter is coming soon. I can feel it, Quinn. And we are not ready."

Quinn slid up behind Eira, taking a place next to her overlooking Winter. "We are," she said simply.

Eira huffed, rolling her eyes at Quinn's tone. She had perfected the caring mother persona. But Eira knew the truth. Quinn didn't care for her. She didn't care for any of her daughters. All Quinn cared about was who would help her stay on the throne left to her with her husband's death. But, the throne belonged to Eira, so long as she defeated her three sisters. And she would. At any cost. "What makes you so sure?"

Quinn was silent for a moment. Then, she lifted a finger to point to the middle of Winter. Soldiers diligently unpacked their bags from their trip to Spring, cleaning up the mess their arrival caused, checking the boundary. "Because those are your people. And they will go to war for you," Quinn said.

Eira pushed back her shoulders, standing up straighter. "I am their queen," Eira said like a mantra.

"You are their queen, and you are going to lead them to Conformity Castle once your sisters are dead. You will be queen over all of Season."

Eira opened her mouth to speak, to agree with her mother, but no words came out. Her body froze. Ice ran through her veins. She couldn't move or talk. She was a silent statue in the middle of the foyer. All she could do was blink.

A loud, whooshing erupted around her. A swirling portal

opened in the room, pulling Eira's frozen body through it. She tried to look back at Quinn, but she couldn't swivel her head enough. The portal was pulling her, its grip too strong to break.

"Don't worry, Eira," Quinn shouted over the noise. "We're ready. You are ready."

Eira couldn't respond. All she could do was listen to the words of her mother until she was dropped onto the icy ground before the giant Tree of Season.

Aviva Davis stood in the center of the small village in Spring, overlooking her people's work. They rebuilt their homes after her mother's attack a few days prior. Even with two of her sisters' help restoring the village, there was much work to be done. Her people hadn't let up, and they wouldn't until this small part of Spring returned to its former glory.

"Princess?" the small child asked Aviva, pulling on her pant leg. "Will you help?"

The girl's mouth twitched nervously. Aviva still wasn't used to being in charge, being looked to. Being a princess. Having people, anyone, be nervous to speak to her. All she had ever wanted was to get away from her foster parents and now that she had, she didn't know what else to do. She didn't know what her freedom could bring, but she knew for certain that she'd never leave the relative safety of Season.

She knelt down to the girl's level. "Of course," she said with a soft smile. The girl grasped her hands, pulling her up to a stand. Aviva followed her through the village.

They stopped at a broken cabin. Its door hung loosely from its hinges. The sides buckled underneath the weight of the collapsed roof. And everything was charred.

The little girl pointed to the cabin. "My house," she said.

Aviva nodded, lifting her hands. The broken pieces of the cabin lifted from their posts, wooden logs floating in the air, repositioning into a new cabin. Trees from the woods drifted through the air, roots and all. Aviva placed them on the sides of the cabin, wrapping their vines and branches around the destroyed logs, steadying them.

"Thank you," the little girl said, smiling up at Aviva.

"Where are your parents?"

She shrugged, looking around her. "I haven't seen them since the queen," she said, her words disintegrating with the quiver of her lips.

"Come on," Aviva said, holding her hand out. "Let's go look."

They walked back to the center of town, hand in hand. Blankets were thrown on the ground near a large pile of wood. Villagers moved lifeless bodies to the blankets, laying out the dead.

Aviva looked away, not able to bring herself to look at the villagers who had died at her expense. Quinn had been looking for her, and she'd hid like a coward. Marge had told her to hide, but still, she shouldn't have. She should've pushed Quinn back sooner. If she hadn't frozen in her spot, Marge would be alive. Most of the villagers, if not all of them, would still be alive. If she hadn't been weak.

"Mama," the little girl pulled her hand away from Aviva and ran toward one of the blankets. She plopped down beside a body, tears falling from her face. "Mama," she screamed as if she could wake her up.

A man ran up to the child and picked her up. The little girl held tightly to the man's neck. Tears dripped from both of their eyes.

Aviva stepped forward to go to the girl, and then she knelt

on the soft, fresh grass. Her body racked with shivers. Her lips quivered and her arms thrashed out at her sides. Her vision went dark. All she could see was the tearing of a portal through the air.

"Princess," the little girl screamed, jumping down from the man's arms and running toward Aviva.

Aviva's lips trembled as she tried to form words.

She was sucked through the portal leaving behind her home and the sobbing little girl.

In the Land of Texas

Orla Fletcher opened the door and walked into a dimly lit room. Someone stood at the window, illuminated by flickering candles and moonlight.

"Hello?" She took a careful step farther into the room.

Whoever it was didn't move.

Orla got closer, inch by inch, waiting for them to say something or turn around. The door swung shut with a thud behind her, leaving her alone with the stranger. Trapping her inside.

"Hello?" She was close enough to touch him. Her breathing quickened as she reached out a hand. Her fingertips brushed against his shoulder. He turned around to face her.

She screamed. Screamed until her throat tightened with hoarseness. She closed her eyes and squeezed. Bright spots burst into the darkness behind her closed lids.

Her body jerked around. Her arms flailed at her sides, her heels dug into a soft surface. Someone's hands wrapped around her arms. She couldn't open her eyes to see who it was.

"Sweetheart," the muffled voice of her mother said.

"Orla?" her father's voice rang in her ears.

Orla finally opened her eyes, just enough to see her parents standing over her in her bedroom. Her mother brought her into a hug, stroking her hair. Orla soiled her mother's shirt with a puddle of tears. "It was just a nightmare," her mother whispered.

Orla nodded against her mother's shoulder. But even though she knew it was only a dream, she couldn't get rid of the image of Brey's lifeless, cloudy gaze.

Orla rubbed at her eyes, trying to stop them from burning. But it was no use. She hadn't slept well in days, and it was definitely getting to her.

She laid her head down on her arms, drowning out the sounds of the classroom. She was a high school senior in her last semester before she graduated. She should be happy, excited to get to her next phase in life. She should be looking forward to picking a college. She had been waiting for this moment, counting down the days until she could put some distance between herself and her overbearing parents. But instead, here she was. Utterly exhausted.

She jumped up, the squeak of her chair like nails on a chalkboard. The memory of Brey burned into her head. The box laid open on her bed. The blood soaked blanket. His glazed eyes. The mangled ends of his neck where he'd been decapitated. It was an image she could not rid herself of. No matter what she tried. It stuck with her.

"Ms. Fletcher, maybe if you wouldn't spend all weekend partying, you'd be able to stay awake during class." Mrs. Phillips said, wagging her finger back and forth.

Some of the students laughed, but Orla couldn't bring

herself to care. Staying awake in class was the least of her worries.

No, being this close to graduating (or not graduating if her grades didn't get better) wasn't her main concern. Being in Texas wasn't her main concern. Her main concern, the only thing she could think of besides Brey's head, was getting back to where she was born.

She needed to go back and help protect the younger sister she'd left behind. She needed to make sure she was okay. She needed to get through the next trials, take care of Eira and Quinn, and figure out how to make it out of all of this alive.

She had to get to Season.

Orla nodded off again, her head hanging between her hands. She jumped up, rattling her desk. Brey's face disappeared behind her eyes. Mrs. Phillips stood over her, her arms crossed in front of her chest.

"How many times do I need to wake you up, Ms. Fletcher?" Mrs. Phillips asked, her voice loud enough that it carried around the entire room.

Orla leaned back in her chair, slipping down the seat. "Sorry," she muttered, looking straight ahead at the whiteboard instead of at Mrs. Phillips.

"Sorry?" Mrs. Phillips said, clicking her tongue as she finally turned, her heels echoing off the floor as she returned to the front of the classroom. "You're going to be sorry when you have to repeat your senior year because you wanted to sleep instead of do the work," Mrs. Phillips said.

Orla rolled her eyes. She was tired. Tired of Mrs. Phillips. Tired of school.

"Now, where were we?" Mrs. Phillips asked, flipping through her textbook.

Orla stared at the board, trying to keep her eyes open, but

they drifted shut over and over again. She jerked awake each time Brey's face appeared.

She rubbed her eyes and yawned. She really needed sleep. But she couldn't sleep, not with the nightmare on repeat.

Orla watched Mrs. Phillips walk back and forth in front of the class in a daze. Her vision went in and out, blurring Mrs. Phillips and everything behind her. A strong, cold wind swept past her. She shivered, unable to control the hair on her skin from sticking straight up. She was freezing.

She jumped up from her desk and ran from the room. "Orla Fletcher," Mrs. Phillips called after her, but Orla ignored her. She kept running until she was outside of the school building. Until she dropped onto the asphalt in a frozen ball.

Orla watched as the asphalt broke away into a portal. Through the portal she could see a shining, golden tree. The Tree of Season. She rolled toward the portal, falling through it.

She landed with a thud, her breath knocked out of her. Finally, her limbs unfroze and she could stretch out. She pushed up from the frozen ground, standing before the Tree of Season.

"Nice of you to join us," Eira said through gritted teeth.

Orla lunged at her. Her fingernails dug into Eira's arms as she grabbed her, hard. "You killed him," she yelled, tears instantly streaming down her cheeks. "Why did you kill him, Eira?" She raised her fisted hand, swinging it through the air. Her knuckles cracked against Eira's jaw. She ignored the pain and raised her other hand into the air.

Eira grabbed her hands, but Orla held on and shook her. She could've gone forever without seeing her sister again. Forever would've been too soon after what she'd done.

Orla threw Eira to the ground, stomping over to her. She swung her foot, kicking Eira's side. Eira covered her face with her hands.

"Orla, stop. " Aviva ran up to her, grabbing her arm. Orla tried pulling free. "Stop," she whispered.

Orla took a breath, letting cool air fill her lungs. "You killed Brey. I'll never forgive you for that." She turned on her heel and refused to look at Eira again.

"Where's Idalia?" she asked Aviva, finally noticing one sister was missing.

"She's coming," Aviva said.

Idalia Gallagher walked through her college campus, a coffee in her hand. She sipped at the warm drink slowly, enjoying being outside in the cold air. She hadn't left her dorm in days, not since Orla had gotten the box with Brey's severed head. Not since they had gone to Season and burned what was left of him.

Guilt mixed with sadness and nerves, balling up in her stomach. Making her want to puke. It wasn't her fault he was dead. Eira had killed him, or at least ordered for him to be slaughtered. But she couldn't rid herself from feeling responsible. Brey had been her and her sisters' one source of knowledge. Their guide to Season. And now he was gone. No one could help them now. No one could help them endure Season and the rest of the trials they still had to face. All she wanted was to live. She wanted all of them to survive.

Idalia sighed and took a long sip of coffee, the heat igniting her insides.

She looked down at her hand. A flickering flame jumped between her fingertips. She watched as it moved from finger to finger, playful, powerful.

"Ms. Gallagher?" she heard from behind her. Idalia shook her hand out, extinguishing the flame before turning around.

"Yes?" she said to the man behind her.

"Aren't you supposed to be in class?" he asked.

"I don't have time for this," Idalia said, rolling her eyes and turning her back. He reached out a hand to catch her. "Haven't you learned your lesson on touching me, Professor Hendrix?" she asked, bringing heat to her body. Ready to burn at will.

Professor Hendrix dropped his hand. "Yes, well, you still need to be in class. I haven't seen you since the semester began. You might think about dropping the class if you're not going to bother showing up."

"I have other things to worry about, Professor," Idalia said, his title harsh on her lips.

"Yeah, like what?"

"Nothing you would believe," Idalia said.

"I believe a lot of things," he said, stepping closer to Idalia. She stepped back. "Like a girl who can shoot fire out of her hands," he said, raising an eyebrow to look at her.

Idalia walked backwards. "I'm leaving," she said, turning and quickly walking to her dorm.

"You're failing my class," Professor Hendrix shouted after her.

Good, Idalia thought, picking up her pace. The coffee sloshed in her cup, threatening to spill. But she didn't care, she just wanted to be away from him.

Idalia's knee locked, and she tumbled onto the ground, her coffee spilling near her. Her body fought against the sudden cold. She tried to call her flames, but they wouldn't appear. She froze, every bone in her body seizing up.

A portal opened beneath her, and she fell through.

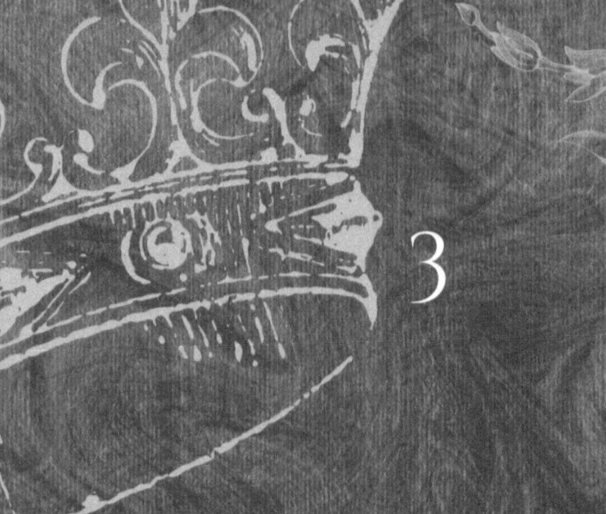

3

In the Land of Season

Idalia stood, brushing off snow. She shivered, her body revolting against her wet, cold clothes. She raised her palms. Flames erupted across her body, turning her into one big fireball. She sighed in relief.

"That's so not fair," Orla said, walking up to Idalia's side once the flames died down. A red tint lingered on her skin, still warming her like a heater.

"I'm freezing," Aviva said, her voice breaking as the quiver of her lips took over.

"It's not even cold," Eira said from the other side of the tree.

Idalia glanced her way. The snow had melted in one spot, a large circle near where Eira leaned against the tree. Skid marks left the ground uneven. Footprints stomped into the earth, leaving a random pathway. Eira's hair stuck up in crazy spikes.

She kept her hands close to her body and took deep breaths as if it were hard to breathe.

"What happened here? Y'all start the fight without me?" Idalia asked, turning toward Orla and Aviva who huddled together. She turned back on Eira. The hair on the back of her neck stood up, and she angled herself a few inches so she could see her older sister in her peripheral vision.

"Something like that," Aviva rolled her eyes. "Think you could share?" she asked, reaching a hand out toward Idalia.

Idalia glanced at Aviva's outstretched hand. "I honestly don't know," she said, afraid to test it out.

Aviva grabbed onto Idalia's arm. She pulled it back quickly, "Ow," she whimpered, holding her hand against her chest.

"Sorry," Idalia said, killing her flame all the way. The red tint to her skin disappeared. Goosebumps prickled her skin with the burst of cold wind around them.

Aviva pouted but raised her other hand. Logs flew through the air, landing next to the three sisters. "Dry them off," Aviva said.

Orla pushed a gust of wind over the logs, removing every drop of snow. Idalia pointed a hand at the pile of logs. It erupted into flames. Orla and Aviva sighed. All three of them huddled as close to the flames as they could without burning themselves. Heat seeped into Idalia's pores. The skin of her face tightened.

"So, what do we do?" Aviva asked, her words clearer without her teeth chattering.

"What do you mean?" Orla asked, not taking her eyes off the burning wood.

"When did you become so outspoken?" Idalia said at the same time, wrapping an arm around Aviva's shoulders. "I don't recall you being like this when we left only a few weeks ago."

Aviva shifted on her feet. "I guess being in charge of Spring has rubbed off on me. They expect a lot from me."

Idalia nodded and dropped her arm from around her sister's shoulders. She couldn't imagine what Aviva had gone through in the last few weeks. After Quinn destroyed Spring, they had rebuilt the majority of the village before she and Orla had to go back to Texas. Idalia hadn't wanted to leave. But her parents wanted her to continue going to college. The semester had barely begun, and she hoped she could drop her classes so she could stay in Season and help Aviva. But hope did little for her. It did little for any of them.

"We're here for the trial, right?" Orla asked.

Idalia nodded. "Must be."

"So, what do we do? No one else is here. Last time Brey and Quinn were here and a ton of the townspeople were crowded around watching," Aviva said, her voice faltering at the mention of Brey's name.

Idalia glanced at Orla, but she wouldn't meet her eyes. Idalia looked around, away from the fire and away from the tree. There was no one in sight. No sounds coming from far off. Nothing except a large patch of black earth by the trunk of the tree–the place she had burned Brey's head until there had been nothing left. She pried her eyes away.

"I don't know," Orla whispered.

"What if we don't have to do this?" Aviva asked, her voice hopeful.

Idalia glanced at Aviva. "I'm pretty sure we weren't called here for nothing," she said. "We have to go through four trials. Brey said it over and over. We have to finish them and then the finale before all of this is over."

"But no one's here," Aviva said, her voice pitched high. "I don't want to be here."

"Neither do I," Orla said, leaning in toward Aviva. "I've missed you," Orla whispered.

"Missed you, too."

Idalia was silent. Hoping, but not hoping, that something would happen. The waiting, the not knowing, was eating at her. Her skin prickled with every brush of wind, every crinkle of a dead leaf. Her ears and eyes strained.

The wind picked up, whipping around her, lifting her red hair into the air. It slapped against her face and she fought to keep it back behind her ears, but it wouldn't stay. Her feet slid, pulling her forward. She dug her heels into the snow. She gritted her teeth as she tried to stop moving, but she couldn't. A force she had felt only a few times before controlled her movements–when Brey had pulled them from this very spot back to the castle after training, when the first trial had ended and they were pulled from Autumn. She had had no control then, and she had none now.

"What in the world," Orla said, her words almost lost in the wind.

Idalia stopped moving just beside the Tree of Season. Her hand lifted toward the trunk of its own volition. A bright light erupted from the tree as her palm connected with the bark.

She covered her eyes with her free arm.

"It's the start of the trial." Eira's voice floated toward them.

4

Eira prepared for the catapult through the air and slid gracefully onto her feet. She stood up, waiting a few seconds until the dizziness subsided. The woods around her were covered in snow, inches and inches deep. Trees were sprinkled with white everywhere she looked. She was home. She was in Winter.

She started toward the town, running as fast as she could, hoping to make it there before anyone else.

Her feet were sure against the snow. She had the advantage of practice over her sisters. She knew these woods like the back of her hand. She knew Winter. She knew her own element. She would survive.

"My queen?" Eira skidded to a stop, a few feet away from the edge of the forest. She could just see the wall she had built outside of Winter.

Eira turned slowly, following the voice. A soldier stepped out from behind a bush. "What are you doing out here?" she asked, authority leaking out of her mouth.

"Queen Quinn sent us," he muttered.

"*Us?*"

"Yes." He nodded. "She stationed soldiers throughout the woods. We're to watch for your sisters."

"Good. So we're ready then?"

"We're ready," he said, barely above a whisper.

"Where is she?" Eira asked, stepping closer to the soldier. He looked at her in confusion. "Quinn. Where is she?"

"In the manor, my queen."

Eira laughed. "Of course she is. Take me to her," she said. The soldier nodded and led the way toward the manor.

"Quinn," Eira said when she entered her mother's chambers. Quinn was perched at the window, overlooking Winter's forest.

Shock registered on Quinn's face, but she smoothed it away quickly. "What are you doing here?"

"The same as you, I suppose." Eira joined her mother at the window. The forest stretched for miles, white blanketing the trees and ground. A few black dots scurried in the distance. "Surviving," Eira said, not looking at her mother.

Quinn huffed. "You're supposed to be down there," she pointed.

"Why?"

Quinn took a step back. "Why?" she asked, her voice rising. Eira didn't budge. "You have to compete in the trial. You have to kill your sisters."

Eira nodded. She couldn't count how many times Quinn had drilled it in her head that she had to kill her sisters. She had to win the trials. She had to survive. She already knew all that. And, she'd win. She would become queen of Season with no one standing in her way. No one.

"The trial is different this time," she said, still keeping her eyes on the many dots in the forest. "Brey is no longer running the show."

"Well," Quinn said. "You should still be down there."

"And I will be, after I finish one small thing." Eira tightened her hand into a fist. The bumpy edges of an icicle formed in the palm she held down by her side.

Quinn faced her. Eira placed a hand on her shoulder. She'd never realized just how similar she and her mother were. Same icy blonde hair, though hers was considerably shorter. Same shade of ice cold blue eyes. Same height and athletic build. They were almost identical. Almost.

Eira pulled her mother forward with the hand on her shoulder and plunged her dagger of ice into her abdomen before Quinn opened her mouth to say anything else. Quinn hunched over, her arms falling over Eira in an awkward embrace. She gasped for breath, looking at Eira in confusion.

"I can take it from here, Mother," Eira said, letting Quinn's body drop to the ground. "I don't need you."

Eira dodged Quinn's hands as she tried to scratch at her. Blood spilled from her mother's mouth, frothing as she tried to speak. Eira only stared until life left the queen's eyes. Until she was sure.

Eira left Quinn on the floor of her chambers, the dagger made of ice slowly melting and mixing with the puddle of blood spreading underneath her.

5

Idalia pushed out her hand, a raging ball of fire flying through the air and into a wall of snow. The snow blackened, a scorched smell drifting into the air. The snow evaporated and Idalia walked through the now empty space.

She stayed low to the ground, crouching as she walked.

"Orla? Aviva?" she whispered harshly, but the cold wind took her words away. Leaving her stranded and all alone.

She trudged through the thick snow, her feet and legs covered in ice. But she was warm. Her body was red with the flame inside her. Her sisters wouldn't be so lucky. She needed to find them before they froze to death.

Orla directed the wind away from her, trying to keep the chill at bay, but her lips were turning blue and she shivered nonstop. She could barely force her legs to move, they were so cold. All she could do was shiver.

Orla looked up, a cracking sound drawing her attention. A branch snapped over her head. She watched as it fell, knocking into the other tree branches on its way down. She needed to move, but she couldn't. Her body was frozen in her spot. She tried to get her legs to move, but they weren't listening. She watched with numb horror as the branch tumbled through the air about to crush her.

Aviva ran, her feet sinking into the snow with each step. She continued pumping her arms and legs, not letting the cold take over. Not letting herself die.

Her breath came fast, fog puffing from her mouth every time she exhaled. Her face was freezing and raw. But, she ignored it. She kept running. She didn't know what she was running to or from. But, she still ran. Not allowing herself to give up.

She skidded to a stop in the middle of a clearing and doubled over, heaving, trying to catch her breath. A trembling raced through her body that she couldn't control. She looked up trying to figure out where she was. But she wasn't familiar with Winter. She left before she had gotten the chance to know the layout. And she had been too out of it when she had run away. She couldn't remember anything. And it didn't help that everything was white.

A branch toppled from the top of a tree, the noise deafening as it crashed into the other branches. Snow cascaded from the limbs, falling like a waterfall. A body stood directly in the middle of the snow drift.

"Orla," Aviva yelled, throwing out her hand. The tree

branches just above Orla's head curled, making a basket to catch the falling branch.

The branch burst into flames as it settled into the nest above Orla's head. Idalia ran over from the opposite direction.

Aviva went to Orla's side, pulling her out from underneath the burning tree branch. "Come on," she said, her hand wrapped around Orla's upper arm. Orla's eyes were glassy, a dazed look taking over her face as she stared at her sisters.

"It's a good thing y'all found me, huh?" Orla laughed shortly.

"Yeah, yeah it is," Idalia said.

The burning tree branch popped and fell onto the snow behind them, the fire extinguishing.

Idalia pushed them farther from the tree. "What were you doing just standing there?" Idalia asked, her voice rising as her face turned redder.

"I'm cold," Orla said, hugging herself.

Aviva swept her hands up and a few roots twisted into seats on top of the snow. Twigs and fallen branches piled together in the middle of their circle. Idalia's hands exploded in flames and lit the fire pit. Orla sighed with relief.

Aviva sat in silence as the world around them darkened. Eira was nowhere to be found. And that was good, maybe they could ride out the trial without seeing her. Maybe they could get lucky, have whatever test was coming for them, not face Eira, and get back to Spring. She needed to get back to her people. There was still so much work to be done there. So much to fix that Eira had broken.

"I have a bad feeling about this," Orla whispered. Her hands were tucked underneath her armpits and she bent so close to the fire Aviva thought her hair would catch fire.

"About what?"

"Being here. In Winter."

Idalia scoffed. "So do I. We're here to die. That's literally the point of these trials."

"No," Orla shook her head. "Winter is Eira's domain. We're here. She doesn't seem to be close to us. So where is she?"

No one answered her. There was no answer. Aviva didn't know where Eira was. And she didn't want to know. She would gladly stay away from her after she had trapped her in the manor in Winter. Aviva had thought they were close, but after Eira betrayed her trust, she didn't know if she could ever get over the way Eira had treated her. Just as her foster parents had. Kathy and Ted had trapped her. Everyone kept imprisoning her.

"What's the plan?" Aviva asked, looking up at Idalia as she reignited the fire.

"How am I supposed to know?" Idalia snapped.

Aviva put her hands in the air as if warding Idalia off.

Idalia took a big breath and ran her hand through her hair. "Sorry, but I don't know what to do," Idalia explained. "I never know."

Aviva nodded. "Well, for now, we just need to make it through the night."

Orla had slumped over and her eyes were closed. Soft noises escaped her lips.

"How does she sleep here?" Idalia asked, shaking her head.

Aviva shrugged. "Maybe because she's too delirious to realize where she is."

It was quiet, except for the crackling of the fire and the wind around them. "We're too exposed here," Idalia said, looking around her.

Trees surrounded them, but the fire was bright, leaving them too bare.

"We can't go without the fire," Aviva said, reading Idalia's mind. "We'll freeze."

"Then we have to hide it." Idalia stood up.

"On it," Aviva said, closing her eyes and pulling her hands up in front of her chest. She circled them together, an intricate dance between her fingers.

The roots underneath a nearby large tree poked through the snow and snaked up and around the trunk. Loose branches stacked over each other, sheltering each side, making a small hut constructed of branches and roots.

"That'll work," Idalia said with a nod of approval.

Aviva laughed. "I've had a lot of practice making buildings," she said.

Idalia bent down and shoveled snow on top of the hut. Aviva helped until it was all white, blending into the snow covered ground. She threw snow on top of the fire pit to extinguish the flames.

Aviva woke Orla up and moved her into the hut, sitting beside her. Idalia took her other side and quickly ignited a small fire in the hut. The warmth from the fire was very present in the small space.

Aviva settled into Orla's side, letting her warmth lull her to a fitful sleep.

6

A buzzing sound zipped by Orla's ear, followed by a thunk. She opened her eyes slowly, her head foggy and her vision not completely working. She shook her head to clear her eyes. Her cheek brushed against something soft. She moved her head to the side, only able to turn so far before her face met the butt of an arrow.

Another arrow flew into the hut, skimming between the branches.

Orla leaped to her knees, tumbling Aviva and Idalia from their pillowy spots on her shoulders. The small fire smothered in the kicked up snow.

"What's going on?" Aviva muttered, rubbing her eyes.

Idalia woke quickly, her eyes darting around looking for danger. She squatted next to Orla, bumping into her shoulder.

"Get up, get up." Orla pulled Aviva away from the trunk they had all leaned against to sleep.

Idalia crawled through the small opening of the hut, staying low to the ground.

"We've got to go," Orla said, pushing Aviva after Idalia. She ducked into the snow just as another arrow flew past her face.

She stared at the three arrows stuck in the trunk of the tree they had been against mere seconds before. They had to get out of here. They had to escape whoever it was aiming at them. And quickly, before an arrow found its mark.

Orla brought up the rear as they ran through the trees, dodging more arrows. An arrow slid across Idalia's arm, slicing it open, and landed in the tree behind Orla. Blood poured from the wound, leaving a trail as they ran.

"Orla," Idalia yelled, looking back at her. Fallen branches ignited in flames all around them. Anything that could burn was aflame. "Throw the branches at them."

"I don't know where they are. I don't know where they're shooting from," she said, ducking as another arrow whipped near her.

"Throw it everywhere," Aviva shouted.

Orla nodded and squeezed her fists together. She listened for the wind all around them, a soft hum in her ears. The different currents made distinct noises as she focused on the closest ones. Fiery branches burst through the air in every direction, a widening circle as she pushed the currents farther and farther away from them. Screams of pain erupted into the cold morning air.

Orla kept running, her calves sinking into the snow. Her heart pumped, her breathing heavy with the cold air. She couldn't see anyone, but she knew they weren't far away. Not if they were close enough to shoot arrows. She couldn't run fast enough. She couldn't put enough space between them.

Orla ran through the tree line into a clearing. Trees were sparse in the middle, but all sides were filled with dozens upon dozens of trees. She couldn't see through the dense trees. But she could see soldiers covered in fur stationed at every tree around them. Orla stopped running, almost crashing into Idalia and Aviva.

"What do we do?" Aviva whispered, her voice filled with fear.

The soldiers held their bows steady but didn't shoot. They had them surrounded.

"I don't know," Idalia said, not taking her eyes off the soldiers in front of her. "But we're not gonna give up that easily," she said, her mouth set firm. "We're not dying here."

Orla held her hands at the ready. Wind whipped around her and her sisters as they stood with their backs to one another, all looking out in a different direction. She would protect them, somehow. Idalia was right. They weren't going to die here. Not if she could help it.

At the sound of a whistle, the soldiers surged into action. They ran full speed toward them.

Orla pushed the wave of soldiers back with huge gusts of wind. They stumbled and fell but struggled back to their feet. So she did it again and again. She turned slowly in a circle, pushing the rest of the soldiers farther away as Idalia shot fireball after fireball, melting the snow beneath the soldiers' feet, and Aviva sent tree roots to tie around their legs. The soldiers were trapped.

The soldiers screamed, their voices mixing in with the wind. But they were stuck. So Orla ran. Aviva and Idalia followed.

They ran through the muddy trench between the trapped soldiers, dodging hands as they went.

On the outskirts of the clearing, Idalia stopped and turned back. Flames licked at her palms. She shot a ball of fire at the nearest soldier. The flame ignited his fur vest. The soldier screamed, his terror filling the suddenly silent air.

"Idalia, what are you doing?" Orla yelled, running back as Idalia readied another flame.

"Stopping them from following us," Idalia said, her eyes locked on soldiers.

"They're not going anywhere," Aviva said, catching up to them. "But we need to."

Orla pushed against Idalia's hand, removing her line of sight from the soldiers. Flame jumped from Idalia's hand to Orla's, her skin searing underneath the fire. She screamed and dropped to the ground. She submerged her hand in the snow, the flames dying.

Idalia jumped away, letting the fire extinguish. "Orla, I'm sorry," Idalia said, dropping to her knees beside Orla.

"It's fine," Orla said through gritted teeth. She pulled her hand out of the snow. It was red and blistered. "Let's go." She stood up, holding her hand against her stomach.

"Where?" Aviva asked. "Where are we supposed to go? Eira has her army in these woods."

"How?" Orla asked, turning in circles. She peered through the trees, looking for something. Her eyes squinted and her face contorted in confusion. It made no sense that Eira had an army waiting for them. The last trial had happened in a dome shaped arena in Autumn. Where was the dome here? Where was the wall that was supposed to keep them separated from the onlookers?

"What?" Idalia asked, slowly standing up.

"There's no wall," Orla whispered.

"Wall?" Idalia said, raising an eyebrow.

"Last time, in the Trial of Autumn, there was a wall separating us from everyone," Orla said, her voice shaking. This wasn't right. Something was different. Terribly different.

Aviva copied Orla, peering through the wilderness. "It's not there," Aviva said. "But, why?"

"Brey," Idalia whispered. "Brey's gone. He must've been the one to set up the first trial. Without him, who knows how these trials will go."

"Brey," Orla whispered. His face popped into memory, and finally it was his whole face instead of the decapitated mess she had been sent. Finally she saw Brey as he was before he was dead before her. But with his death, there was no telling what could happen. What had Eira done? What consequences would come from his untimely demise? Her thoughts came fast. She could feel heat rising in her body as she realized what was happening.

"Eira's going to kill us," Orla said into the cold air.

Silence crowded in, smothering them.

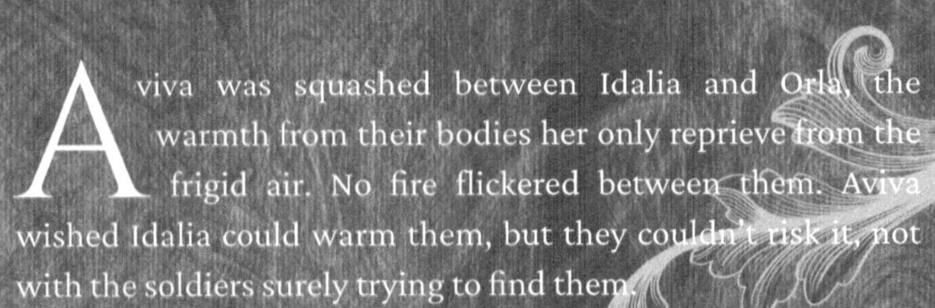

7

Aviva was squashed between Idalia and Orla, the warmth from their bodies her only reprieve from the frigid air. No fire flickered between them. Aviva wished Idalia could warm them, but they couldn't risk it, not with the soldiers surely trying to find them.

"If-if there's no wall," Orla stammered against her chattering teeth, "can we leave?"

Aviva felt Idalia shrug her shoulders. Her answering wince rang in Aviva's ear, too loud for her liking. She was trying hard to concentrate on other sounds, on the footfalls of the soldiers. If they were coming, she needed to know. They would need time to get away.

"Who knows?" Idalia asked.

"We could try," Aviva said. "We could go to Spring. It's nice there," she said, drifting off. Her eyes fluttered shut and the images of Spring, warm and green, floated behind her eyelids.

"We need to do *something*," Idalia said, shaking. "I can't keep us warm without hurting y'all. And if we don't warm up, we're going to freeze to death out here."

Aviva rubbed her hands up and down her legs. But she could hardly feel the motion since her legs were numb. Her whole body was numb.

"We need to find Eira," Orla said through gritted teeth.

"I don't think we should worry about Eira," Aviva said, snapping back to reality. "She's probably holed up in her manor in Winter all nice and cozy."

"Aviva's right," Idalia said. "Eira sent her army. She's not out here herself."

Aviva's stomach growled, interrupting Idalia. "I'm hungry," Aviva sighed. "And thirsty."

"We need food and water," Orla said. "Shelter, too."

Aviva nodded in agreement.

"Yeah, but where are we going to find those things?" Idalia asked.

"Spring," Aviva said wistfully as the image of her small cabin appeared in her mind.

"Do you know how to get there?" Orla asked. "Because everything looks the same to me."

Aviva shook her head. "I can't remember," she said with a solemn look on her face. When she had escaped from Eira's manor not long ago it had been dark, too dark to see anything that would lead their way now. She tried remembering, but everything was muddled in her mind. The adrenaline of running blocked memories that would be helpful.

"We have to be close to Winter, right?" Idalia asked. "Why don't we just go there?"

"Go toward Eira?" Orla's mouth hung open. "Why on earth would we go toward Eira?"

"Because we don't know how to get to Spring and we need food and water. Today," Idalia said.

Aviva chewed her dry lips. Her stomach gurgled again. She wiped her nose on the back of her hand as snot attempted to run down her face. "Yeah," Aviva whispered. "I think she may be right."

Orla blew air out of her nose and crossed her arms over her chest. "Fine, which way?"

"That I don't know," Idalia said, standing up.

Aviva stood with her to look around. But all she could see were trees. There was no beacon of light for them to follow like there had been in the Trial of Autumn. Nothing to suggest Winter was close. Nothing to help them.

"Use your flying thing," Aviva said. "Go look," she shrugged, pointing to the sky.

"Fine." Orla rose to her feet.

Standing next to Idalia, Aviva stared as Orla summoned a wind current and soared toward the sky, high above the tree line. She turned in circles, scouting the four cardinal directions. Aviva bit her lower lip, nerves and anticipation threading through her. Anxious energy filled the atmosphere, soaking up through the ground and her boots to thrum through her veins. Even the earth felt discontent in this barren place, as if it too waited for what their sister was sure to bring.

"That way," Orla yelled, pointing east.

Before Aviva could fully digest her sister's words, Orla let out a scream that curdled Aviva's blood.

"Orla!" Aviva yelled, watching, frozen as Orla tumbled through the air.

Orla whipped back and forth, flailing as if she was trying to find a current to stand on, full speed, through the trees. Aviva couldn't do anything to help. Her eyes tracked Orla as she fell through the sky. She could only watch as she landed in a blanket of snow, ice shooting up around her.

"Ow," Orla groaned, turning on her side and grabbing her stomach. Tears sprang to her eyes.

Aviva knelt down next to her, finally unfrozen, her body shuddering. "Are you okay?"

Orla didn't respond.

"Orla?" Idalia said, standing over them.

Orla held herself in a ball. Aviva leaned in close to her, placing a gentle hand on her arm and turning her over so she could hear the mumbles coming from her mouth. "Eira...she's coming."

"Coming?" Aviva asked.

Orla nodded. "She's got another army," she said with a ragged breath. "We need to hide."

She rolled onto her back, slowly stretching out her limbs. Aviva noted the tight line of Orla's lips as she leaned her head against the snow, her brown hair soaking up all the moisture.

"Where?" Aviva said, her eyes growing larger as she looked up at Idalia. Where could they go? They had barely escaped Eira's other army.

"I don't know," Idalia said, slumping in on herself.

Aviva looked back at Orla as if she had an answer. And apparently, she did. Orla lifted a wobbly hand off the snow covered ground and knocked Idalia off her feet with a gust of wind. Idalia wavered a few inches above the forest floor.

"Orla, what are you doing?"

"We're hiding," Orla said, looking up into the trees. Idalia rose higher and higher into the air until she landed on a tree branch so far above, she was just a speck in the sky. "Your turn," she said, turning a hand toward Aviva.

Aviva braced herself, ready for the current to take her into the air. She stayed as still as possible, her eyes refusing to look downwards as she climbed higher off the ground. She plopped near Idalia on a sturdy branch. Orla followed close behind.

"It's the best we have at the moment," Orla sighed. She peered over the side, looking toward the ground. She waved her hand in a small circular motion. The wind picked up snow, scattering it around, covering their footprints. She leaned back against the tree trunk.

Aviva cupped her hands toward her chest, balling her firsts. The branches pulled in all around them, cocooning them up high in the tree.

8

Eira marched into the clearing, a swirling mass of snow hovering over her head. Her army matched her every step. Soldiers surrounded her on all sides, covering her. Making sure she'd be the one to survive. Making sure their queen would end up Queen of Season.

She stopped and listened. The whine of the wind pierced her ears, drowning out every other sound.

She raised her arms high above her head. The snow on the ground lifted, floating up into the air, circling around her, and joining the trial's storm. The blizzard was in full force. A smile spread on her face at the sheer size of the storm. Tree branches cracked in the wind, threatening to break apart.

Eira dropped her arms, and the snow fell harder around her. She loved the feeling of ice pricking at her skin as it tumbled through the air. "Let's end this," she said with a wicked grin.

Aviva's eyes opened. She could only see darkness, and she could only feel coldness.

She wiped her cheek, hand gliding across her wet skin. She looked up, confused. A blanket of snow sat on the branches that made the top of the cocoon. "Oh," Aviva said, raising her hands to cover her face as her shelter buckled under the weight of the snow.

"Wha-what is it?" Idalia said, flailing her arms and wiping at her face. Her body turned red as heat ran through her body.

"Idalia," Aviva said, jumping away from her sister.

The branches near Idalia caught on fire. Smoke filled the cocoon, suffocating them.

"Idalia, stop," Aviva said between hacking coughs. Her eyes watered.

"Sorry," she muttered.

Orla grabbed handfuls of snow from the cocoon's floor and threw it over the flames, but it did little to halt the fire.

A snap sounded. Aviva screamed as the branches underneath her broke away and fell. She tumbled through the tree, the leaves like mini razor blades cutting every inch of skin they touched. She landed in a pile of snow, her breath catching in her throat.

Aviva groaned, clutching at her leg. She pushed herself up, her stomach flipping on itself. She was going to be sick.

A stick pierced clean through her calf. She braced her leg, bit her lip, and yanked it out. A hole in her calf squirted blood. She squeezed the wound, blood running through her fingers. Her vision blurred and blackened. She reached over and knotted her shirt in her mouth, ripping the sleeve from its seams. She quickly tied it around her calf, half blinded by the colorful dots behind her eyelids. She fell back onto the snow.

Idalia melted the snow around her. She laid in a puddle of water and looked up at the sky. Her eyes could barely focus on the snowflakes floating around her or the white blanket that covered every inch of the sky. She couldn't breathe. All she could do was wait for the feeling to come back into her limbs. She was numb, but at least she wasn't cold.

Orla rolled to her side, holding her stomach with one arm, and pushing up with the other. Her breaths came in heavy waves, each one pounding against her chest. She felt achy and bruised all over. Blood dripped from her nose, soaking the white snow.

"Well, hello, sisters," Eira said, walking toward Orla. She held a spear in each hand, their points glistening.

"Eira," Orla said, trying to stand up. She slipped against the snow. "What are you doing?" she asked, finally climbing to her feet. She didn't like the whine in her voice, the fear slipping out as Eira got closer. And she couldn't see her sisters behind her, didn't know if they were okay. But she pushed the fear and pain away and stood up straight.

"I'm ending this," Eira said, a devilish smile spreading over her face. She shot her hand out, the spears barrelling through the air toward Orla.

Orla raised an arm, protecting her face, squeezing her eyes

shut. She waited for the spears to meet flesh, to slice through her.

Screams erupted around her. She peeked over her arm. Two of Eira's soldiers were sprawled on the ground, spears sticking out of their bodies. A rippling current of air pulsed in front of Orla, protecting her.

Eira huffed and pulled more snow from the ground.

The wind around Orla rattled, and the snow fell in heavier sheets. The sky darkened, making it impossible to see more than a few inches in front of her. Orla could feel the air grow hungrier as the storm picked up. This was it. This was the trial. It had to be. It was almost over.

"Go, attack," Eira yelled at her soldiers.

Orla braced herself for the onslaught, pushing a wall of air out from her body.

The soldiers took off, running through the storm. The screams of the soldiers mixed with the howling of the blizzard, filling the air with terror.

Orla fought for a foothold in the piling snow, turning her back on the soldiers, on Eira. She had to protect her sisters–the ones not trying to kill her.

A few feet away, Idalia laid in the snow. "Get up," Orla yelled as she rushed over and pulled at her.

Idalia didn't budge.

"Come on," Orla said, using all of her strength to lift Idalia to her feet. She grunted with the effort, her side burning with pain. She blinked back tears, but Idalia was standing.

Arrows and ice spears bounced off Orla's shield of air as she moved toward Aviva. She continued pushing air into her current, trying to keep it strong.

"Here," Idalia said, bending and lifting Aviva to a stand. She wrapped one arm under her armpit, and Orla did the same on the other side. They hobbled away as fast as they could.

A spear of ice shattered against a tree trunk in front of them. "I can't do this for much longer," Orla said, refocusing on the shield, patching the holes that pierced the wall of air. They had barely made it a few feet.

Aviva swiveled her head back toward Eira and her army.

Trees tumbled down behind them. Tree after tree crashed to the earth, the loud thunks deafening. Orla silently thanked Aviva for the assist.

"Where do we go?" Aviva asked, wincing as she turned back around. "What do we do?"

Idalia pulled her necklace from her neck, snapping the closure. "We go home," she said as she held the golden Tree of Season necklace in her palm.

Orla fumbled for her own identical necklace that hung delicately on her neck. Light burst from the necklace, burning her palm, but she ignored the burn.

Aviva held her palm out, necklace facing up. Idalia grasped her hand, stacking her necklace on top of hers. Orla squeezed both their hands, her necklace sandwiched between the back of Idalia's hand and her own palm.

The beam of light grew larger and larger, blinding them. The storm around them stopped, and the air died.

9

Eira skidded to a stop before colliding with a fallen tree. She waved her hands to shoo away the ice storm. She could finally see in front of her, the blanket of white disappearing around her. There was nothing obscuring her line of sight. Nothing stopped her from getting to her sisters except twenty downed trees.

She looked straight ahead, where she was sure her sisters should have been. But there were no sisters. All she saw was piles of snow, discarded trees, and footsteps that ran away from her and stopped in the middle of the field.

"Where are they?" she said, her face turning red as she held her breath in anger. She turned in circles, searching every direction. She hadn't seen them sneak behind her. She hadn't seen them go anywhere at all. "Where did they go?" she screamed.

"I'm not sure, my queen," one of her soldiers said, looking around like a lost puppy. His eyes skirted around her face, too nervous to look directly at her.

"Find them," Eira yelled. Icicles shot up from the piled

snow, taller than she was. They encircled her. Their points glistened in the sun. She took a big breath, and stepped around the sharp edges. She turned her back on the empty clearing and marched back home to Winter.

In the Land of Texas

"Is it over?" Aviva's soft voice floated toward Idalia.

Idalia opened her eyes and looked around. They weren't in Season anymore. There was no storm. And Eira was nowhere to be seen. "Yes, I think it is," she said. "For now."

She unwrapped her arms from around her sisters and took a step back. They were in the middle of her campus courtyard, right outside of her dorm. Students milled around, going from one class to the next, not paying any attention to them. No one noticed three girls pop into existence.

"What do we do now?" Orla asked, hugging herself.

Idalia shrugged. "I don't know," she whispered. Her head swam as her body adjusted to being back in Texas. Her hands shook by her sides. "I guess we go back to normal."

"What is normal?" Aviva huffed. She looked side to side. "I shouldn't be here," she said.

"I don't know if any of us should be here anymore," Orla said.

"We belong to Season," Aviva nodded in agreement.

Idalia looked at them, battered and bruised from yet another trial. It was true, they didn't belong in Texas. But, it was their home. And Season had turned into their nightmare.

"I should go," Aviva said, stepping away from them. But she tripped, her bad leg slipping out from under her.

Idalia's body sagged with exhaustion, dropping beside Aviva with a *thunk*.

Her vision went black. She couldn't feel the snow underneath her. And, she couldn't hear anything except for the sound of a faraway ambulance.

In the Land of Texas

A viva looked up at the ceiling, bright lights blinding her. She wanted to shield her eyes but couldn't. Several people in green scrubs rummaged around her. They all talked at once. She couldn't understand the words. All she could hear was a beeping sound to her left.

Beep... Beep... Beep...

Over and over again. Aviva tried turning her head to the side to locate the machine making all the noise, but a hardened neck brace stopped her. She lifted an arm. It felt weird hovering a few inches above the stretcher, like it wasn't attached to her body. A nurse gently pushed her arm down and made quick work of inserting an IV.

"Hey," an older woman said from Aviva's shoulder. "What's your name?"

Aviva opened her mouth to answer. No sound came out.

Nothing. And then she screamed as the nurses started working on the hole in her calf.

Her eyes fluttered shut, everything turning black. Her head swam, and she lost feeling all over. Her eyelids were peeled back and a strobe of light flashed across her face. Strong hands dug into her chest. A breath she didn't know she was holding escaped, and she breathed again. The world came back into view slowly.

She couldn't focus on anything or anyone as the nurses ran around the room in a dizzying rush. After what felt like hours, most of them cleared out. They pulled the rails up at Aviva's side and pushed her out of the room. She watched as lights on the ceiling flickered by as they rolled her down several hallways.

She tried to keep her eyes open, to figure out where she was, what was happening. But her eyes kept falling shut. Her breathing was shallow. She was numb.

A mask was placed over her nose and mouth. She breathed in deeply. Her body relaxed. Her heart slowed. Her eyes shut again.

Idalia pushed herself up into a sitting position.

"Be careful," a nurse sitting at a desk beside the hospital bed said, barely turning her head to look at her.

"I'm fine," Idalia said, holding her wrapped arm out in front of her body until she settled into the uncomfortable bed. The nurse clicked her tongue, but Idalia ignored the noise. "Where are my sisters?" she asked.

"Sisters? The girls you were brought in here with?" the nurse asked, finally turning away from a monitor.

Idalia nodded. The nurse tapped against a tablet for a few seconds before looking back up at Idalia. "One is in surgery," she said before tapping away again. "And it looks like the other is still here in the ER."

Idalia held her breath. Her hands clenched together so tight her nails cut into her palms. And heat began rising. She leaned her head back, trying to focus. Focus on anything besides the flames attempting to burst from her body.

"Are you all right?" the nurse asked, stepping closer to the bed.

Idalia nodded. "Fine," she said through gritted teeth.

The nurse nodded in return. "Would you like some water? I'll go get you some water," she said before disappearing behind the sliding glass door.

Orla sneezed, blood flying from her nostrils. "Ow," she cried, reaching up to touch her nose. Blood stuck to her fingertips. Her skin was tight and bulging with a swollen knot. It pulsed under her fingers.

"Here," a nurse said gently, placing a cold pack on her nose and dabbing at the blood on her face. "The doctor will be here shortly," she said.

Orla nodded. And then waited and waited.

Finally, after what felt like hours, a doctor swung the curtain open. He rolled a chair beside Orla's bed. He clicked through a tablet before looking up at Orla. "How are we doing today?"

Orla eyed him, one eyebrow raising. "Just great," she said, sarcasm dripping from her words.

"Right," the doctor laughed. It was a low, hollow laugh.

One that seemed practiced. "Well, let's take a look here." He set the tablet off to the side and moved the cold pack from Orla's face. He nodded. "Yep, definitely going to need to be reset," he said to himself while lightly touching her nose.

"Ow," Orla winced, pulling away from his hands.

"Okay, so your nose is broken. For the best outcome, we'll need to set it soon. We can use a nasal spray to numb the area. After we reset it, we'll pack it. It should heal in a week or two. Are you allergic to any medicine that you know of?"

Orla shook her head.

"Okay, I'll write up a prescription and be back shortly to reset the break." He stood up, pushed the curtain aside, and left.

A few minutes later, the curtain moved again and the doctor strolled back in with a nurse and all the materials he needed to fix Orla's nose. He made quick work of the procedure. A few minutes later, Orla was taped up with gauze inside and outside of her nose. Her head swam with nausea as she leaned against the reclined hospital bed.

"Looks good," the doctor said with a nod of approval. "You'll have quite a bit of bruising, but it should heal nicely in a few weeks."

Orla nodded weakly and closed her eyes. The doctor left the small curtained area, but the nurse hung around cleaning up his mess. The left side of Orla's body dipped as the bed gave away slightly when the nurse leaned over next to her. "We'll have discharge papers ready for you soon," she whispered, careful not to jostle Orla too much.

Orla nodded again and let herself drift off into a fitful sleep.

II

In the Land of Season

Eira watched as Winter changed. The snow melted away leaving the gazebo in the middle of the town clear for soldiers to stand guard. She leaned against her windowsill, looking out at the square. Her townspeople milled around on streets lined with budding flowers. Spring was coming, and Eira did not enjoy it.

She turned abruptly and marched out of her chambers. She ignored the maids cleaning her manor and walked through the huge front doors and onto the large wooden porch. A few rocking chairs sat to either side, swaying in the soft breeze with no one to hold them down.

"My queen," a guardsman said, kneeling down in front of Eira. Eira tipped her head in acknowledgement before passing by him to get to the gazebo.

Eira lunged up the concrete stairs. The huge roof panned

out, protecting her and a few soldiers from the sun. She could feel the ice in her bones starting to melt from the heat that Spring brought with it. She straightened and wiped at the sweat building on her forehead. She slid her fur jacket off her shoulders and held it out. A small woman behind her eagerly took it and stepped off to the side.

"My queen," muttered the soldiers as they noticed her arrival. They fell to their knees one by one. Their foreheads touched their hands upon their knees. They knelt still, unwavering. Motionless rock statues waiting for their queen's command.

Eira had always wanted people to listen to her, to obey her every word. Growing up in the foster system had left her hungry for control. But without Quinn to boss them around, these people had become almost too needy. She shouldn't have to tell them how to think or what to do.

"Rise," Eira said with a dismissive wave of her hand.

They stood and gathered around her, creating a barrier between her and the townspeople as if she needed protection from such weak people. She needed no such thing. All she needed was her mastery over water, and it was strong as ever.

A man covered in fur pelts despite the growing heat made his way to the center of the pack. His face was shallow, void of emotion. It was a face Eira knew well. "Jedrek," she said, holding out a hand to touch his arm.

Jedrek didn't shy away from the touch, but Eira could tell by the rigidness in his body he didn't welcome it either. "My queen," he said, his lips stretched into a tight line. He bowed his head slightly. "We were just about to set out again, is there something I can assist you with?"

"No, Jedrek," Eira smiled coyly. "Nothing but obeying my command and finding my lovely sisters." The sarcasm dripped from her tongue, settling over the group.

"We have been searching nonstop. There is no sign of them anywhere near Winter. Perhaps they went to your home realm."

Eira rolled her eyes. Of course her sisters went back to Texas. They couldn't handle the Trial of Winter, but how did they escape? How did they survive her storm? "You best make damn sure they aren't anywhere in Season before making that assumption."

Jedrek nodded, "Of course, my queen."

Eira marched away from the soldiers, leaving the gazebo just as fast as she had entered. "Donovan," she called, not bothering to look behind her. She heard footsteps pad against the ground shortly after.

"My queen," he said, matching pace with her and following her back to the manor.

"I need your advice."

"I would suggest not angering the captain of your army," Donovan said, stopping beside Eira.

Eira laughed. She liked Donovan and his quick wit. Out of everyone in Winter, he aggravated her the least. "That is not the advice I asked for," she said.

Eira turned to look over her town again. It was a great town. Not too big. Manageable. Beautiful. And it was all hers.

"What advice do you seek? Is it in regards to your mother's untimely death, perhaps?"

Eira looked at her advisor, her eyebrow raised. "No, I would say her death was very timely."

He met her eyes but said nothing.

She sighed, a deep and long sigh that covered them with tension. "How do I get my sisters to come back to Season so I can kill them?"

12

In the Land of Texas

Aviva was cold, her limbs growing purple with each bitter kiss from the frigid air. Snow flurried around her, disrupting her vision. She couldn't see her hand outstretched in front of her.

A warmth spread from her calf down to her ankle. Blood poured from an open wound down her pant leg. She kneeled down to peer closer. A bloodied stick lay a few inches away, discarded. She placed her hands over the bleeding hole, holding tight to stop the blood from pouring out, but it wouldn't cease. She looked around furiously.

"Aviva," she heard in the distance.

"Hello?" Aviva called, trying to find the source of the voice. "Idalia? Orla?" she yelled through the wind.

In the distance, Aviva could just barely make out a spot of

light. "Help," she screamed, afraid to move and hurt her leg even more. "I'm over here."

She watched as the tiny pinpoint of light grew larger and larger until it was right in front of her. The light was a fire and it danced on top of Idalia's hands. Aviva's body stopped shivering, taking in the great heat. "Thank goodness," Aviva sighed.

Idalia didn't speak, she only stood in front of Aviva with her hands outstretched.

Suddenly, the wild wind stopped. The snow still poured from the sky but no longer in flurries. Orla stepped up from behind Idalia. She didn't speak either. She stood next to Idalia, both of their faces blank and their eyes dead.

"What's going on, guys?" Aviva asked, her voice pitching with worry. "Why are y'all acting so weird?"

Her sisters both stepped forward, reaching out a hand. Fire and air blew toward her.

Aviva jumped straight up in her hospital bed, clutching at her chest. Her heart pummeled against her ribs and she couldn't catch her breath. She looked around the room but couldn't focus on anything. She barely recognized her surroundings, all of the machines swooshing and beeping beside her.

"Hey," Idalia said.

Aviva jumped away from her touch.

"You okay?" she asked, worry creasing her forehead.

Aviva stared at her, unable to form words. She watched Idalia's face etch with worry with each shuddering breath. "Yea," Aviva finally muttered. "Weird dream," she added.

"These meds will do that to you," Orla said, nodding toward the machines she was hooked up to.

Aviva finally took in her surroundings. A few machines connected to her body by wires. A few others were turned off and pushed against the back wall. A door with a large window pane was to the right of her bed. Orla sat in one of the two chairs lined on the wall. A painting hung over Idalia's head on the opposite wall. A small TV was mounted in the corner. Something was playing, pictures flashing across the screen, but no sound came out.

Aviva tried pulling her legs up to her chest to stave off the sudden chill that ran through her body. She never liked hospitals. Or doctors of any kind. There were always too many questions and too many lies told the few times her foster parents took her to a doctor.

Her left leg didn't move under the mound of packing and wrap covering her calf. She reached down to feel the material. Pain shot through the leg. She leaned back against the pillow.

"They stitched you up," Orla said.

"You lost a bit of blood so you had to get a transfusion, but the doctor said you should make a full recovery if you stay off of it for a while and let it heal properly," Idalia said, stepping back from the bed.

Aviva nodded. Her head spun, and she felt out of control. "What happened to your face?" she asked, staring at the cast on Orla's nose.

"I broke it when I fell," she said, rolling her eyes. "Ow," she winced, as she reached up to lightly touch the cast.

Idalia took a seat next to Orla.

"What even happened out there?" Aviva asked, relaxing against the pillow and closing her eyes. She was exhausted, and she could barely remember why.

"I don't know how she did it," Idalia said under her breath. "How did Eira get her army in the trial? And there wasn't a wall like there was during the Trial of Autumn. It makes no sense."

Orla shrugged. "Who knows? She needs to be stopped."

"Yeah," Idalia said, sarcastically. "Because we can stop her in our condition right now." She ran a hand through her red hair.

"You don't look hurt," Aviva pointed out with a small shrug.

Idalia raised her arm. It was wrapped with a small piece of gauze. "This is about it," she said. "Don't know how I managed that with everything Eira threw at us."

"We have to figure out how she did it," Aviva paused. "And how she got so strong. Or we're all going to die," Aviva said. Her voice was flat, monotone. There was no emotion behind her words because there was no question. They would die if they didn't stop Eira.

"What we need to do," Orla leaned forward, whispering, "is figure out what we're going to tell the cops."

Aviva's eyes snapped open. Cops. There would be cops involved. Cops were already after her for killing her abusive foster dad after he attacked her. She couldn't be here. She had to leave.

Aviva pulled the IV out of her hand and the patches off her chest. She swung her right leg over the edge of the bed and scooted to the end of the cot. She leaned down and used both hands to push her left leg off the bed. She placed both feet on the ground. A cold shock ran through her body when bare toes met the icy tiles covering the floor. Her left calf screamed with pain, but she ignored it and tried taking a step.

"What are you doing?" Idalia said in a hushed voice, running to her side.

"I can't be here," Aviva said. She pushed Idalia away and put her weight on her bad leg. She crumpled to the floor. The cast didn't allow for any movement in her limb.

"What are you talking about?" Orla asked, rising from her chair. "You can't exactly walk out of here," she said.

"Y'all don't understand," Aviva said, grunting as she pulled herself up and leaned against the hospital bed. "If the cops come I'm going to be arrested. I killed Ted," she said in a hurried whisper. "I can't be here," she repeated.

"You don't know if the cops know," Idalia said, standing only a few inches away from Aviva. Her hands were outstretched.

"Kathy knows," Aviva said, "and the cops are going to call our parents if the doctors haven't already."

"How do you know your foster mom knows? You left right after," Orla said.

Aviva shrugged in defeat. "Even if she doesn't know for sure, she would tell the cops it was me. She'd do anything to get rid of me. And I gave her the perfect reason."

Orla touched her arm lightly. "You had every right to kill him, Aviva. He was dangerous."

"Yeah, well, the cops won't care much about that," Aviva said, not meeting her sister's eyes.

"Okay," Idalia said.

"Okay?" Aviva repeated. Her eyebrow lifted in confusion.

"How do we get you out of here?" Idalia asked, turning in circles as if looking for an escape route in a hospital room with only one exit. "And where do we go?"

I3

Idalia rolled a wheelchair through the hospital room door. Aviva and Orla eyed it suspiciously. "And you think no one will stop us?" Orla asked while helping Aviva out of the bed and into the chair.

Idalia shrugged. "Won't know until we try, but what other option is there?"

"Let's just get this over with," Aviva said, wincing as her bandaged leg was jostled against the wheelchair. Orla grabbed a blanket from the bed and tucked it around Aviva, hiding the cast.

Idalia took a big breath and then opened the door. She pushed Aviva down the hall with Orla walking to her left. She tried to maintain a good pace, not too fast or too slow. Something inconspicuous. Just taking a stroll through the hospital.

They passed a nurses' station. A few nurses manned the computers, clicking through files or something, but none of them stopped them. Idalia pulled up short in front of the elevators. Orla reached out to push the button, and they waited until the elevator stopped at their level. The elevator was empty and Idalia rolled Aviva inside. A ding sounded as the doors closed. Idalia took a breath.

The elevator ride down seemed to be agonizingly slow. Each floor closer to the ground sent a shiver down Idalia's spine. This was a dumb idea. She knew it. Her sisters were hurt and probably needed more care from the doctors. But she also knew Aviva didn't have the luxury of time. Aviva couldn't just sit here and wait for cops or Kathy to show up. She didn't have anyone in her corner. No one besides herself and Orla. So, Idalia was going to do whatever it took to keep her safe. To keep both of her sisters safe.

The final ding sounded and Idalia grabbed the handles of the wheelchair. Her knuckles turned white as the doors slowly slid open.

"Idalia," Orla said, swatting at Idalia's hands.

Idalia looked down. The rubber handles of the wheelchair were burned. She shook her hands out, the flames disappearing. "Sorry," she said, her voice catching in her throat. She had to get a grip. Control herself before she accidentally burned the whole hospital down.

"Come on," Aviva said, urging them through the open door.

Idalia grabbed the charred handles and pushed Aviva out into the lobby. No one stopped them as they rolled outside.

Orla and Aviva both looked at Idalia as she pulled the wheelchair to a stop on the curb. "What?" Idalia asked.

"Where's your car?" Orla asked.

"You think I drove here?" Idalia asked with a laugh, tilting her head to the side and staring hard at her sister. "We have to catch a cab or something," she said. She stuck her head out into the street looking both ways to find a vacant cab.

Orla hit herself on the forehead. "Ow," she said, wincing when the force moved her nose underneath the cast. "I totally forgot," she laughed.

"Yeah, so easy to forget we just collapsed outside of my dorm room and were brought to the hospital because we were attacked by our other sister in a fantasy land," Idalia said under her breath.

"Kinda wish it was that easy," Aviva said. "Can't believe the mess we got ourselves into."

Idalia pulled up short. "We didn't get ourselves into anything. We were forced into a world we know nothing about because our biological parents wanted to test a theory," she said, raising her hands in a flurry. If her father hadn't sent them away as kids, they wouldn't have been in this situation. They would've been prepared for the trials. They would've known about their powers. They would be succeeding instead of absolutely failing at each and every turn. She couldn't stand the thought of how different things would've been had King Quilo left tradition alone. And now it was her responsibility to change it even more, to figure out a way to survive. She had to figure out how to stop them all from dying.

Orla swatted at her. "Look," she said, pointing to a yellow and black cab a block down.

Idalia waved the cab over and watched as it rolled to a stop in front of them. Orla helped her lift Aviva out of the wheelchair. They awkwardly stumbled toward the cab. Orla opened the door and let Aviva slide onto the leathery seat. Orla slid in next to her, and Idalia squished into the last very small spot. She left the wheelchair on the curb, told the cab the address of her dorm, and watched as the hospital disappeared from view.

In what felt like seconds, the college she attended rolled into her sight. She directed the cab driver to the back, by the dorm rooms, and then waited for him to pull to a stop a few feet away from her dorm. "Thanks," she said, tossing the driver a wad of cash she found in her pocket and opening the door. She ignored the driver's stare as they stumbled from the cab.

She could only imagine how they looked to him. Orla and Aviva broken and wrapped up. Her with no damage anyone could see, only mental and emotional. All of them looked dehydrated and exhausted. What a sight it must've been.

Idalia was careful not to scrape her bandaged arm as she practically carried Aviva up the stairs to her room and sat her on the couch. She plopped down beside Aviva and tried to catch her breath. She tried to rein in her whirling thoughts.

"It's been a crazy few days, huh?" Aviva asked, her head resting against the couch. Her eyes were closed and her lips were turned up into a smirk.

"Something like that," Idalia said, standing up.

"I'm just so tired," Orla said, slouching down onto the couch and wrapping her arms around herself.

Aviva followed suit, laying down while letting her bad leg hang off the couch. They both closed their eyes. Idalia watched as their breaths got slower and deeper. When she was sure they were asleep, she snuck into her room and fell on the bed. In a matter of seconds, she was asleep too.

14

Orla stirred. A handsome face shifted into view. She watched as the face took shape. Brown hair, only a shade darker than her own, fluttered in a wind Orla couldn't feel. Dark brown eyes bored into Orla's soul. She recognized the face. She would've known it anywhere.

Orla jerked awake. She covered her mouth with her hand, choking back the beginning of sobs.

"What's wrong?" Aviva asked, slowly pulling herself up into a sitting position and rubbing at her eyes.

"Brey," Orla cried.

"Brey?" Aviva asked sleepily.

Idalia padded into the living room.

"I keep having these nightmares," Orla said, tears rolling down her cheeks. "He died because of us," she whispered, shaking her head.

She stood up from the couch. Her chest rose and fell quickly. Energy surged through her. And she needed to let it out or it would suffocate her. She needed to get rid of the image of Brey's severed head. But she couldn't. She could only relive it over and over.

"He died because of Eira," Idalia said slowly. "It's not our fault."

Orla sniffed back tears. "I know," she said, turning away from her sisters. "I know that." And she did know it, but it didn't stop the guilt that ate at her. It didn't stop her from blaming herself, wishing she had been able to do something, anything to change what happened to him.

A ringing phone broke the tension in the room. Orla turned to find it, but it was nowhere in plain sight. Idalia dropped to her knees and searched the floor, looking underneath the couch and chairs. Orla rummaged through the scattered papers on the kitchen table.

"It's yours," Idalia said, grabbing Orla's phone from between chair cushions. She tossed the phone across the room to Orla.

"Hello," she said, bringing the phone to her ear. Her mother's frantic voice came through the speaker.

"I'm okay, Mom," Orla said, turning her back on her sisters. "I lost my phone... I'm sorry, Dad... Fine, okay... Be home in a little bit..." She could barely get a full sentence in as her parents kept talking over her.

She disconnected the call and looked at her sisters. Idalia was still rummaging around her dorm while Aviva sat on the couch staring blankly at the wall.

"I have to go home. My parents are pissed."

"Ah, here it is," Idalia said, pulling her phone out from behind the TV stand. "What's going on?" she asked, keying back into the conversation.

"I have to go home. My parents have been calling me for days apparently," Orla said. She scrolled through her phone. There were several missed calls and texts from her parents.

"I'm in so much trouble," she whispered. A deep sigh racked through her chest.

Orla made her way to the door, twisted the doorknob, and then stopped and turned around. "I don't even have my car. It's at the school. Can you give me a ride?" she asked, looking at Idalia.

"I'll stay here if it's okay with you. I don't really have anywhere else to go," Aviva said to Idalia.

"Yeah, of course," Idalia nodded. "I'll be right back."

Orla followed Idalia out of her dorm and into the parking lot to her car. They sat in silence as Idalia drove Orla home, into an assault she was sure would happen.

"Oh my god," Orla's mother said when she walked through the front door. Her eyes were puffy, and her cheeks were tear streaked. "What happened to your face?" she asked, coming up to her and gingerly touching at the bandages around her nose.

"Ow," Orla said, swatting at her mother's hands. "I fell and busted my nose, so I went to the doctor," Orla lied.

"Your eyes are all swollen, sweetheart. Are you sure you're okay?" she said, letting her hands fall to her sides.

"Yeah, the doctor said it'll heal in a week or so. I'm fine, Mom," Orla said, pulling her mother in for a quick hug. She sniffled against Orla's shoulder.

"I've been so worried about you," she said softly, her words mumbled.

"I'm glad you're home safe," Orla's father said, stepping closer to Orla. "But you have a few questions to answer."

Orla gulped nervously, glancing toward her father. His face

was set, his eyes hard. He was mad. About as mad as she had ever seen him. "Okay," she said against the frog in her throat.

"Not just for me. The police have some questions as well," he said.

"Oh," Orla said.

Orla's father pulled a chair out from beneath the kitchen table. Orla walked quietly over to it and sat down. She folded her hands in her laps and waited for her parents to sit down across from her. Her father leaned forward, his elbows resting against the table. They waited. "So, do you want to clear anything up, or are we supposed to just assume that you ran away from home without telling us?" her father asked.

"Uh," Orla mumbled, trying to come up with an explanation for disappearing for days.

"And why did you leave your car in the school parking lot? We had to go pick it up," her mother exclaimed. "What is going on?" she asked, with a hand on her chest.

"Sorry, Idalia picked me up from school and we just got carried away," Orla said, twiddling her thumbs under the table.

"And you didn't think we should know that?" her father asked. His face turned red with anger. "Have we not grounded you enough over these last few months?"

"I'm starting to think Idalia and Aviva may not be the best people for you to be around," her mother said, looking over at her father. Her father nodded in agreement.

"What? No, that's not fair. You can't tell me who I can hang out with," Orla said, rising to stand. "You can't keep me from the only biological family I have." She crossed her arms and planted her feet firmly on the floor, holding her ground.

Her mother and father both took deep breaths, shocked at her outburst. But, she was right. Idalia, Aviva, and Eira were her only real family. The only tie she had outside of her adoptive parents. The only people who had the same blood coursing through their veins.

A knock sounded on the front door. Her father stood and left the kitchen. Her mother sat unmoving across the table. Orla waited, her breath holding in her throat. She could hear the faintest conversation from the front door. Then, boots walking across the floor.

"This is Officer Marks," her father said when they walked into the room. "It's time to answer those questions." He took a seat back at the table and motioned for Officer Marks to do the same. Orla stood over the three of them, all sitting and looking up at her.

"As your father said, I'm just here to ask some questions. Your disappearance from class had us all very worried. We just want to make sure you're okay and not getting tangled up with something or someone who doesn't have your best interest at heart," Officer Marks said calmly. Orla eyed him carefully, waiting to see if he had more to say, but he leaned back after his spiel. He looked directly at her, not bothering to include her parents in their conversation.

Orla huffed. "I left school early to hang out with some friends," she said with a roll of her eyes. "They picked me up, and I forgot to get my car afterwards." She could feel the stares from the three of them. None of them believed her. But that was fine. They didn't have to believe her, they just had to stop questioning her.

They sat in silence, the tension growing until Officer Marks stood up and nodded. "Thank you for your time," he said, extending his hand. He held a card out to Orla. She took it quickly.

"If there's anything else you want to add to your story, you can call that number," he said. He turned away from Orla and faced her parents. "If I have any more questions to tie all of this up, I'll let you know."

Her parents nodded. Officer Marks walked back through the house, Orla on his heels to close the door behind him. He grabbed the door just before stepping outside and turned back to Orla. He pointed toward her face. "What happened there?" he asked, his head cocked to the side.

"I fell," Orla said shortly.

"Hmm, well, keep an eye on it. Looks like it was a nasty fall," Officer Marks said before finally letting Orla shut the door. She watched through the window as he got into his patrol car and sped away from her house.

Orla walked back through the house, passing through the kitchen. "I know," she said, throwing her hands into the air when her father opened his mouth to speak. "I'm grounded," she said, leaving them in the kitchen and going to her room. She closed and locked the door behind her. She pulled her phone out of her pocket, clicked on Idalia's number, and paced around her room until she answered.

"Hey, how'd it go?" Idalia asked in a hushed tone.

"The normal interrogation," Orla said, finally planting herself on the edge of her bed. "A cop stopped by."

Idalia gasped. "What did the cop want?"

"To know why I left my car at the school. Didn't seem like he knew anything about leaving the hospital or Aviva."

"Good," Idalia said, sighing with relief.

"I'm about to hole up in my room for a while. But let me know if anything changes over there," Orla said.

"Yeah, okay. Bye," Idalia said.

A click ended the call and Orla leaned back against her bed. She had missed the comfort of her own room. The warmth of her bed. She snuggled up against her pillows and blankets, falling asleep instantly.

15

A viva jerked awake, sitting up straight against the couch in Idalia's dorm. A loud banging continued on the door. "Campus police, open up," a booming voice said through the wood.

Aviva pushed herself to a stand, wobbling on one leg. She hopped away from the couch and fell. Idalia rushed into the living room and helped her stand. Idalia led her to the bedroom, straightened her hair and clothes, took a deep breath, and left her to go answer the door. Aviva leaned against Idalia's bedroom door, waiting for the voices to filter in.

"Good evening. Are you Ms. Gallagher?" the campus cop asked after the squeak of the door opening.

"Yes?" Idalia said.

"Mind if I come in?"

"What for?"

"I got word of an incident outside of your dorm. You and two other girls passed out and were taken to the hospital? Is that right?" Papers rustled. *Must be looking through a report of some kind*, Aviva thought. Aviva held her breath and strained her ears. Blood pounded against her eardrums making it harder to hear the conversation. Her hands started to sweat.

"Yes, and?"

"I saw that you made it back today. Just wanted to do a well check," the cop said.

"I'm well, thanks."

"And the other two?"

"They don't go here, so is it really the campus's concern?"

"It is, actually. When we have three girls leave the campus in an ambulance, we all become very concerned."

No voices filtered through the wooden door for a minute. It was one of the longest minutes of Aviva's life.

"Sorry for the disturbance," he said.

"That's quite all right," Idalia said.

Aviva heard the sound of the door shutting and Idalia's footsteps against the floor. She scooted away from the door and tried to get her breathing under control.

"Well?" she asked when Idalia opened the bedroom door. She couldn't stop the fidgeting of her hands beside her.

"It was nothing," Idalia said with a wave of her hand.

"It wasn't nothing," Aviva said, her voice rising. "The cops are searching. They went to Orla's. Now they're here. Next thing I know, they're going to show up at Kathy's doorstep and then start hunting me." The air in her lungs evaporated, and she clutched at her chest.

Idalia bent down to Aviva's level, wrapped her arms under her armpits and managed to get her to sit on the bed, one leg straight out in front of her. Idalia sat beside her.

"It's going to be fine," Idalia said. "They're not arresting any of us. And we won't let them take you either, Aviva. We have your back," she said, putting her arm around Aviva's shoulders.

Aviva nodded even though she didn't believe a word. Orla

and Idalia wouldn't be able to do much of anything if the cops came after her for killing her foster dad, Ted, and then running away. They wouldn't send her to another foster home. They'd put her in jail. The only way out of this nightmare was to go back to Season and face a different type of monster.

Aviva and Idalia sat in silence for a while. Finally, Idalia stood and gave Aviva the room to sleep. But, Aviva couldn't relax. She couldn't avoid the feeling that everything in her life was on the verge of exploding. She rummaged through Idalia's nightstand and found a piece of paper and pen. She scribbled on the paper and then set it on the nightstand, placing the corner of the lamp on top so it wouldn't move.

Aviva pulled her necklace off and stared down at the golden circle in her palm. The Tree of Season was represented in gold. A different colored stone nestled in the notch where each of the four roots snaked away from the trunk. And four daughters, each with the power of a different element, made up Season.

Aviva focused her thoughts on Season, imagining herself back in Spring where she had been before the Trial of Winter had forced her away. She was happy in Spring. She belonged. She had a home and some sort of family. She was happy there. At least for a little while.

The smell of Spring rose in the air–luscious green grass; big, round trees; fresh water. The warmth in her palm grew until her whole body felt on fire. But, it didn't hurt. It wasn't painful. It was peaceful, a warm embrace. Aviva's eyes remained closed until she could feel the dewy earth of Spring underneath her.

16

Idalia rolled over and plummeted to the floor of her living room. "Crap," she muttered, picking herself up and rubbing her face. She was tired, no doubt. But she couldn't get restful sleep. She couldn't get into a deep enough sleep to forget about everything that was going on. She just wanted to forget for a little while.

"Aviva?" Idalia called out into the still room. She tiptoed through her dorm and leaned against her bedroom door. She didn't hear a sound. She turned the knob and peered inside.

There was no lump on the bed. Nobody anywhere in the room. Idalia held her breath and swung the door open. She walked around the room as if Aviva was playing hide-and-seek. She lifted the comforter and looked under the bed. Nothing.

A slip of paper stuck under the lamp on the nightstand caught her attention. Idalia blew out a breath and looked at the note. Aviva's handwriting was scribbled all over it.

Sorry to do this again.
Aviva

"Sorry to do this again?" Idalia said, anger filling her. The paper burned to ashes in her hands. She shook the fire out and took a deep breath. She really needed to get things under control.

Idalia went back to the living room and found her phone. She paced as it rang.

"Hello?" Orla's sleepy voice said.

"Aviva's gone again."

"What do you mean?"

Idalia rolled her eyes. "I mean, she left. She disappeared. Again." Her voice rose with each word as did the beat of her heart. Warmth gathered on her palms.

"Calm down," Orla said. Idalia huffed in response. "Where would she go?" Orla asked.

Idalia shrugged even though Orla couldn't see her. "I guess back to Season like last time."

"Great," Orla groaned. "So what's the plan?"

Idalia threw her hands up in frustration. What was the plan? What could they possibly do? Eira was in Season ready to attack, probably trying to hunt them down again. Aviva was gone, too scared to stick around in Texas. But they couldn't leave her to deal with Eira alone. They had to protect their little sister. One way or another.

"We have to go after her," Idalia said.

Without even a second pause, Orla's voice came through the phone, "Okay, I'm coming."

Orla left her room in a hurry, a piece of paper fluttering to her bed. The note to her parents wasn't going to be good enough for them not to get mad at her. But she couldn't do anything else. She had to leave. She had to go after Aviva and help Idalia. She had to put an end to her oldest sister. She had all of these things to do that her parents would never understand.

She tiptoed out of the quiet house, put her car in neutral and rolled it out onto the street. A flashback of the night her and her friends had snuck out, doing the same thing she was doing now–pushing her car farther away from her house– clouded her memory. The same night where the Tree of Season necklace came to her and her whole life changed. The night she had a vision of Season and her sisters. The night where the beginning of her new life started.

She shook the nostalgia out of her head and jumped into her rolling car. She turned the ignition and drove away.

17

"**M**y queen," Jedrek called from across the garden. Eira sat on the bench, enjoying the fresh air of Winter. The captain jogged toward her. She stood when he reached her.

Jedrek inclined his head and caught his breath before speaking. "I just received word your sisters have been spotted in Season. Aviva of Spring was alone. Orla of Autumn and Idalia of Summer were seen together."

Eira rubbed her hands together, nodding her head in excitement. "Excellent," she said, a smile spreading across her lips. She puffed out her dress, the skirt fluttering across the stone walkway lining the garden. She walked around a bush of red flowers she couldn't name. The smell floated up toward her, filling her nose with a sweet scent. Things were looking up for her. Her cheeks ached as her smile spread wider. She turned around, winding around another bushel of flowers.

Jedrek stood at attention, his legs locked, his arms down beside him. He stood tall and firm. Eira cocked her head to the side.

"My queen?" Jedrek asked when she raised an eyebrow at him.

"What are you still doing here?" Eira asked, her voice rising. Her cheeks turned red. "Go find them and bring them to me," she all but yelled in his face.

He gave a stiff bow and hustled from the garden, grabbing men along the way. Eira watched them all disappear. Her chest pounded. She walked around the garden unable to contain her excitement. Her hands shook at her sides. Tingling spread from her toes up her body.

Her sisters were back. Let the fun begin.

18

Aviva stood in front of burning pyres, leaning heavily onto a wooden staff. Her injured leg throbbed beneath her, but she would stand until the last embers disappeared into the smoky air.

"My princess," a small girl said, coming up to Aviva.

Aviva looked down at her. She had dirt smudged all over her scrawny arms and face. Aviva held out her hand and the little girl grabbed a hold of it tightly. "Why did this have to happen?" the little girl said, her voice breaking as she looked over the burned remains of the wooden structures where many of her neighbors had been put to rest.

Aviva grunted as she bent down to the girl's level, careful not to put too much weight on her injured leg. A spark of pain shot through her calf as she settled onto her knees. "Look," Aviva said, turning the girl's face away from the fire. "Sometimes things don't make any sense. Sometimes destruction happens," she said, waving a hand over the small village, "but that is not what matters. What matters is what we do after the storm. And we are going to repair our village. Will you help?"

The little girl nodded quickly, excitement building in her eyes. Aviva pointed to a set of men past the bodies waiting to be burned, past the makeshift tents, toward the bushes surrounding the village. They were at work putting new cabins together. "Go see if they need your assistance," Aviva said.

The little girl nodded and ran off, splashing through the puddles littering the ground.

Aviva stood in silence for a while. The smell of smoke no longer registered in her mind. "Princess," a frail man said, coming up behind her.

"Yes?" Aviva asked, not taking her eyes off the pyres. The flames were almost gone. The souls were almost released.

"This was Marge's," the man said, holding out his hands. A small bracelet made of twine sat in his palms. A golden charm in the shape of a rock hung from the twine. "I'm sure she would want you to have it," he said, offering it to her.

A tear threatened to fall down her cheek, but she sniffed it away. She took the bracelet and held it gently in her hands. "I can't accept this," she said, pushing it back toward him.

He nodded his head. "She would've wanted you to have it," he repeated.

"She didn't have any family?"

He shook his head sadly. "No, they died throughout the years. The happiest I had seen her in a long time was when you arrived. She had waited all her life to meet the princess who would take Season back for us."

Aviva twiddled the bracelet in between her fingers. "I'm sorry," Aviva whispered. She wasn't sure if she was talking to the man or to Marge.

"There is nothing to be sorry for, Princess Aviva. Marge was the rock of our village, and there is no one she would rather have take her place than you." He turned to watch the pyres smolder with Aviva. The villagers Eira and her army had killed in her search for Aviva had all died trying to protect her even though in a few months and a few more trials, she might not even survive herself. But now, she would protect them. She had to for Marge.

She tied the bracelet around her wrist. The charm dangled, warm against her skin. "Let's get to work," she said to the man.

He nodded and led her to a group of people sitting down in the middle of the village. They all turned and watched as Aviva scuttled up to them, her bad leg dragging a little behind her. It hurt, bad. But, it couldn't be any worse than what the people of this small village felt since Eira attacked them and ruined everything they had ever worked for.

"What's there left to do?" Aviva asked the group.

One man stood in the middle of the mass of people. "We need to build these cabins," he said, a hand out to the bare ground around them.

"And find food," another said from amongst the crowd.

"We need to get more water stored," a lady said.

Everyone nodded. "We need protection around the village. Something more than bushes," another man said from the back of the crowd.

A murmur erupted from the group. They all nodded, and yeses were heard throughout. Aviva held her hand up to quiet them, half expecting it to go unnoticed. But they all closed their mouths and looked up at her. "I will take care of the cabins," she said. "You divide into groups to find food, water, and begin building a fence around the village."

"Yes, my princess," they said collectively. They rose and gathered into groups, each one setting out to do their tasks. Hunting parties were sent out for the food. Ladies grabbed buckets and readied storage for more water. Men began digging around the border of the village to set up the fence.

Aviva turned toward the cabins. Old, burned wood was scattered haphazardly on the ground. She let her wooden staff fall to the ground beside her as she raised her hands into the air. The earth opened before her, sinking the old cabins into the ground. Then, new, strong trees sprouted from the ground. They intertwined with each other making large coverings. Smaller trees rose underneath them, shaping out the walls of the many cabins. Walkways between the cabins appeared out of the dust. A small village of tree houses stretched out before her.

Her arms dropped to the side, a heavy sigh escaping her lips. Energy fled from her body. She bent slowly to pick up her staff.

"Wow," she heard from behind her.

She turned to look. A small boy, hiding behind an empty barrel, had his mouth hanging open. When Aviva met his eyes, he ducked behind the barrel.

Aviva walked slowly over to him. "Hey," she said, bending down to his level.

He peeked out from behind the barrel again, looking at her wide eyed. "That was..." he paused, stopping to search for the right word. "How did you do that?" he said instead.

"I'm one of the Four, so I have special powers," she said.

"Amazing," he whispered.

Two men sprinted toward them. Aviva stood up quickly. "My princess," one said when they reached her. He bent over, his hands on his knees to catch his breath. "Your horse," he said between gasps, "is back."

Aviva followed them as quickly as she could while adjusting to the feeling of the cane. A warm feeling spread through her as she drew nearer to the edge of the village. Just past the bushes, Aviva could make out the black head of her horse. "Milo," she said, her voice giddy with excitement.

"We didn't know if he would return. He ran as soon as you were pulled into the Trial of Winter," the man said.

Aviva took a step closer to Milo. The horse neighed, bobbing his head up and down. His black mane flapped in the wind. She placed her hand on his dirty nose. Milo nuzzled against her palm. The horse leaned against her, pushing his weight onto her body. She hugged his neck, burying her head into his mane. She smiled. Milo was her favorite, most precious, thing she had ever been gifted, and he was home.

19

The portal opened and Idalia raced toward Conformity Castle, Orla close behind her. She ran up the large stone staircase and burst through the front doors. A few maids turned to look at her as she entered the entrance hall.

"Anyone seen Aviva?" Idalia asked the maids milling around. They all shook their heads no.

"Where could she be?" Orla asked, reaching Idalia's side.

"Only place would be Spring, right?"

Orla nodded. "That makes sense, but how do we get there?"

Idalia looked at the necklace in her palm. "You portaled us to Spring before."

Orla stepped up to her, grasping her hands tightly. Idalia's necklace warmed against her skin, a light glow emitting from their palms. She closed her eyes and envisioned Aviva. And Spring. She had to be in Spring. Where else would she have gone? She definitely wouldn't have gone to Eira like she had last time.

Minutes passed and Idalia felt no change in the air around her. She opened her eyes.

"We're still here," Idalia said.

"I don't know how this works," Orla said, pulling her hands from Idalia's. "I can't control where it takes us."

"Well, I guess we have to find our own way to Spring then." Idalia turned away from Orla and headed up the spiral staircase. Orla followed. They traveled to the top, and walked down several hallways before stopping at a closed door. Idalia didn't bother knocking, she just walked right in.

The room was just how she remembered it. Papers and books were tossed around everywhere. There was no real order or organization. Brey must have still been searching for answers when Eira killed him. He obviously hadn't found any before he was decapitated.

Idalia took a big breath and laid her hands on the desk in the middle of the room. She could almost feel the warmth radiating from the wood. She could almost feel Brey's essence. As if he was standing right there beside her, pointing to the things she needed.

She rummaged through the papers quickly, not wanting to be here one second longer than she needed to be. She didn't need the reminder that Brey was no longer with them. He couldn't help them anymore, and they needed more help than ever.

"Here," she said, pulling a rolled up paper from underneath stacks of books. She flattened the map. It was a little different than the map Brey had given her the first time they needed help finding Aviva. There were more details etched into the paper. Hand-drawn landscaping. Villages designated by boxes and trees in the shape of *X*s. Brey's name was smudged at the bottom corner. He had drawn it.

Idalia traced her finger along the map. Last time they went east to go to Winter. This time they would need to go south.

"Come on," Idalia said after rolling the map up and heading toward the door. She pulled Orla away from a box of things on the opposite wall.

"Where are we going?"

"To see if we can get a ride south."

They hurried down to the stables and set out to hunt down their sister.

Lady, Idalia's chestnut horse, stomped her feet when she entered the stables. "Good to see you again," she said, kissing the soft fur on his head. She strapped a saddle on her back and mounted.

"Let's go to Spring," Idalia said, leaning down to whisper into her horse's ear. Lady took off running around the stables. Samson, with Orla on his back, followed close behind.

Idalia's hair whipped behind her as Lady picked up speed. She went from a canter near Conformity Castle and through the gardens to a fast gallop on the outskirts of the castle. They broke through a clearing, hills rising up in the distance.

Idalia saw the glimmer of the Tree of Season as they left the castle behind. It was a huge golden tree. She remembered the first time Brey had shown all of them the tree. She had felt a pull from it as if it were beckoning her. She could still feel it. The necklace hanging around her neck, a golden representation of the tree and its seasons, grew hot. She threw thoughts of the tree out of her mind and focused.

"What if we're too late?" Orla called, her voice getting lost in the wind.

"We can't be," Idalia shouted. She leaned down, ground her heels into Lady's sides, and held on as Lady galloped away.

Orla swatted low hanging branches out of her way as they traveled through a forest. "Where are we?" Orla whispered, leaning toward Idalia. They had slowed way down after hours of riding. Orla's legs were beginning to cramp and she desperately needed something to drink.

Idalia shrugged. "South," she said. "Hopefully close to Spring now."

They let the horses find their way through the forest. Orla looked up to see a large fence made of rock and tree trunks. "Aviva," Orla said. Idalia nodded in agreement.

Orla slid off her horse's back and led him to the makeshift gate. It was open. She peered into the village. People huddled in groups. Some stripped meat from animals, some poured water into huge barrels, and some gathered kindling into large piles.

She stepped through the gate, and a swarm of men with spears and knives rushed them. Idalia brought flames to her hands and Orla gathered the air into a gust beside them.

"Princess Idalia, Princess Orla," a man said, coming up to them. The men behind him dropped their weapons. "To what do we owe this honor?"

Orla shook away her element, the hum of the wind disappearing around her. "We're looking for Aviva."

"Do you intend on hurting our princess?" the man asked, dragging his feet into a fighting stance.

"We would never hurt her," Idalia said.

Aviva popped into Orla's sightline, leaning heavily against a cane as she worked her way through the crowd. Orla pushed past the people near her and ran toward Aviva, hugging her tightly.

"You had to leave again?" Idalia asked Aviva when she joined Orla's hug. "Really?"

Aviva shrugged. "It's not safe in Texas."

"It's not safe here," Orla exclaimed, holding Aviva at arm's length.

"I'd rather face Eira than be sent to prison," Aviva said. She unhooked herself from Orla's grasp and turned away. "Now, come. Let's find y'all a place to stay." She led them to the many cabins intertwined in trees.

20

Eira sat quietly beside Donovan as they rode in the back of a carriage. Eira's pure white horse, Willow, pulled them, trudging through mushy grass. Her hooves clanked against stubborn rocks on makeshift roads. They'd been riding for a while, but Willow didn't seem the least bit exhausted.

Soldiers marched around the carriage, shielding Eira from possible threats but also obstructing her view. Peeking through the carriage's window, Eira could make out large trees erupting from the earth so close together there would be no room for the carriage to fit.

"My queen," Donovan said, turning to face her.

"Yes, Donovan?"

He mulled over his words for a moment, the bumping of the carriage accentuating the wait. "What is the point of this adventure?" he asked. There wasn't a seed of anger or disappointment in his voice, only curiosity.

"To find my sisters, of course." She paused, letting the bouncing road comfort her, calm her. Eira continued, "Jedrek said they were back in Season. The only logical place Aviva would be is in Spring. I have no idea where Orla and Idalia would go besides Spring to be with Aviva."

Donovan nodded his head as she talked. "Of course," he said.

"It would be a better use of all of our time," she said, waving her hand to encompass all the soldiers and horses around them, "to catch them all together. Make this season shorter than planned," she said with a shrug.

"And you think you can take on all three of them at the same time?" Donovan asked.

Eira's eyes flared with anger. Her jaw clenched as she spoke, "I am far stronger than they are. I have been in Season longer. I have exercised my powers. Season is mine and nothing will stop me from getting it. Nothing."

"Yes, of course, my queen," Donovan said, turning to look the other way. "I only wonder if it would be smarter to pick them off one by one." The words were barely a whisper, but they flew on the wind to Eira's ears. She rolled her eyes. She had made the decision to go ahead and search Season for her sisters, she wasn't going to turn back now.

Willow slowed as Jedrek came up on the side of the carriage. He leaned down from his horse to speak to Eira. "We are nearing the first village. What is your command?"

Eira set her jaw and pushed back her shoulders. "Tear it down."

21

Aloud horn woke Aviva. She sat up in her makeshift bed, throwing the blanket off her. Orla and Idalia stirred on the floor. A knock sounded on the door. Aviva stood slowly to open it, her leg aching as she managed to get across the room.

"My princess Aviva," a man said when she opened the door. His face was red and sweat dripped from his forehead.

"What's going on?" she asked.

"We got word from surrounding villages that your sister Eira has started invading. She's going through Spring tearing everything down," he stuttered. Tears welled in his eyes.

Aviva's hand tightened on the doorknob. Why did Eira have to ruin everything for her? Why did she have to take away the only place she'd ever been able to call home? Why couldn't she be like a normal big sister, instead of trying to kill all of them?

"Don't worry," Aviva said, her eyes determined, "I'll take care of it."

The man nodded before running to the next door. Aviva

watched for a minute as the man told the family the same thing he had just told her. Panic filled all of their eyes. The mother of the family rushed inside and gathered a few things before taking up her smallest child and following the man to the next cabin.

"What's happening?" Idalia asked when Aviva finally shut the door, turned around, and leaned against it for support.

"Eira," Aviva said, a hiss between her teeth. "She's destroying Spring."

Orla stood up, shaking off the rough night of sleep. "What do you want us to do?"

"We have to stop her," Aviva said, her hands balled into fists at her side.

Orla and Idalia nodded their heads in agreement. "Let's do it, then," Idalia said, standing up with them.

"Yeah, let's put a stop to Eira," Orla agreed.

Aviva looked at them, her heart bursting. She couldn't decipher the meaning of the pounding in her ears. All she knew was that they were no longer going to let Eira decide how things were going to go down. They were going to hunt the hunter.

She quickly gathered her belongings and left the cabin. On the way out of the small village she stopped a young boy. A few minutes later, he met her at the gate with all of their horses.

Aviva constructed a step out of mud to help her reach Milo's back. She slowly lifted her leg into place, letting it fall into the stirrup. She winced at the movement, but a few minutes of working with her element had a brace strapped around her leg to offer more support.

The young boy looked up at Aviva. "What are you going to do, princess?"

Aviva glanced down at him. She smiled tightly. "I'm going to make sure Eira doesn't harm any more of my people."

The boy nodded and stepped back allowing the horses to gallop away.

Aviva led Idalia and Orla through the forest. They dodged low hanging tree branches, vines, tree trunks sticking up from the ground, and piles of slippery dirt. Their horses were sure-footed as they raced away from the small village Aviva had just restored.

They broke out of the forest and onto a dirt road. They rode in silence for a while, passing by several small villages that hadn't yet been destroyed. Eira hadn't made it that far into Spring. *It must take a while to burn a village to the ground,* Aviva thought, her mood souring as the minutes dragged by.

The sun slowly disappeared from the sky, fading behind far off hills to the west. The darkness brought a change of temperature. The wind snipped at them as they whipped through Spring.

Aviva brought Milo to a stop at the edge of a village. She slid off his back, the brace for her leg still holding firm. Idalia and Orla copied her.

All three of them walked into the village, horses in tow.

Aviva pushed open a wooden gate. It creaked loudly on its rusty hinges. She used Milo as her cane to walk slowly into the village. Their footsteps were the only sounds around. No fire crackled in the dark night. No children laughed. No hushed conversations between adults. There was nothing besides her sisters and their horses.

"This is weird," Orla whispered as they walked farther into the village.

Aviva's eyes took a while to adjust to the darkness. She stumbled over and around fallen items of clothing, weaponry, and leftover food. Idalia drew a flame to her palm, lighting the dusty walkway.

"Very strange," Idalia said as they turned a corner to see a line of cabins spreading through the village. All of the homes were vacant. Everyone was gone.

"They must've fled," Aviva said. "Eira has to be close now."

Aviva led them along the road until they reached a small barn. She pushed the door open. It was warm inside, covered with hay, and buckets of water were placed around the room. "We'll rest here for a while, then. Head out again in the morning," Aviva said.

Orla and Idalia nodded and disappeared farther into the barn.

Aviva stood in front of a barrel, splashing her face with water. She took a sip from her palms. The fresh water felt so good, the liquid running down her dry throat.

Orla and Idalia joined her after a few minutes. They drank and cleaned themselves the best they could with only water.

Aviva winced at the sight of Orla's nose after she removed the bandages. Underneath, dark bruises splattered across her face. Aviva was glad she hadn't busted her own nose. She couldn't imagine the pain. Even her own calf seemed mild in comparison.

Orla's stomach growled. She clutched at it and grimaced. "I could really use a burger right about now," she said, licking her lips.

Idalia nodded in agreement. "Yea, me too," she said, a small laugh escaping. "Don't think we could pop back into Texas real quick to pick one up, huh?"

Aviva resisted the urge to roll her eyes and instead waved her hands in the air, water droplets flying around as she tried to dry her body. Orla sent a gust of wind around the barn, drying off every drop on them. "Thanks," she said. She stepped back from the barrel and her sisters. "I'll go see if one of the cabins has any food."

She walked away. A few seconds later, her sisters' footsteps sounded in the silent night. She didn't speak to them as she crossed the doorstep of an empty home. All three went inside and rummaged through the cabinets. There were only a few stale pieces of bread and left out jam.

Aviva gathered the food into a worn cloth bag and went to another cabin, and another, grabbing all the edible food she could find. When she was done, and all the cabinets had been picked through, she met up with her sisters outside of the first home. They each had a few things in their hands. A couple of apples, a half a loaf of bread, an almost empty pot of honey. But no meat or anything of much substance.

Orla sighed at the finding. "I could really go for that burger."

Idalia nodded in agreement.

Aviva's jaw clenched and she turned on her heel to stomp away.

"What's wrong with you?" Idalia asked, jogging to catch up to Aviva.

Aviva whirled around. Her face was red with anger, her fists clenched around the handle of her bag of food so tightly her knuckles were white. "No one asked y'all to come," she shouted. "Go home if you want to. I don't care. Just don't stick around complaining about being here," she said. Her voice echoed around them in the empty village. "Just leave me alone," she whispered and turned to head back toward the barn.

Orla stuck out her hand and grabbed Aviva's arm. "We're not leaving you alone. We're here to help," she said softly.

"You're not helping," Aviva said, yanking her hand away and stalking off.

She found a warm spot of hay and sat down, eating a few pieces of food in silence. She tried keeping her eyes open, tried to watch for any movement or sound that wasn't her sisters or their horses in the back of the barn. But her leg hurt, her eyes burned, and she was exhausted.

Aviva struggled to breathe. She thrashed her limbs into the air, clawing at the hands around her neck. She opened her eyes. For a split second, she thought she was back home in Texas with Ted. He hovered over her, eyes bulging with anger, face beet red. But her eyes adjusted to the darkness around her.

A man in a dark blue hood stood over Aviva. His hands were wrapped tightly around her neck, and he leaned against her, adding pressure. Tears sprung to Aviva's eyes as she struggled against the man. "For my queen," he said, leaning close to her ear. Aviva landed a kick to his knee, and stumbled to a stand, her bad leg aching. He gathered himself quickly, before she could manage to get her legs working together, and rushed her again. His fist connected with the side of her face.

Aviva fell to the ground, clutching her jaw. She put a hand up and scooted back against the floor of the barn. Her back hit the wall. She closed her eyes tight as the man ran toward her.

A loud cracking sound made her look up. A large tree root burst through the flooring of the barn. The root shot into the air as the man ran toward Aviva. The man collided with it, unable to change directions fast enough. Blood pooled at his feet and dripped out of his mouth. Aviva gasped at the sight.

She scrambled to a stand again. She couldn't take her eyes off the man as he took labored breaths.

Deeper in the barn, Aviva heard rustling. A burst of flame shot out into the open area. The horses bucked in their stalls, standing on their hind legs and whinnying loudly. Aviva left the man to die as she awkwardly ran, her leg still tight in a brace, toward the commotion.

She ducked as another flame ignited a stall door to her left. "Idalia," she called.

In the very back of the barn, in the last stall, Orla and Idalia wrestled two men. Orla blasted them with air, pushing them out of the stall and into Aviva. Aviva tumbled backwards. She got to her feet quickly. The two men stood in between Aviva, Idalia, and Orla. The sisters glanced at one another.

At once, they sent their elements hurtling toward the men. Earth, fire, and air mixed together to blast the offenders. Their screams filled the barn.

Aviva dropped her hands and ran toward a stall. Her horse pawed at the door. She unlocked it and let him out. She pulled herself onto his back and looked back at her sisters. "Let's go," she yelled. Her sisters mounted and followed her lead out of the barn and into the night air.

She couldn't tell if the pounding in her ears came from the three horses galloping away from the barn or from the adrenaline rushing through her veins.

"Aviva," Orla yelled, her horse catching up to Milo.

Aviva turned to look over at Orla. She was pointing behind her, back toward the barn. Aviva whipped her head around to look. Idalia was bringing up the rear, but she held a fireball in one hand. Aviva moved to look around Idalia. One of the men was stumbling out of the barn, clutching at a badly burned arm.

"Leave him," Aviva shouted.

Idalia looked back at the man one last time before letting her fire die out around her palm. "Eira must be close," she said, pushing her horse to get into line with Aviva and Orla.

Aviva nodded. "We need to lead her away before she gets to the next village."

"Yeah, but how are we going to do that? She just had her people try to kill us," Orla shouted, her free hand waving.

"I don't know," Aviva said, biting her tongue.

Silence covered them as their horses leapt into the forest and navigated the dark woods. Idalia broke the silence. "We need to get somewhere safe, first."

"We need to see where Eira is," Aviva said almost at the same second. "We need an advantage."

Aviva dug her heels into Milo's side, and he shot forward, leaping over fallen logs Aviva could barely see. Milo knew the area far better than Aviva ever could. "Take us somewhere good," she said, leaning forward to get close to his ear. Milo's ears twitched at her words and he switched directions, leading them closer to where Aviva presumed Eira to be.

22

Eira waited by a fire pit. She was warm, a little too warm for her liking. Being in Spring was nothing like being in Winter. She missed the comfort of her manor. She had grown used to her plush bed. She was unaccustomed to the hard ground she had to sleep on while traveling.

She shook her head in disgust. She had never thought she would be one of those people who enjoyed the finer things. After aging out of the foster system, she thought she would never have nice things of her own. Much less a whole town and hundreds of people who followed her blindly. It was a nice change, no doubt. But for some reason, it made her feel like a fraud.

"My queen," a small guard said, running up to her and disrupting her sour thoughts.

"Are they back?" she asked, standing and towering over the guard. He looked up at her, his face white as the snow back home.

"Just one, my queen," he said.

"Just one?" Eira asked, following him away from the fire.

He gulped before speaking again. "Yes, my queen. Only one has returned."

Eira's fists clenched tightly together. She followed him silently around the camp until they came to a tent. Inside, Eira could hear the painful cries of a man. The healer was tending to him, muttering under his breath when Eira slid the heavy material aside.

One of the three guards she had sent to scout the next village lay on a makeshift bed. Blankets piled under him to offer some reprieve from the hardened earth. She didn't know his name. She hadn't bothered to learn any of their names. Not until they proved useful, and apparently, this guard and the ones who were with him were anything but.

"My queen," the guard said. It was a struggle for him to speak...a struggle for him to do much of anything by the looks of it.

Half of his body was a mangle of blood, blisters, and hanging skin. The arm that was not severely burned looked broken, twisting at the elbow.

"I take it you had a run in with my sisters?" Eira asked the guard.

He tried to nod but winced in pain instead. Eira nodded herself and turned away, walking out of the camp. The small guard followed her outside. She turned to face him. "Kill him," she said.

The guard's face went blank. "But, my queen..."

Eira waved her hand dismissively. "We should end his suffering," she said, making her voice softer. Trying to convey some sort of emotion for the poor man who lingered on death's door.

The guard straightened up. "Yes, my queen," he said, before walking back into the tent to whisper to the healer. Eira walked away from the tent, the sounds of a guard dying behind her.

Donovan waited for Eira outside of her own tent. He had a somber look on his face. "Cheer up," Eira said when she approached. "My sisters are close."

"Yes, but at the expense of three men," he said, lifting the tent flap for her to pass under.

"No worries, my dear Donovan," Eira said, a smile spreading on her face. "We have many men to take their places. And my sisters have no armies to fight with."

Donovan nodded his head. "Of course," he said, barely above a whisper.

"As soon as day breaks," Eira said, settling into the blankets and pillows her guards had arranged on the floor of her tent. "We will find my sisters and we will end them."

Eira sat high on her horse as her guards led the way around the forest. Scouts were sent in every direction looking for her sisters. Eira's eyes were glued to the scenery, watching for any movement in the edges of the forest. But she saw none for what seemed like hours.

"Movement to the right," a guard called to his fellow soldiers, scooting in closer to her side.

Eira swiveled her head just as a deer shot out from behind a bush. Willow reared and Eira clutched at the reins, holding so tight her hands turned white. "Woah, woah, woah," Eira said. Willow pounded into the earth. She pranced in a circle before finally settling back down. "That's a good girl," Eira said, rubbing a hand against the horse's slick neck.

"Are you okay, my queen?" the guard asked.

Eira looked over at him. He was a few paces away, giving Willow her space. "Yes, I'm fine."

The guard nodded and turned back to the path. They followed the grass-covered road in silence. A few minutes passed. The leaves on the trees fluttered to Eira's right again. She pulled tight on Willow's reins, readying for another deer to spook her horse.

A beautiful black horse, smaller than Willow, sprinted across their path. Two more horses followed it.

Eira's guards went crazy. They jumped away from the horses, falling onto one another, scrambling to their feet. Eira jerked Willow's reins and kicked her sides. "After them," she yelled to her horse and small army.

Eira leaned down closer to her horse as Willow darted after her sisters.

23

Aviva pulled the reins, and Milo galloped off the road and back into the forest. She heard the hoofbeats of her sisters' horses behind her. But she didn't look back. She kept straight ahead, leading her sisters away from Eira's army and all of the villages in Spring.

A whizzing erupted next to Aviva's ear. She slid to the side, barely escaping the point of Eira's ice dagger. The dagger shattered into a million pieces against a tree trunk.

She glanced behind her. Idalia and Orla spread out, speeding through the trees, with Eira bringing up the rear to make a diamond. The glint of another ice dagger caught Aviva's eye. She threw a hand backwards toward Eira. Her horse stumbled as a thick tree root shot from the earth just in front of her. Eira screamed in frustration.

Aviva raced toward a clearing, the trees thinning the closer she got. Orla and Idalia weaved through the forest, escaping seconds after Aviva did. Their horses skidded to a stop just before dropping off a ledge.

"What do we do now?" Orla called to them, her words broken by her rapid breathing.

Aviva backed Milo up and turned him to face the forest. "We stop Eira," she said, sliding off Milo's back. Orla and Idalia dismounted and joined her in the middle of the clearing. Their horses pawed at the ground nervously.

They waited as Eira made her way through the forest. Willow cantered into the clearing. "Well, well, well," Eira said, an impish smile spreading across her face, "what do we have here?"

"It's time to end this, Eira," Idalia said, bringing flames to her hands and stepping forward. Aviva could feel the heat from the fire even from a few paces away.

Eira slid down Willow's broad back, shook two ice spears into her hands, and strolled toward her sisters. "It sure is," she said. She flung her hands outward, sending spears flying through the air.

Idalia blasted one with fire, melting it before it reached them. Orla swiped the other away with a blast of air. Aviva squatted down, putting her hands to the earth, feeling the roots underneath. Sensing the power her element offered her. The roots snuck through the ground and wrapped around Eira's ankles.

Eira blew out a frustrated breath and tried to pull her legs free. The roots tightened around her calves. She reached down and blasted the roots with ice until they crumpled around her, shards of ice littering the grass. Spears formed in Eira's hands. She shot them through the air, toward her sisters.

Eira knelt down, digging her hands into the earth.

Aviva shot up to her feet, her connection to the earth splintering as each piece of grass and root turned to ice and died under Eira's fingertips. Ice spread through the clearing until the whole field was covered. Aviva's feet slipped, the ice hard to balance on. The horses neighed worriedly behind her.

"How did she get so strong?" Idalia asked through gritted teeth as she planted her hands on top of the ice. The flames around her palms grew smaller and smaller the longer she tried to force her fire to melt the ice.

Orla braced her feet against the ice and straightened. "She's been in Season for a while now. No telling what she's been up to."

Aviva slipped and fell, hitting the ground hard. Her calf screamed in pain. She closed her eyes for a millisecond, a tear threatening to fall. But she pushed herself back up. "Does it really matter? We have to stop her."

Aviva righted herself again, Idalia and Orla at her side. Their hands were outstretched, their elements ready for when Eira closed the distance.

Eira stopped walking. She was far enough away that her sisters' powers couldn't reach her. They were weaker than her. They hadn't embraced Season, not like she had. Trying to maintain two lives would be their downfall, and having no life to go back to would be Eira's advantage.

Eira produced spear after spear and threw it in their direction with little time to see if she hit a mark. Her arm grew sore from the constant movement, but she didn't stop. She barely noticed that her sisters were destroying each spear with less and less accuracy. She barely noticed that Idalia could hardly bring a flame to her hand to melt her ice. She barely noticed Aviva struggling to uproot the earth under the thick ice. She barely noticed Orla falling backwards onto the ground, an ice spear sticking out of her chest.

Eira froze, the spears dropping from her hand. Aviva and Idalia dropped to their knees beside Orla. Orla's blood blanketed the earth, covering everything in red. Then Orla took her last shuddering breath.

Her lips pulled taut across her face. She stepped closer to her sisters. Using Orla's death as a distraction, she sent a layer of ice toward them.

"Stop!" Aviva yelled, waving a hand in front of the ice flying through the air. Nothing happened. No roots punched through the ground to shatter the ice, no tree trunks hurtled toward Eira. Idalia shot fireballs into the ice, melting it just in time before it reached them.

Idalia pulled Aviva from the ground, and without a word, pushed her off the cliff. Idalia wrapped her arms around Orla's still body, and jumped over the edge.

Eira's mouth hung open at the sight of her sisters leaping into the unknown. All she could hear was their screams as they plummeted to whatever was below.

24

Idalia kept her arms tight around Orla's lifeless body as they hurtled through the air. The ground below them approached faster with each millisecond. Idalia fought against the wind, trying to keep herself right side up. She turned her head, forcing it to the side where Aviva was tumbling over backwards.

"Aviva," Idalia yelled, her voice lost in the wind. "Aviva," Idalia called again. She reached her hand out, keeping one arm tight and secure around Orla.

Aviva moved her head an inch, her eyes meeting Idalia's.

"Your necklace," Idalia shouted. "We need to teleport."

Aviva moved her hand unsteadily in the air. She grabbed a hold of her necklace. A small light emitted from her palm.

Idalia moved through the air, trying to get closer to Aviva. Aviva stretched one arm toward Idalia. Time stood still. Slowly, a portal opened beneath them. Very slowly. The light from their necklaces grew as they fell to the earth.

Idalia and Aviva's hands touched an instant before they hit the ground and slipped through the portal.

In the Land of Texas

Idalia picked her head up. Blood trickled down her forehead and dripped onto the concrete under her. Her arm was slung over a limp body, but her eyes wouldn't adjust to see the face next to her.

"Idalia," Aviva croaked, lifting herself up on her elbows.

Idalia shook her head, trying to get rid of the muddled feeling in her body. She pushed herself into a sitting position carefully as she assessed her condition. Her elbows and knees had scraped against the concrete, her bicep was sore from the cut of Eira's spear and holding onto the body while hurtling through the air; but otherwise, she was uninjured. She pushed her hair back behind her ears and looked at her sister.

"Where are we?" Idalia asked no one in particular, looking around. Stone walls lined both sides of them. An overflowing trash can was haphazardly discarded beside a black door a few feet away from them. They were in the middle of an unidentifiable alleyway. The only sounds came from far away, cars honking in the distance.

"I don't know," Aviva said. She scooted closer to Idalia. "I was a little distracted when we were portaling."

Idalia put her arm around the limp body beside her and pulled her into her lap. Her bicep burned with pain, but she ignored it as she brushed the hair off Orla's face.

Orla's eyes were closed. Her clothes were stained with blood, a massive spiral of crimson red near her chest. She didn't move, not even as Idalia jostled her in her arms. Idalia's fists tightened in Orla's sleeves. She leaned down to place her lips on Orla's forehead. "I will make Eira pay for this," she whispered against Orla's hair.

"Idalia," Aviva warned.

Idalia fought back tears. She squeezed her eyes shut, colorful dots appearing behind her lids. A burning smell lifted into the air, filling her nose and making her throat tickle with the need to cough. Sizzling erupted under Idalia.

"Idalia," Aviva said again, her voice more urgent. She ripped Idalia's hand off Orla's body.

Idalia opened her eyes to see her hand engulfed in flame. She jumped away from Orla's body just as her clothes set on fire. Aviva scrambled back from the mess.

Idalia got to her feet as Aviva looked around for something to put out the fire. There was nothing. But that was okay. Idalia put an arm out to stop her searching. "It's better this way. We would've never been able to explain what happened."

Aviva slowly nodded, standing up shakily and turning toward Orla's body.

Smoke rose high into the air, billowing out from the alleyway. Idalia stood shoulder to shoulder with Aviva and watched as their sister burned. A gust of wind picked up the ashes, swirled them around Idalia and Aviva like a hug, and spread them into the air. One final breeze was Orla's goodbye.

25

Donovan stepped up beside Eira as she leaned over the edge of the cliff. She could not see all the way to the bottom, could not see if her sisters were splayed out on top of the rocks she imagined would be hidden in the darkness. Donovan pulled her back from the ledge. "We cannot risk losing our queen to the depths below."

Eira rolled her eyes but took a few steps back. She called a guard a few feet away. He shuffled over to her and bowed his head. "Yes, my queen? How can I be of service?"

"I need the bottom of the cliff searched. My sisters may be down there."

The guard looked over at the wide expanse of rock, the blackness swallowing up the earth below. His face grew whiter, and he swallowed a hard lump in his throat. "Of course," he said, bowing again and turning to find a few willing guards.

Donovan scooted closer to Eira's side. "Is it smart to send out a search party? These men might not return."

Eira watched as the guard gathered volunteers. They all went to the edge of the cliff to peer over the side. They talked quietly to each other, trying to figure out how to get to the bottom, then gathered supplies and started down the cliff. One guard had a felt wrap secured tightly around his waist. They lowered him down the cliff, and he carefully used the rocks to climb the side of the mountain. His foot slipped off the rock, and he stumbled, grasping for footing. The guards holding him up heaved backwards to keep him steady.

"So be it," Eira said, turning away from the guards. "Knowing whether or not my sisters are dead is far more important than a few men." She walked toward their camp without looking back.

The night grew even darker. Eira sat close to a fire, the embers licking at the now dry grass at her feet. The ice she had coated over the field earlier had melted into the ground, leaving it soft enough to sit on as Eira waited for news from her guards. Donovan sat across from her, his legs crossed and his hands folded neatly in his lap. He said nothing.

The silence hung over Eira. Her skin began to tingle the longer she sat idle. She needed to do something. Needed to be productive. She pulled her legs to her chest. She leaned toward the fire, getting her hands as close to the flames as she could without burning her fingers. One hand was practically in the fire before she felt the sting. She pulled her hand back.

It was red. Eira brought ice to her hand, freezing away the pain.

"You are unsettled?" Donovan said, looking over at Eira.

Eira looked up from her hand. "No," she said.

"What is bothering you, my queen?"

Eira avoided eye contact. "It shouldn't be taking this long," she said looking over toward the cliff where her guards had disappeared hours ago.

"It takes time," Donovan said solemnly.

Eira looked over at him. He hadn't moved the entire time they sat down. "Is something bothering you, Donovan?" He met her eyes. The sadness she saw in his eyes dissipated the second he looked at her. Instead, a neutral look took over his face.

"We do as you wish, of course. But I do believe we should save our own people," he said.

Eira's jaw clenched tightly as she tightened her hands into fists. She didn't like being criticized. Not even in this offhanded way Donovan had about him.

"There are other ways to garner the same results without putting your soldiers in harm's way."

"What ways?" Eira asked tightly.

Donovan sighed. He ran a hand roughly against his pant leg. He opened his mouth to speak, but shouting distracted Eira.

She stood and turned toward the noise. Her soldiers rushed to the side of the cliff. Many of them peered over the side. Some reached their hands down into the darkness. Heavy breathing filled the night air. Eira wrapped her robe tightly around her and marched over to the commotion. Just as she arrived, her soldiers pulled the men from the side of the cliff onto safe ground.

She waited expectantly as the men caught their breaths.

The hushed whispers quieted when Eira leaned down next to a soldier sitting just inches away from the edge of the cliff. "What did you find?" she asked, her voice silky sweet.

The man struggled to breathe, his chest rising and falling rapidly. It took several more moments for the man to be able to speak. Softly, he said, "Nothing, my queen. No one was down there."

Eira shrieked in frustration as she bolted upright. "Useless fools," she screamed through gritted teeth. She shot her hands out and a heavy blanket of ice knocked the man off the edge. All she heard as she turned back toward the camp was the shocked gasps of her soldiers and the man's screams echoing against the cliff walls as he tumbled to the dark below.

26

The dorm was dark. Blinds shut, curtains pulled tightly to cover every inch of the window. Aviva sat on the edge of the couch, her fingers drumming against her knees in an unsteady beat. Her skin prickled with each sound that echoed outside of the room. Her eyes darted back and forth, memorizing every inch of her sister's living room.

"Relax," Idalia told her. "No one's coming to get you here."

"You don't know that," Aviva said, her voice rising louder than she intended. "The cops aren't looking for you. They're after me," she said, covering her face with her hands. Her shoulders shook with the force of her tears. She inhaled sharply, pulling the emotion back into her body. "I'm not safe anywhere," she whispered.

Idalia sat on the couch beside Aviva and pulled her in for a hug. Aviva resisted the urge to shrug her sister off; and instead, leaned into her chest. They sat in silence for a few minutes.

When Aviva's body relaxed, Idalia stood up from the couch. She walked through the living room and opened the fridge, a small light emitting into the dark space. "I'm gonna have to go to the store," Idalia said, staring at the empty shelves of the fridge. "Anything particular you'd want?"

Aviva shook her head. "No thanks."

Idalia's footsteps blended with the drumming of Aviva's heartbeat. The constant thudding was all she could hear as Idalia left her alone in the dark. Aviva's body itched to move, to run, to leave. But she found that no matter how much her brain yelled at her to go, she couldn't lift herself from the couch. She was glued to the cushions. Her legs ached with the strain of her torso leaning against her thighs. After a while, the burning in her legs lessened to a dull drum. Aviva listened intently to the world outside of Idalia's dorm. Every sound made her heart jump. Every slam of a dorm door, every muffled conversation, every light breeze that ran along the building put Aviva on edge.

She wasn't safe in Texas, sitting alone in Idalia's dorm. And she definitely wasn't safe in Season with Eira hunting them down. Where could she go? What was her best option? How could she survive?

Aviva wiped away the tears that fell along her cheeks. She barely registered that she was crying. What caused the tears, she couldn't quite pinpoint. It was a culmination of things. It was every piece of her life fitting crookedly together. The jagged remains of her puzzle left her confused as to what to do next.

If she hadn't been given up by her father, a king of a faraway mystical land, she wouldn't have been put up for adoption. If she wouldn't have been in foster care, she wouldn't have had to kill her foster dad. If she hadn't killed someone, she wouldn't be running from the cops. And if she wasn't running from the cops, she could stay in Texas and be safe from her sister.

But who was she kidding? Her life had never been easy. It had never made much sense. And now, she would die. Either in jail or by her sisters' hands. Because if Eira didn't kill her, Idalia would have to. There was no way Aviva would bloody her hands even more. There was no way Aviva would be queen of Season.

27

Eira watched as Winter appeared before her. At first, the white speckled roads were mere lines in her sight. But then, she noticed the grass poking out from under the melting snow. Winter was holding on to the cold as long as it could.

She lifted a hand off her horse's saddle and pointed it at the road she and her men traveled on. The snow hardened under her. The horses neighed, filling the air with a sweet noise as they tramped their hooves deeper into the frigid snow. A smile crept onto Eira's face. She was the commander here. She was in control. Of her powers, of her place, of her people. She had never felt better.

"My queen," Jedrek said, kicking the sides of his horse to keep up with Willow. "You're sending search parties out?"

"Yes," she said curtly, turning her eyes back to the road. The tall gate opened as they passed through into town.

"If I may ask, what makes you think your sisters will come back to Season?"

"Ah, Jedrek. My youngest sister has gotten herself into some trouble back in Texas. She'll be coming back shortly if she isn't here already. And Idalia won't let her out of her sight for long after what happened to Orla," Eira paused. "I may have not known my sisters for very long, but I do know they'll stick together until the end. They'll make it easier for me to kill them both."

Jedrek remained silent for a moment as they strolled past the townspeople. The look of displeasure was evident on his face. He didn't try to hide it. Eira didn't mind, though. What he wanted didn't matter. The only thing that mattered was herself and staying alive until the end.

"May I head the search parties?" Jedrek finally spoke up, avoiding eye contact when Eira looked over. She fumbled with words. She hadn't expected him to want to go, least of all lead the hunt for her sisters.

When she remained unable to talk, Jedrek continued. "I know the lands far better than anyone else. I am certain we can find your sisters' whereabouts."

Eira nodded her head in agreement. He was the most knowledgeable person in Winter besides Donovan. Her stomach twisted at the thought of letting him go, of giving him something he asked for. "Unfortunately," Eira started. Jedrek took a deep breath, waiting for the blow. "I need you for another task."

Jedrek nodded, his body slumped in resignation. "Of course. Anything for my queen."

"I want you to give Aviva a surprise when she returns to Spring."

Jedrek raised an eyebrow. "A surprise?" he asked, trying out the foreign word.

Eira nodded vehemently. "Yes, a surprise. Something to shock her when she returns. I want you to make her wish she had never abandoned her people."

Jedrek nodded but remained silent. Eira slid off Willow when they stopped in front of her manor. She patted the horse's neck before a stablehand took her away. She walked into her manor with a confident stride.

Her army was going to find her sisters. And if they couldn't, they would at least destroy everything in their path. She rubbed her hands together, a vicious smile spreading her lips.

28

Idalia pushed a cart around the grocery store, grabbing boxes of food and random snacks. She spun the lid off a soda and drank a sip as she loaded her cart.

She wasn't paying too much attention to what went into the cart. She let her growling stomach decide. Cookies, candy, donuts, soda, chips. Junk food. And a few bananas for good measure. After what seemed like forever since a good meal, Idalia was starving. And she bet her sisters felt the same.

Sister. Not sisters.

A crippling sensation swept through her body as the thought of Orla surfaced in her brain. Orla wasn't back at Idalia's dorm waiting with Aviva. Orla wasn't safe in Texas away from Eira. Orla was dead. Idalia had failed her.

"Excuse me," a woman said, pushing her cart around Idalia. Idalia shook her head and sucked back the tears rimming her eyes. Now wasn't the place for a breakdown. Not in the middle of a packed grocery store. And now wasn't the time. She had to put the guilt and sadness behind her so she could take Eira out. She had to make Orla's death mean something. Make it count for something. She had to make it impossible for Eira to be the queen of Season.

Idalia's hands tightened around the cart's handlebars. She took a few shuddering breaths before pushing her cart down the aisle again.

She walked to the front of the store, weaving around people to get to the checkout. She needed to hurry and check on Aviva. They needed to refuel, rest, and plan how they would take Eira down. It was top priority. No distractions until it was done. Idalia had to put all her focus on destroying her older sister.

Idalia froze just as she exited the store. Every hair on her body stood up. Beads of sweat prickled on her forehead. Her heart beat hard against her chest.

She couldn't be seeing this right. There was no way. There was no way she was seeing Orla's parents walking toward her. She gulped as Mrs. Fletcher caught her eye. Mrs. Fletcher's hand rose to her mouth. Her other hand wrapped around Mr. Fletcher's bicep.

Mrs. Fletcher pulled her husband across the parking lot to stand before Idalia. Her eyes were red with dried tears. Idalia could see the pain in them. They were the eyes of someone who was missing their daughter. Who had no idea what was going on. Who had unanswered questions.

"I-Idalia," Mrs. Fletcher stumbled over her name. Her voice was scratchy as if she had just finished crying for the millionth time that day. "We've been trying to reach you," she mumbled, placing a soft hand on Idalia's arm.

Idalia gulped hard against the lump formed in her throat. "My phone is broken. I haven't gotten a new one yet."

"Oh, of course," Mrs. Fletcher said, a small smile crossed her lips that didn't meet her eyes. "Have you seen or heard from our Orla?" she asked, barely above a whisper.

Idalia's heart stopped. Her blood throbbed against her temples. Colorful spots appeared before her eyes. She let out a shaky breath. She shook her head slowly. "No. No, ma'am," she stuttered. Her voice was weak. Each syllable hard on her own ears. The lie cut through Idalia, but the truth was too much. She couldn't bring herself to crush Orla's parents even more. They would never see their daughter again. It was better for them to not know Orla had been murdered. Murdered by her own sister. Murdered for a crown none of them could save themselves from.

Mrs. Fletcher's eyes dropped. She pulled her hands up to her chest and took a huge breath. It rattled her shoulders. Mr. Fletcher put his hands on his wife's back, trying to comfort her. But even he looked troubled. "All right," Mrs. Fletcher said weakly. "If you hear anything..." she trailed off.

"Oh, of course," Idalia said. "I'll let you know."

Orla's parents nodded and walked slowly into the store. Idalia was frozen in her spot. Her hands shook against the handlebar. She closed her eyes.

A car's horn blared next to her. Her eyes snapped open. She raised a hand in a small wave as she walked into the crosswalk and found her car in the parking lot.

29

In the Land of Season

E ira ran her hands roughly against the material of her pants. Her palms were sweating despite the cool breeze Winter offered her. She unclenched her jaw and turned away from the soldier who delivered bad news. Her fists closed. She itched to release her power, but she withheld. No use in offing another soldier. If she kept at it, she wouldn't have an army to command.

"My-my queen," the soldier stammered from behind her. "I am sorry," he said. Without even looking at him, Eira knew he was trembling in fear from his kneeling position.

"Find Jedrek," Eira said simply. She didn't even bother to turn around. "Find Jedrek and Donovan. Tell them I am returning to Texas to locate my sisters. Tell them if my sisters make it back to Season before me to kill them. And if I discover that my sisters are already here in Season, I will kill anyone and everyone who could not catch them before me."

The soldier gasped. Eira stalked away.

In the Land of Texas

Eira stood up, rolled her shoulders back, and shook off the remnants of the portal. It had been a while since she had portaled. So long since she'd been in Texas that she had forgotten what dry heat felt like. Immediately, sweat formed on her forehead and dripped down her neck. She slid her jacket off her arms and threw it against the alley's wall.

Carefully, she surveyed her surroundings. She took a few steps out of the alley to assess where she had landed. Eira had found that she couldn't quite remember where she had last seen her sisters in Texas. She had barely been able to picture Texas at all.

A chiming doorbell rang on her right. Her eyes followed the sound.

A large window let her peek inside a coffee shop. The coffee shop, Eira realized as she took in the familiar area, was where Orla had worked.

Now if only she could remember how to get to Idalia's college from the shop. The tree shaped necklace burned on her skin, itching to portal again. It would be easier, but Eira couldn't trust it. Not when she didn't know exactly where she wanted to go. Instead, she let the necklace sear her skin as she walked down the sidewalk past the coffee shop.

A street sign caught her attention. *College Road.* It couldn't be a coincidence. She stopped walking and waited for the cars before hurrying across the crosswalk. And then she froze.

Eira hadn't noticed the cop car parked on the other side of the road. She watched as the uniformed man took a close look at her. She turned her back toward him and fought the urge to run. *Remain calm*, she told herself over and over.

She dared a peek over her shoulder just in time to see the cop pick up his radio and flip on his lights.

The siren blared in her ears, smothering the pounding of her footsteps against the pavement as she ran down the sidewalk. She pushed past a few college kids. They yelled after her, but she ignored them. She kept running and running. She knew the cop car was right beside her, she could feel it in her bones, but she couldn't take the time to look. Couldn't waste the seconds and slow her pace.

Instead, she turned a sharp corner and followed another sidewalk. At the end of the sidewalk, she could make out a tall building that could only be a part of the college.

"Stop right there," a booming voice said from behind her. She didn't stop.

Her feet slid against the concrete as she dug her heels in. She breathed hard, her chest rising and falling rapidly. A cop car had slid onto the sidewalk, blocking her in. A cop behind her, a cop in front of her, and she could hear the sirens of more police cars speeding toward them.

A young man stepped out of the car in front of her, using the door as a shield as he aimed a pistol at her. His voice wavered as he yelled, "We have you surrounded. You have nowhere to go."

He was right. She didn't have anywhere to go. She wouldn't be getting out of this one, not easily.

Eira took a steadying breath. It wasn't going to end here. She wasn't going to let some useless men in uniforms take her down. Not when she was more powerful than them. Not when she could destroy them in an instant.

She raised an arm.

A loud explosion erupted around her as ice shattered from the force of the bullets pelting into her wall of frozen water. She raised her other arm and a million spears of ice flew through the air until they collided with one of the cops who dared shoot at her.

She barely recognized the sound of the sirens, her ears pounding with blood, as more cars pulled up around her. In a sweeping gesture, she wiped the sidewalk clean of the police. Screams echoed in her ears. She took off running.

30

Aviva hobbled past the fence of a small village in Spring. A loud crunch was all she heard as the black, dead leaves snapped under her foot. A faint burning smell wafted in the air around her. It was quiet. Too quiet for what should have been a busy town on the outskirts of her territory.

The sound of her footsteps echoed against the walls of the village as Aviva drew closer. She put a hand against the wall to steady herself at the sight of what was left.

The village had been torn apart. No structures remained. No huts. Nothing. The ground was soiled with ash. Charred remains of cabins laid at her feet. The burning smell stung her nose. On the far side of the village, a few huts were still burning, crumpling into heaps on the blackened grass.

But where were the people? No one huddled in the shadows. There were no bodies littered about. They were either captured or forced to evacuate.

Aviva stood. She balled her fists up, her fingers digging into her palms. She wiped angrily at the tears flowing down her cheeks.

"You won't win, Eira," she whispered harshly. Her voice floated around her. The only living thing in the small village. "You won't get away with this."

She turned on her heel and marched out of the village, leaving the gate swinging on its hinges.

Aviva trudged down the road, stopping at each village along the way. At each stop, she only saw destruction. Where was everyone?

She splashed cool water on her face from a stream in the forest. A few droplets trickled down her chin and plopped to the grass below. She set her eyes on the road, pushed her feet to keep walking despite the deep ache in her calf. She was going to find her people.

She had to. Even if it was the last thing she did.

31

In the Land of Texas

Eira raced toward the huge buildings at the end of the street. She ignored the sirens' yells. She ignored the people jumping out of her way as she rushed past them. She had to make it to the university. She had to find her sisters. She had to destroy them and take Season for herself.

She skidded to a stop as familiar buildings popped into view. The dorms. One of these was Idalia's, Eira knew. She just couldn't recall which one exactly. She swiveled in circles looking for anything to point her in the right direction, but there was nothing. She inched closer to the buildings, stepping onto the paved parking lot. Idalia's car wasn't in front of the building.

She stepped back onto the grass and waited. Waited for something, anything to lead her the right way.

"Eira?" a voice growled from behind her. Eira whipped

around, two spears forming in her cold hands without so much as a thought. She chunked them in the direction of the voice before catching a full glimpse of the person.

Idalia ducked just as the spears clinked off a car beside her. "What are you doing?" Idalia shouted as she kept her fists clenched, refusing to let her flames explode. Even though anger radiated within her. But she had to control it. They couldn't do this here. Not in front of all of these people.

Another spear sliced the air beside her ear, grazing the tip. Blood trickled down her face. She raised a burning hand to her cheek to wipe the blood away.

"I'm taking what's mine." Eira sneered as she approached.

A wall of ice, so thick Idalia couldn't see through it, hurtled toward her. Her control faded. She let the flames reign. Fire met ice. Both elements dwindled until nothing was left. A large puddle laid in between the sisters.

Idalia ducked behind a car. Icicles shattered against the metal. She shielded her eyes from the sharp edges. She put her hand against the pavement of the parking lot and sent a flame toward Eira. It encircled her, lighting her up. But Eira didn't scream, she barely moved as the fire engulfed her. Slowly, inch by inch, the fire died around her. Eira stepped closer to Idalia, her body a blue so cold it was like she was made of water. She had become her power. She had become her element.

Eira clapped her hands together, a flurry of ice twisted toward Idalia. Cars lifted from the ground, swirled in the air, and dropped in an entirely new place. The air turned frigid in an instant. People screamed and ran away from the chaos.

Idalia stood up, no longer shielded by the cars. She turned

away for a second as sirens rang in her ear. The police were coming. They couldn't be here. She turned back to face Eira. She opened her mouth to speak, to tell Eira they had to leave when a sudden, sharp pain shot through her raised hand. The pain radiated from her hand all the way up her shoulder. Blood bubbled on her skin, the cold forcing it into lumps. It fell in heaps to the ground below.

Eira blinked out of existence as Idalia crumpled to the ground. She clutched her necklace with her good hand, her damaged arm falling uselessly at her side.

One second, she lay on the hard pavement, her blood soaking her clothes. The next, warm grass blanketed her, pulling her into a deep sleep.

32

A warm breeze rustled against Idalia's nose. Her eyes blinked open. Seconds then minutes passed before she could see the landscape around her. The world grew darker with every labored breath. Idalia groaned and rolled onto her back, stifling a scream as her arm rubbed against the earth. Her shoulder jostled with each nudge from a horse's nose.

Idalia reached out a hand to rub the spot between the horse's eyes. A sigh of relief escaped her mouth as she recognized the animal. "Hey, Lady," Idalia whispered. "How do you always find me?" Her words were lost in the breeze. The world around her disappeared as pain seared through her arm.

A second later, Idalia's vision came back. Lady nudged her again. Idalia shook her head slowly. "Okay, okay," she said, her voice faint.

Lady pushed Idalia up into a sitting position, standing strong behind her. Idalia rested for a moment, trying to quiet the thumping in her head. The world spun around her, faster and faster until she felt she might puke. Lady neighed in her ear and blew another breath out of her nostrils. Idalia stood carefully, leaning heavily on her horse. She pulled herself onto Lady's back, groaning as she slid into place. She bent down, practically lying on her horse's back, unable to hold on with both hands. She gripped her horse's reins with one hand and clicked her tongue until she took off into a canter.

"Take us home," she whispered. She wasn't sure if Lady heard her. She wasn't sure of anything as blackness swallowed her.

Idalia could feel herself slipping, going down, down, down into the earth. A breeze sounded in her ear, swishing like waves in time to the faint beating of her heart. It was so soft. Like it wasn't even there. Like she wasn't even there anymore. She was cocooned in the blackness, a warm blackness.

"My lady," came a faraway whisper. The words were distorted through the pounding in her ears. She couldn't lift her head or open her eyes to see anything around her. All she could do was wait for the next wave of pain.

Idalia groaned as she slid from her horse, her legs no longer working to keep her steady. She fell and fell. The ground never met her.

"My lady," she heard again. The voice was closer, she could feel the breath, but the words were escaping her. She couldn't understand them. Couldn't get a grasp on them. Or on anything around her. "What has happened?" the voice asked.

Idalia floated through the air, unaware of her surroundings. Unaware of what had happened or what was happening. The only thing she knew was the roaring pain that burned through her arm again and again. She pitched to her side, slipping from hands. She clutched at her arm, her eyes squeezing tight as another round of anguish rushed through her. She kept her shoulder rigid as she held her arm across her body. She tried breathing, tried catching a breath. They came faster and faster until she couldn't catch them. The pain was too much.

"Healer! Healer!" the voice screamed. The words bounced in Idalia's head. It was all she saw before the blackness stole her away again.

Burning. Burning. Burning. All Idalia could feel through the blackness. Her whole body blazed to a crisp.

Idalia attempted to open her eyes. Her eyelids fluttered and drooped, too heavy to open fully. She tried again and again. Noises floated around her. Clinking and clanking. People moving around. Hands touched her, a small break in the burning before it started all over again.

There was screaming. Someone was screaming. She was screaming.

Idalia finally forced her eyes to open.

The small flickering of a flame put everything in shadow. A dark figure stood over her. A face appeared before her eyes. "My lady," the woman said softly. "Are you with us?"

"Where-where am I?" Idalia asked, her voice barely above a whisper.

The woman placed a hand on Idalia's forehead. The heat

from her forehead radiated off the woman's palm. "You're in Summer. You're home."

Idalia tried sitting up, pushing against the cot with one arm. She let out a groan as her head swam and her vision blurred. The woman pushed her lightly back down. "Stay still," she said. Idalia obeyed, her muscles aching too much to do anything else.

The woman slowly worked to wrap a bandage around Idalia's arm. Idalia gritted her teeth, trying to keep the screams inside. But it hurt. Every little movement hurt. And she was dizzy. It didn't matter how still she was, her mind raced against waves she couldn't see. Idalia pushed her head back against the cot as hard as she could. Her uninjured hand tangled into the soft sheet wrapping the cot. Her mouth opened.

A scream rippled through the small hut as the woman dripped an elixir onto Idalia's hand. She watched as it seeped through the hole in her palm.

She was going to throw up.

Another lady Idalia hadn't noticed rushed to her side with a bowl of water. She dipped a cloth into the bowl, rang it out, and placed it on Idalia's forehead. Before the lady could turn away, Idalia caught her wrist. "Find Aviva," she said. "Find Aviva," Idalia repeated.

Her hand dropped from the lady's wrist. Her head rolled to the side. Blackness claimed her again.

33

Eira plummeted to the ground. The force of the portal had knocked her off her feet. Several soldiers hurried to her side. She raised a hand, waving them away, as she pushed herself up from the ground.

"Are you injured?" a soldier asked her, stepping closer.

Eira dusted off her clothes, ash falling to the earth. "I'm fine," she said through gritted teeth. "Get Jedrek and Donovan. Send them to my room."

The soldier nodded and hurried away. Eira spun around, anchoring herself to her whereabouts. She marched through the yard to her manor, a trail of burned debris left in her wake.

"Run me a bath," she instructed the first servant she saw upon entering the manor. The small girl led Eira to her room and started a warm bath. Eira dropped her dirty clothes and sat in the bubbly water. The servant picked up the mess and left her to bathe.

A few minutes later, a knock sounded on the door. Eira didn't bother to open her eyes as she said, "Come in."

Jedrek and Donovan strode into her room. It took them a

second to notice the open bathing room door. They both looked away from Eira lounging in the tub, barely covered by bubbles. They grumbled apologies.

After a few silent moments, Eira cleared her throat. "My sisters," she started, tapping her fingers on the side of the tub. "My sisters are in Season."

Jedrek stepped forward and bowed his head. "My queen, I assure you they are not. We have searched nearly every town within riding distance. They are nowhere to be found."

Eira chuckled. There was no humor in her laugh. It hung in the air, bitter as crushed mistletoe. "You will search again. They are here. And they will not be returning to Texas, this I assure you." Jedrek stepped back in line with Donovan as if the blow of her words were forceful enough to send him sprawling.

Jedrek nodded. "Yes, my queen."

Eira's closed eyes fluttered. She breathed in deeply letting the fragrance from the bubbles waft into her nose. The deep menthol scent cleared her sinuses, cleared her thoughts. "Find my sisters. Do whatever you have to do to find them. Bring them to me." She took a steadying breath. "I will end this."

34

Aviva leaned against a broken wall. The only thing remaining of the next town that should've been alive and well in Spring. But every town she'd come across had been destroyed. She had no inkling where her people were hiding or if there were any left. She had no idea if Eira had left anything behind.

She shuddered against the cool breeze of the night. She pulled one leg close to her chest, wrapping her arms around it while the other lay flat on the ground, the pulsing beat of pain in her calf a steady rhythm. She clamped her jaw tight. No shivering. She couldn't let the shivering take over.

She was fine. She was all alone, but she was fine.

Aviva closed her eyes. The sun began to rise, but her body ached from all the walking she had been doing over the last few days. She needed more rest. She needed more food, too. Her stomach grumbled in agreement. But she ignored it. She ignored the sun's warm rays on her face. She ignored the hunger. She ignored everything and slept.

A tap on her shoulder woke her. She jumped up and put her fists in front of her, blocking whatever blow was about to fall.

But there was no impact. Only a small crowd of people wearing red hoods. Aviva stumbled back a step, her back pressing flat against the wall. They watched every breath she took, every small movement she made, every thought that crossed her mind.

Aviva touched her hand to the wall, feeling the earth beneath the structure. She readied her powers, focusing on the feel of Spring all around her. She let the crisp air blow against her face. Let the smell of the grass waft into her nose. Let the earth rumble and turn in on itself, readying to bury all of them.

One of the hooded people stepped to the front of the crowd. *Dumb move*, Aviva thought centering her thoughts around the person. *Easy target*. Aviva could easily make the roots underfoot shoot from the ground to surround the figure in seconds. She could bring the earth to a storming roll to push back the others, to separate them. Isolate this person. She would do it. She would do it all if they made a wrong move.

A flick of the hooded person's wrist had Aviva shooting vines through the air. They wrapped around the person just as the hood fell down around their shoulders. A small smile played on the unfamiliar girl's lips. "Hello, Lady Aviva," she said, completely unfazed by the vines tightening around her sides.

The rest of her group remained still, watching Aviva. She couldn't see their faces, the large hoods obscuring the view, but she could feel their wary stares on her.

"Do I know you?" Aviva asked through clenched teeth. She took a small unsteady step away from the wall. She didn't want to be stuck too close if the others pounced. She needed an escape route.

The girl shook her head. "Of course not," she started,

stretching against the vines and mumbling. Aviva didn't loosen them. "But we have a mutual friend it seems."

Aviva's eyebrows pinched together in confusion. Friend? She barely had any. Let alone anyone wearing red hoods. Red. Like the dress Idalia wore on the night they burned their father's corpse. Red like Summer.

"You're from Summer?" Aviva asked, all the pieces clicking into place.

The girl smiled a wicked smile again. "Your sister says hello."

Aviva let the vines drop. The girl smoothed out her red cloak and stretched her arms far from her body. They were not a threat, Aviva decided. At least not yet. Not with a bigger enemy still out there. Not with Eira trying to ruin the trials and kill them all like she'd killed Orla. Aviva's fists tightened at the thought, at the flash of Orla's face in her mind. She took a steadying breath. In, out. In, out. She kept breathing until the anger and sadness dissipated just enough, and she could release her clenched fists.

"Lady Idalia requests your presence," the girl said. "We were told to fetch you." The girl motioned behind her to the rest of the silent people.

"And you thought you needed a small army?" Aviva asked, finally taking the time to count the crowd.

The girl laughed. "You can never be too sure with you four. Your powers get the best of you sometimes," she said, eyeing the vines at her feet. "Come now," the girl said, motioning for Aviva to step closer. Aviva took a small step and halted.

"How do I know this isn't a trick?" she asked warily.

The girl shrugged. "You don't."

Aviva took a steadying breath, trying to slow her racing heart. It beat wildly, almost to the point of pain. Idalia wouldn't hurt her, she kept repeating to herself. Idalia wouldn't trick her. And these people with their red hoods and tanned skin did look like they came from Summer. She had to trust someone. And who better than Idalia, the only true sister she had left? But still, her leg shook as she balanced awkwardly on her outstretched step.

"Lady Idalia is hurt," a whisper came from the crowd.

With that, Aviva's feet set into motion and she walked the distance between her and the crowd.

Aviva broke out into a sweat, her whole body covered in dripping water. Her clothes clung tightly to her body. It was bad enough that she was dirty from her time in Spring, but now the sweat congealed all the dirt together in one big mess. She needed a bath.

"We're here," Sara said. She'd introduced herself and some of the others on the ride to Summer.

Aviva slid off Milo's back, her feet landing on the crisp earth. Leaves cracked underneath her. She patted her horse's head and waited for the others to dismount.

"It's strange," Sara said, looking over at Milo.

"What is?" Aviva asked.

Sara motioned toward her horse. "Your horse found you in the middle of nowhere."

Aviva shrugged and stepped away from Milo. "He always knows where to find me when I need him." She watched as the rest of the hooded crowd walked into the town before them. Sara waited a step ahead. Aviva patted Milo once more and said, "Now don't go anywhere," and made to follow Sara. Milo neighed at her back.

Sara led Aviva past tents set up on the border and small

houses filled with families, past buildings selling all sorts of merchandise, and straight to the town's center. She didn't stop to let Aviva gawk at anything, urging her along the footpath to the largest building. A stone tower speared into the sky, a small room with windows facing each direction occupied the very top. Aviva guessed that was for the lookout. She guessed whoever stood in that room could see for miles and miles.

The building wasn't a mansion like what Eira inhabited. No, it was a heavily fortified complex. The people of Summer didn't play at keeping their princess safe.

Aviva swallowed, her throat dry as they stepped inside. The sound of screaming stopped her dead in her tracks.

"Come," Sara said, pulling Aviva forward. They raced through the building, as fast as Aviva could limp, going up and up the winding stairs. They only stopped when they reached a room with a wide open door on the fifth floor.

Women in red robes ran in and out of the room, their faces drawn. Some carried buckets of water, some clean, some murky with blood and dirt. Aviva stood out of the way as Sara ran into the room. The screaming turned to muffled sobs. Aviva stepped into the doorway.

Idalia lay on a bed, her face soaked in sweat despite a woman wiping her forehead. The other women tended to her arm. They were rewrapping it, from her shoulder all the way to her hand. She whimpered as a woman tightened the bandage on her hand. Sara leaned down to Idalia, whispering in her ear. Idalia finally looked up and met Aviva's worried eyes. "Don't worry," Idalia managed through clenched teeth. "It looks a lot worse than it is."

Aviva only nodded and stepped further into the room.

A few minutes passed as the women finished and cleaned up the mess. A few minutes passed before everyone but Sara and Aviva remained in Idalia's room.

"Wh-what happened?" Aviva asked through trembling teeth. Idalia was pale, paler than normal. Her ghost white skin stood out against her flowing red hair.

"I'm fine," Idalia muttered. "It was a lot worse. It's healing," she said, glancing toward Sara who nodded in agreement.

"Should we go back to Texas? Go to a hospital?"

"No," Idalia said, her body lurching forward as she exploded upwards. She groaned and nestled back into the pillows. "No, I can't. I can never go back," she whispered.

"What happened?" Aviva asked again.

Idalia sighed, "Eira." Because one word was enough. That word said it all. Eira had done this as she had done everything else. She opposed them at every turn. She fought against them any chance she got. Eira was the problem. She always had been. She would never be on their side.

Idalia launched into the whole story, telling Aviva how they had fought each other on the grounds of the campus, how police had come, how Eira had sliced through her arm and disappeared. Aviva's hand clenched at her sides the whole time, anger brewing in the pit of her stomach.

"We need to stop her," Idalia said, finally taking a breath.

Aviva nodded in agreement. "We do, but you can't."

Idalia's mouth dropped open. She tried speaking, but Aviva interrupted. "You are hurt. You probably can't move from this bed," Aviva said with a dismissive wave of her hand. "Can you even use your hand? Can you make fire?"

Idalia looked down at her wrapped hand. She squeezed her eyes together, her brows furrowing. A few moments of silence, of waiting, filled the room. Sweat dripped down Idalia's face.

"That's enough," Sara said, laying a hand on Idalia's uninjured arm.

"No," Idalia yelled, her voice high with worry. "No, I have

to be able to use my power. We have to figure out how to stop Eira."

"You have to heal," Sara said lightly.

Idalia fell back against the pillows, an exhausted breath escaping her lungs.

"We will. We'll figure it all out," Aviva said. "But right now, you have to get better and I have to find my people. I have to go back to Spring."

Idalia looked over at Sara, "Go with her. Help my sister find her people and bring them all back here."

"Lady Idalia–" Sara started.

"Go," Idalia said, her voice forceful. "That's an order."

35

Eira flipped through the pages of a book. She hadn't realized just how boring it was to wait. Back in Texas, she had always been on the run. Fighting to survive. Here she had several people who took care of everything. Who made sure she ate, slept, bathed. She didn't have to worry about her next meal or finding somewhere new to sleep. Here she was dying of boredom.

Horse's hooves clobbered the gravel road outside her window. She jumped up from her seat to take a look. Donovan sat atop a fine horse, several men riding behind him. They stopped just in front of Eira's porch. She hurried from her room to meet them.

Donovan slid off the horse and bowed low as Eira approached. The others followed suit. "Any news?" Eira asked as soon as she got into ear shot.

Donovan stood tall. "The villages of Spring have all been destroyed. They are uninhabitable. The people of Spring will have to flee."

"And my sisters?"

"No word yet. Jedrek is still searching for them."

Eira hissed. "Aviva should've been in Spring. Where is she?"

"We are not certain, but..." Donovan began.

Spears of ice shot out of Eira's hands. She clutched them tightly. "Are you sure of anything at all?" she yelled. Onlookers stopped to stare, but Eira didn't care. She had given them one job. One job to find her sisters and they had failed. Again.

"If you cannot deliver my sisters to me then I am going to have to go find them myself," she said, her face set in determination. She had failed herself, allowing others to do her work. Delegating. It was pathetic. She was pathetic. She had forgotten the one simple rule she had learned in Texas: don't trust anyone. She would take matters into her own hands.

"I would advise against it," Donovan said.

"Good thing you don't have a say," Eira said and stalked back inside.

Donovan told the others to tend to the horses before he followed her.

He waited until they were both inside, in a room all alone. "My queen," he said, bowing his head slightly. Eira turned to look at him. "These things take time. Jedrek will find your sisters, and you will put an end to the trials. You will be queen of Season. But, it takes time."

Eira huffed. "I don't have time."

"You do," Donovan said. "You are well protected and cared for. You have time. Let us continue the search for your sisters."

Silence engulfed the room. Then, a sigh as Eira finally said, "Fine."

Donovan nodded, pleased with himself. Eira rolled her eyes. "But," she said, watching as Donovan's face grew wary. "Prepare my forces to march on Summer. We destroyed Spring. We're going to do the same with Summer."

Displeasure swept across Donovan's face. Eira knew what he was thinking. She knew he didn't agree with destroying the other territories. But her sisters left their people unattended, which made it too easy. She didn't care that Donovan was probably right when he had told her weeks ago that destroying Spring would make it harder to control them when she became queen of Season. But she wouldn't have to control them if they were all dead.

A smile crept on her face as Donovan said, "Yes, my queen."

36

The room was quiet once Sara led Aviva away. Idalia breathed in deeply, closed her eyes, and focused. Or tried to. But the sound of bustling outside her room distracted her.

She had to close the door if she was going to focus. She sat up slowly, giving her body time to adjust to the new position before scooting to the side of the large bed and kicking her feet down. She didn't know how long it had been since the fight with Eira, but it was long enough that her body felt foreign in a vertical line.

Idalia braced her good arm against the bed and rose to her feet. Colors swam before her eyes in no discernible pattern. She waited for them to disappear before she shuffled her feet against the wooden floor.

Idalia heaved in a breath as she reached the door and shut it with a bang. The noises from outside disappeared. She was left in silence.

She turned back around, surveying her room. The bed was against the wall, stuck in a corner. It was laid with several pillows and light blankets. A window allowed natural light in. Two chairs sat on either side of the door that led to the bathroom. Books rested atop the various nightstands and dressers. It was all decorated in fine reds, oranges, and yellows. The whole room looked as if it was engulfed in flames.

Idalia pushed against the door and walked unsteadily to one of the chairs. She nestled down into the seat. It wasn't nearly as comfortable as the bed, but she was tired of laying down. Tired of being useless and broken.

With a huff, Idalia placed her wrapped hand on top of the chair's arm. She shook her head in disgust. She couldn't believe she had let Eira hurt her, couldn't believe she hadn't been strong enough to stop her. How was Eira so strong? How had she mastered her powers when Idalia couldn't even conjure hers anymore? She unwrapped her arm, letting the dressing fall to the floor.

Idalia sucked in a breath as the jagged scar was unveiled. Her palm was marred by an uneven circle. A single scar ran from her palm, up her wrist, and continued to her shoulder. The scar looked like the aftermath of lightning hitting a tree. It's what it had felt like too. Idalia trembled at the memory.

She balled up her fist, gasping as pain shot through her arm. She squeezed and squeezed until her knuckles were white and the pain was a distant thought. She practiced opening and closing her hand until she no longer felt the stretch and tear of ligaments and tendons. She practiced until her hand was numb and sweat fell down her cheeks.

Idalia stretched her hand out, shaking the numbness away. She tried bringing her flame to her palm, but nothing happened. She shook her head and tried again.

And again. Nothing. No flame appeared in her hand. No burning scent or flickering orange ball. Nothing.

She tried her other hand. Instantly, fire burst from her

palm. It crawled up her arm and engulfed one side of her body. She relished the warmth, in the feeling of being on fire. She pressed her palms together, gritting her teeth as an ache shot through her scars. She released her hands and for a millisecond, flame played on the scarred hand. But then it sputtered out and died.

"Ugh," Idalia yelled in frustration, slamming her good hand against the side of the chair. Her whole body diffused, the fire ebbing away.

Her bedroom door flew open and a small girl stuck her head in frantically searching the bed. It took the girl a minute to realize Idalia was sitting in one of the chairs. The girl bowed when her eyes met Idalia's, and her face turned bright red. "Sorry, Lady Idalia," she muttered. "I thought you were hurt."

"No," Idalia said, "not hurt. Just unable to fully use my element it seems."

The girl nodded. "It'll take time."

"Everything does," Idalia said, rolling her eyes.

The girl chuckled. "Yes, well scarred tissue doesn't connect as easily with the elements. You have to work around it."

Idalia's eyebrow raised in question.

The girl stepped forward. "May I?" she asked. Idalia wasn't too sure what she was asking, but when she nodded, the girl walked over to her. She grabbed Idalia's palm lightly turning it so her palm faced upwards. She ran a finger against Idalia's palm. "This," she said tapping the center, "will not connect. This, though," the girl said, tracing around the angry red scar, "is fine." She dropped Idalia's hand. "Work around it," she shrugged.

Idalia looked at her palm. The ugly scar was there, but there was plenty of healed, uninjured skin around it. She touched that part, felt the vibrations underneath. Idalia closed her eyes and imagined her flame dancing on the outskirts of her palm, not touching the center, not touching the damage.

The girl clapped and jumped up and down. Idalia opened her eyes to see a ring of fire on her palm just as she had imagined. A smile broke out on Idalia's face. "Thank you," she whispered, looking through the fire to the girl.

"Mara," she said in answer.

"Thank you, Mara," Idalia said, watching her flames burst into the air around them.

37

Aviva was thankful for the rain as it pelted against her face, a welcome relief from Summer's torment. Milo shook his head, slinging the raindrops off his mane.

"Spring is strange," Sara called from her horse. Aviva glanced over at Sara. She rode next to Aviva, but a step behind leaving Aviva as the leader of the small pack of Summer people. "The rain," Sara said, moving her hands through the water. "Summer doesn't rain. Not like this." She turned her face upwards, letting the rain drench her.

"In Texas, it's usually only hot or raining. Really no in between," Aviva said.

Sara thought for a minute, opened her mouth, and then clamped it shut as if she thought better of speaking whatever was on her mind.

"What?"

Sara glanced at Aviva. Aviva's eyebrows raised in question, so Sara continued. "I've just always wondered why King Quilo sent the Four away. I always wondered why he changed laws to separate you from each other."

Aviva remained silent even when a red hooded boy hissed Sara's name in warning. She didn't know the laws or her father well enough to speculate, so she didn't bother trying.

"The trials worked. They always have. Without them, we have war. Without structure, we have destruction."

Aviva nodded her head in agreement. "War is coming. Eira is coming. She destroyed the villages in Spring. She'll be upon Summer next."

"You and Lady Idalia will stop her," Sara said matter of factly.

"And what will happen if only Idalia and I are left at the end? Who will die then?" Aviva snapped. She didn't want to think about putting a stop to Eira anymore. She only wanted to find her people and go far, far away.

Sara set her mouth in a line, her answer better left unspoken. Aviva didn't want to think about who would win the whole thing if only her and Idalia were left. She knew Sara would do anything to ensure Idalia was crowned. Their people would do anything to secure Season featured their desired climate. The people of Summer would want a permanent summer. The people of Spring would want spring forever. And the people of Winter would want all of Season to be frozen over.

She also knew she would never lay a hand on Idalia.

They remained silent as they rode through destroyed town after town. Sara didn't comment, but Aviva saw her eyes go wide as they entered the first village. Only crumbles remained. There were no buildings, no cabins, no tents, no marketplace. Everything that was a landmark in the village laid in a heap on the muddy ground. Aviva sent up a silent thanks to the rain for disguising the tears falling down her cheeks.

Days passed. Silent days as they continued searching each village for any clue on where all of Spring's people went.

They camped on the outskirts of a village. Sara and her companions sat around a small fire. Aviva sat on a fallen tree trunk a few paces away. She watched as Sara joked with her people. Their smiles showing with their hoods hanging round their shoulders.

Aviva's stomach ached with sadness. She hunched over, taking her eyes off the happy scene. She couldn't bear the sight when everything around them was a mess–when everything was always a mess in her life. She couldn't stop the intrusive thoughts from gathering in her head. "I'm going for a walk," she called over to Sara. She didn't wait for a response.

Aviva stepped farther into the forest. The low hanging branches and their leaves scratched against her. Thankfully, her leg hurt less and less as the days went by. Her limp was barely noticeable now as the muscle had healed itself.

She passed the trees all the horses were tied to. Milo neighed softly as she brushed a hand down his neck. "Good boy," she whispered. Milo leaned down to nibble on the grass at Aviva's feet.

She kept walking, letting the moonlight guide her.

Aviva tried pushing all the thoughts out of her mind as she ducked under low lying branches and stepped over fallen twigs. But as she walked farther and farther away from Sara and her crew, the harder the thoughts became to evade.

Eira had to be stopped. There was no question about it. If she wasn't, Season would end up all but destroyed. Already, she had changed Season and the laws Season's people had abided by for centuries. Already, she had pummeled a fourth of this world. But once Aviva and Idalia defeated Eira, they would have to complete the trials. One of them would have to kill the other.

Aviva's stomach turned at the thought. She would not kill Idalia. She didn't even know if she'd be able to end Eira. Even despite all she'd done. Even despite Eira destroying the only place Aviva could call home now that she could never return to Texas.

Aviva was stuck in Season. Stuck with a sister set out to kill her and another one she would never hurt.

A twig cracked a few feet away. Aviva's body stilled. Her blood ran cold. Dread filled her every cell. Blood rushed to her ears, pounding so loud she couldn't hear anything else. Her hands froze at her sides.

A figure stepped out from behind a tree, and before Aviva could even recognize what it was, she let out a scream to alert Sara and the group. A scream so powerful she was left huffing afterwards. She took a breath, gathering her hands into fists, but the figure lifted hands into the air.

Aviva's thoughts finally clicked together, and she dropped her hands.

A small boy stepped closer to Aviva. "Is it you?" he asked, his voice only a whisper. "Is it really you?"

Aviva dropped to her knees. Eye level with the boy, she said, "Yes, it's me. Are you alone?"

The boy shook his head. Just as he did, tiny heads popped up all around them. Children. Hidden.

Aviva's heart swelled at the sight. She had found them. She had found her people. Some of them, at leasts. At last.

Thundering footsteps sounded behind them. Shouts filled

the silent air. The children ducked down, their bodies disappearing among the twigs and grass. Aviva turned toward the sound. She could hear the soft whimpering of the children behind her as the noise grew louder. She spread her feet, planted herself firmly in the grass. She would stop whoever was coming. She would protect her people.

Sara pulled back on the reins and skidded to a halt right in front of Aviva. She jumped down from her horse as her company followed suit. "Lady Aviva, are you all right?"

Aviva exhaled, her chest burning. "Yes, I'm fine."

"We heard the call. What are you doing out here?" Sara surveyed their surroundings, double checking for danger.

"I told you I was going for a walk."

Sara huffed. "Someone should've escorted you."

"On a walk?" Aviva laughed.

"Yes, on a walk," Sara said, her face set in stone. "You are Lady Idalia's sister. If anything were to happen to you..." she trailed off.

Aviva fought the urge to roll her eyes. So much was happening to her. And nothing would stop it.

Sara lifted her finger and pointed behind Aviva. "You found them?" she asked in disbelief.

Aviva nodded and turned to face the children who were standing straight up. She left Sara to go back to the boy. "Are there others? Or are you all that is left of Spring?"

The boy shook his head. "There are more. We are headed for them now."

"I'm coming with you," Aviva said. The boy nodded.

"Us, too," Sara said. Aviva glanced at her, opening her mouth to object. "Lady Idalia ordered us to help you find your people and bring you all back to Summer. So let's find them and go home."

The boy watched as Aviva finally nodded. "Fine," she said. He motioned to the rest of the children.

"Follow us," he said and led them all farther into the woods.

38

Bells rang in the early night. Idalia rushed from her bed to the large windows. Summer was darkening as the sun disappeared, but she could just make out the group of people on horseback. Her sister had returned.

She flew through the tower until she was standing outside, a few guards around her. She waited, her foot tapping lightly against the ground. A small flame bounced around her, jumping from one arm to the other, down a leg, across the ground, and up the other leg. She laughed as the flame tickled her body, running across her shoulders.

The bells rang again, closer.

"Nice work," Mara said, stepping up to Idalia's side.

Idalia took her eyes away from the horizon for just one second to smile and said, "All thanks to you."

Mara shrugged. "I had nothing better to do while my sister was gone."

"Sister?"

Mara's face broke out into a sloppy smile as Sara came into

view. She jumped from her horse and ran toward Mara. They both laughed as they hugged each other.

Aviva slipped off Milo and walked slowly toward Idalia. "Now that's a happy reunion," Aviva said, barely meeting Idalia's eyes.

"We could reenact if you'd like?" Idalia said.

Aviva glanced at Idalia's serious face. They both let out a laugh. The longer they looked at one another, the harder they laughed. Until they were buckling at the knees and holding their stomachs. "Stop making me laugh," Aviva said, clutching Idalia's shoulder.

"I'm not doing anything," Idalia managed through hiccups of laughter.

Slowly, the laughter died down. Idalia stood up fully. "So, did you find them?"

Aviva nodded. "They're coming."

Sure enough, several clusters of people found their way to Idalia's tower. They wore all shades of green and brown. The people of Spring.

"Find a place for all of them," Idalia said. She didn't take her eyes off the growing crowd of Spring people. She just watched as they all huddled together, standing a few feet apart from the people in red.

Sara and Mara broke apart from one other. Slowly, one by one, they gathered groups of people and led them through Summer. Idalia and Aviva waited until everyone from Spring had been escorted to a temporary lodging. Then they walked back into the tower quietly.

"How'd you find them?" Idalia asked when they were seated in the chairs in her room.

"By pure luck," Aviva said, rubbing her eyes. "A boy found me and led us to the rest. They were hiding in the trees on the outskirts of Spring."

"Crazy," Idalia mumbled. "Eira really destroyed Spring?"

Aviva nodded. "Destroyed everything. There are no villages. No houses. All the land is ravaged beyond use." Aviva closed her eyes and rested her head against the chair. "It's useless. She made Spring useless."

Idalia didn't respond for a while. She didn't know what to say to that. Eira had taken away Aviva's home, something she knew was important to Aviva. Something she had gone years without. How low must she be willing to go to destroy a perfectly harmless section of Season? All of it, all of the trials, Orla, everything would be a waste if Season was destroyed in the process.

"You want to clean up and rest? I can get a room set up for you if you want," Idalia finally said.

"You got your powers back, I saw," Aviva said, opening her eyes and looking toward Idalia.

"Yea. A little. Mara and I had been working on it while y'all were gone."

Aviva nodded. "Good. I'm sure we'll need it."

Silence overtook them. Idalia sat back in her chair, thinking of what may come. How Eira could be stopped. *If* she could be.

"Yea, I'll take that shower," Aviva said, standing up after a while.

Idalia showed her to the room next to hers. Once Aviva was settled, Idalia went back to her own room, fell on the bed, and closed her eyes.

A knock woke Idalia. Sara stood on the threshold when she managed to open her eyes and get to the door.

"I apologize for the interruption," Sara said, a blush creeping onto her cheeks.

"No worries," Idalia said, fighting back a yawn.

Sara stepped into the room. "I just wanted to update you on the housing for the Spring people."

Idalia nodded.

"We have most of them situated. We had to room several together, but they didn't seem to mind. I think they like being together," Sara said.

"Of course they do," Idalia said. "Their homes were ripped away from them. They need some sense of familiarity."

"We will do everything we can to keep them comfortable here."

"Good," Idalia said, settling back into her chair. Sara took one look at the other chair. Idalia followed her eyes to see that dirt crusted the fabric everywhere Aviva had sat earlier. Sara remained standing.

"Lady Aviva informed me that Lady Eira may attack here next," Sara said, her hands clasped together behind her back.

Idalia nodded. "That seems highly likely. She doesn't want to complete the trials. She wants to take us both out and claim Season for herself."

"Our people will suffer if she comes here. This tower is the only fully fortified building, which would leave everyone else vulnerable to Lady Eira's attack."

"We don't have another option, do we?"

Sara hesitated. "We do."

Idalia's eyebrows rose. She leaned forward in her chair. "Well, what is it?" she prompted.

"A mountain cave."

"A cave?"

"Yes," Sara said. "We have been preparing for your return

for quite some time now. We possess a highly fortified mountain. It is stocked and ready to go; it has been for a while."

Idalia sucked in a breath. "Why would I need a cave to hide in if the Four have always completed the trials like they were supposed to?"

Sara shrugged. "This time is different. You and your sisters did not grow up here, or even together. We did not know if you would follow tradition."

"It seems you were right to think that," Idalia said, rubbing her chin. She sat quietly for a moment, thinking. A mountain cave. It could hold Eira off, possibly. Or it could trap them all and make them easier to kill. "Does Eira know the whereabouts?"

"No. No one besides a few of us here in Summer does."

"And would it fit us all? With the people of Spring?"

"Lady Idalia, we can't protect them forever. If it comes down to just you and Aviva."

Idalia waved her hand. "Will it fit us all?"

Sara nodded. "Yes, if we make a few adjustments."

"Good, then do that," Idalia said. "How long will it take to get ready to move?"

"Not long."

"Great," Idalia said.

She stood up after Sara left and went to find her sister.

39

S ara led them toward the mountain. Aviva sat up straight on Milo's back, peering over his head to see the mountains jutting from the ground far away. They reached into the sky, their tops hidden in the clouds.

"This is a little crazy, isn't it?" Idalia called over to her.

"All of this is crazy," Aviva answered. "When did this become real life?"

"When our old one ended."

Sara slowed down. "There," she pointed. In the distance she could just make out a small crevice in the mountainside.

They rode as close as they could get with their horses before having to dismount and walk.

"Are they going to be okay here?" Aviva asked, patting Milo.

"Yes, there are many herds of wild horses that roam through here. They won't give us away," Sara answered.

Aviva nodded. She laid her forehead against Milo's head. He snorted against her. "Bye, Milo. Don't go too far."

She left Milo and followed Sara and Idalia along the mountainside. She took careful steps through the rocky path. But she almost fell from misstepping over the thousands of tiny rocks littering the ground. Her leg ached a bit, not as bad as when she first hurt it, but enough to know it still wasn't fully healed. Trying to maintain balance while navigating the ground was hard to do with her slight limp.

"Sorry," Sara said from in front of her, her feet sure against the terrain.

"How often do you come here?" Idalia asked, placing a hand against a boulder to step over a pile of rocks.

"Every few weeks," Sara said with a shrug. She stopped walking just before she reached the crevice. "Had to make sure everything would be ready to go."

Aviva stopped beside her and Idalia. She turned to watch the mass of Spring and Summer people follow their footsteps and crowd the small opening. The soft murmuring from the group stopped when everyone reached the crevice.

"One at a time," Sara instructed before disappearing into the rock.

"You first," Aviva said, pushing Idalia toward the hole in the rock. Idalia glared at Aviva. Aviva coughed out a nervous laugh and shrugged. "You're the big sister, big sis."

Idalia rolled her eyes. "Fine," she said, stepping into the mountain.

Aviva watched until she couldn't see Idalia anymore. She watched until she absolutely could not put it off any longer. She stepped into the dark.

The walls pressed in, sweeping the breath right out of her lungs. It was too dark. The rocks on either side were too close, scraping against her. She couldn't move. This was not a cave. It was a cage.

She was all too familiar with the way cages felt. With the way they made her feel small, powerless. How they left her all alone. Aviva was used to the feeling. Scared of the feeling.

She did everything in her power to not face it. She had killed the person who used to put her in cages, but she still felt helpless.

Here she was. Stuck. Always stuck.

"Hey," Idalia called through the tunnel.

Aviva could barely hear her. It was like she was under water. Everything was muffled. She couldn't breathe. And she would die.

"You okay?" Idalia asked, her voice echoing around Aviva.

Aviva wanted to say no, but her mouth wouldn't work.

A burning yellow-orange flame erupted at the end of the tunnel. "Follow the flame, Aviva."

Aviva took a ragged breath. She placed one foot in front of the other. Again and again. Somehow, she managed to make it to Idalia's flame. She collapsed against her sister, extinguishing the flame. "You're okay," Idalia whispered, holding her tightly.

After a few moments, Aviva stepped back and wiped her tears away. Idalia brought a flame to her hand again, guiding the rest of their people into the cave.

"I told you we would need the fire," Aviva whispered to Idalia as Sara led them deeper into the mountain.

Aviva stopped to gape a few minutes later when Sara stepped through a small doorway and revealed a massive room with several stone tables throughout. The ceiling was so high it disappeared into the darkness above. Several torches were placed along the walls. Sara made quick work of lighting them as she moved around the room.

"The kitchen is through there," Sara said, pointing toward a break in the rock. "And bedrooms are down the halls on that side," she said, pivoting to locate the dark hall of bedrooms leading away from the main room. "We'll have to double up on some rooms."

"I'm sure that'll be fine," Idalia said, turning in slow circles to take in the grand room. "This is fascinating," she whispered.

Sara nodded. "My pride and joy. A stone fortress just for you."

Idalia smiled.

Aviva was quiet, taking in the view. They had to be deep in the mountain. She could feel the hum of the earth all around her. Solid rock formed on every side, a true fortress. A fortress that would keep out Eira. A fortress to keep them safe. Keep all of them safe.

Sara walked away and began instructing the others on where to go, what rooms to share, what to start cooking in the kitchen. Idalia watched her closely. Sara had become the leader in her absence. She had prepared for everything. She was the heart of Summer.

Idalia slipped down the dark hall of bedrooms with Aviva at her side.

Aviva clutched Idalia's hand tightly as they walked into the darkness. Idalia gritted her teeth against the pain shooting through her arm. Her hand was not fully healed from Eira's attack, and it was especially noticeable when her sister had a death grip on it.

Idalia reached out her good hand and lit the torches as they walked down the hallway. Illuminating each step with small flickering flames. Holes in the rock lined the hallway, leaving a gaping view into the rooms. Some holes were covered with blankets to give the sense of privacy. Some were left wide open, but the rooms were empty.

They walked and walked until they reached the end of the

hall. They moved around people as rooms began to fill up, their people settling into their new home.

"There you are," Sara said, walking up from behind them. "Most everyone has been assigned a room."

"Good," Idalia said, nodding hello to a few kids who ran past them.

"I'll take you to your room now, if you're ready," Sara said. When Idalia nodded in response, Sara continued, "I hope you don't mind, but there's only one room fit for one of the Four." Sara grimaced as she said it, shame contorting her face.

"That's quite all right," Idalia said, throwing her arm around Aviva's shoulders. "We don't mind sharing, now do we?"

"Not at all," Aviva said, her voice quiet.

Sara nodded and stepped in front of them. "Right this way, then."

Idalia and Aviva followed Sara through a maze of hallways that all looked identical. Each hall was punctuated by the small torches lining every hallway. Some were already lit as more people got settled. At the end of an unlit hallway, Sara stopped. She pulled a key from her pocket and worked it into the only real door Idalia had noticed in the whole mountain.

Sara swung the door back on its hinges and walked inside the huge room. She walked the edges of the room and lit a few torches. Then, she stepped aside.

The room was very large. The huge bed barely took up any space at all. A couch sat on one wall, a fur blanket draped on the side. Chairs lined another wall as if meetings took place in this very room. Idalia turned in circles surveying the heavily decorated room.

"Wow," Aviva mouthed, running her hands over the fine bedspread.

"We can bring in another bed, if you need," Sara said, stepping toward the door.

Idalia laughed. "That bed is plenty big. Biggest bed I've ever seen."

Sara nodded, a small smile creeping on her face at her approval. "I will leave you to get settled then," she said.

Idalia watched Sara turn and begin to close the door. "Actually," she said. Sara halted. "Could you call a meeting? We need to discuss our next steps."

"Yes, of course, Lady Idalia."

Aviva stepped forward. "Could you also gather my people?"

Sara looked at Idalia who gave her approval. "Yes, gather both of our councils and let's meet."

Sara nodded and left, leaving Idalia and Aviva alone to wait for her return.

"What are our next steps?" Aviva asked, still running her hands over the bedspread.

Idalia huffed and plopped onto the bed. It bounced under her. The blanket was so soft under her fingertips. It seemed so delicate to be in a place made of rocks. "That's what I'm trying to decide," she said, settling into the mattress and wrapping the blanket around her shoulders. "It's not like I've ever had to decide things in a war." A small laugh escaped her lips.

"Right," Aviva said, sitting next to her. "This is kind of ridiculous if you think about it. Two girls from Texas having to decide how to handle the downfall of a whole world."

"Mmm," Idalia mumbled, leaning back and closing her eyes. "I'd so rather be back in Texas going to college and moving on with my life."

"Even I'd rather be back in Texas," Aviva said. Aviva sat still for a moment. "Actually, I don't think I would. I'm sure Season is better than going to jail for murder."

"I don't know," Idalia said, her voice thick with tiredness. "Jail won't kill you."

"True, but one of my sisters will."

A great pause shifted over the room. Idalia fumbled for something to say, something reassuring, but there wasn't anything. There was no reassurance. Because Aviva was right. One of her sisters would kill her, or she would murder again.

Idalia hopped up at the sound of a knock on the door, grateful for the disturbance. Sara stood just outside with her hands behind her back. She bowed her head just a little. "They're ready for you."

Idalia dropped the blanket and glanced behind her at Aviva who slid off the bed. They followed Sara out into the hall. Again, they walked barely lit hallways, turning randomly. There was no way Idalia would ever be able to find her way around without Sara's assistance. At least not through the back tunnels where they seemed to go deeper and deeper into the cave.

The only noise Idalia made as they walked was the echo of her shoes off the rocky walkway. Whoever was at the end of the journey would definitely hear her coming. And maybe that was the design of the place. Nowhere for hidden onslaughts to happen. Nowhere someone could sneak by. Nowhere to hide besides the darkness.

Sara led them to a big room with no decoration hanging from the walls. The space was occupied by several seats, all but two occupied by older men and women.

Idalia walked to an empty chair. Aviva headed for the other. Sara took up her place next to Idalia's chair. Every pair of eyes turned to her as she settled into the cushions. "Thank you for being here," she said, her voice trembling a bit as her nerves racked her body. "As we discussed earlier," Idalia said looking over at Aviva, "we haven't ever been in a situation quite like this. I believe we'd benefit from suggestions of what to do next."

The men and women looked at one another, and a hushed murmur grew over the crowd as they talked quietly to the people next to them.

"We need to stop Eira," Aviva said, her voice ringing strongly through the room. "Help with that," she instructed.

The men and women nodded, and they went to work.

40

Eira stood at the edge of Winter, watching, waiting for anything to happen. No one ran through the gate with her sisters in tow. No one came forward to offer her information on how and where to find the remaining two problems that stood in her way to become the queen of the only home she ever had.

She inhaled sharply as the gate slowly crept open. She stood off to the side, her hands clasped together in front of her. A horse galloped through the opening and turned sharply after the rider noticed her.

Jedrek sat proudly on top of his mount, ever the resilient soldier. The horse neighed as it neared Eira and stomped its feet as Jedrek pulled the reins. Eira watched as the gate closed behind him, no sisters to be seen.

"You have failed, yet again," Eira said, looking up at Jedrek.

"Season is wide. We will find them," Jedrek said, his shoulders rolling back.

Eira huffed a laugh. "Unlikely," she said, turning and marching away. Jedrek followed on his horse, but Eira paid him no mind. Instead, she walked straight to the stables and snapped at the stablehands to get Willow ready for a ride. They jumped into action.

Eira's beautiful horse was led outside of the stable minutes later, fully adorned in blanket and saddle. Eira mounted her horse with little effort and clicked her tongue. Willow walked toward the gate. "Tell Donovan I've gone to retrieve my sisters myself. Don't wait up," Eira said over her shoulder to Jedrek who clung to his horse's reins.

Eira left Winter behind, the sounds of her people disappearing as Willow galloped. The wind caressed her as they plunged through the dense forest surrounding Winter. She didn't know exactly where she was going, only that she would ride until Summer was under her. Until she spotted her sisters. Until she could finally bring them to Winter to end them and become queen.

Minutes, hours, days passed in a blur as Season transformed around her. Dusting off the wintery domain, the ground under Willow's hooves became harder with the heat. Humidity clung to her exposed neck and face. Sweat beaded on her forehead and rolled down her cheeks. Willow's coat was coated with slick sweat as they trudged through the brush.

They stopped only when it was necessary for Willow to rest and eat. Eira didn't so much as give her time to recuperate before mounting her horse again and riding farther away from Winter. She kept them hydrated with melted ice in her hands. Kept the heat as far away as she could with a few splashes of cold water over their bodies.

Eira enjoyed the silence her companion brought. No need for talking. Or directing. Commanding. No need for anything besides sitting upon Willow's back and keeping her eyes on full alert for any type of movement that might be her sisters.

Finally, Willow slowed.

Eira swiped a hand across her forehead. It came away wet. She pulled Willow to a stop and slid off the horse's back. She grabbed the reins in her hands and pulled Willow behind her as she made her way through the thin underbrush.

She was quiet as she marched through the forest, her steps nearly silent even over branches and twigs. The buzzing of insects surrounded her as she walked. She swatted a few away. Willow shook out her mane and the bugs flew away. With each step they took, the forest grew thinner and thinner. So thin that Eira could make out the outskirts of a town.

Summer. Finally, Summer was in view.

Eira stopped at the edge of the forest, still hidden by trees and bushes. She waited a few minutes for movement, for people to come out, for anything to point to life in Summer.

But there wasn't anything. Nothing moved, not even a bug or bird. No one left their dwellings. No one made a noise.

The silence grew louder and louder until Eira's skin crawled and she couldn't take it anymore. She left the cover of trees and stepped out of the forest and into the road that separated her from the town. The road was well traveled, that was easy for her to tell with the many footsteps smushed into the hard ground. But still, no one was there.

The town was empty. And her sisters were nowhere to be found.

41

Aviva kept her hand on the rock wall as she navigated through the cave. She followed the sounds of people chatting. Her chest tightened as the walls pressed in around her, but she kept walking, trying to steady her breathing.

The drumming in her ears shielded the noises she was trying to follow, making it harder to find her way.

A distinct laugh cut past the thrumming in her veins. Her breaths eased a bit as she rounded a corner and saw her sister in the middle of a group of Summer people, all clad in vibrant reds. They smiled and cheered, enjoying themselves in their cave with their lady.

Aviva stood on the outskirts of the room, much like the rest of her people from Spring who sat along the walls and whispered quietly with one another.

"Glad to see you managed to make your way around," Idalia said, her sing-songy voice echoing off the walls as she walked toward her.

Aviva pushed her hair back from her face, a few beads of

sweat gliding into her hair as she did. "It's rather confusing down here."

Idalia nodded and leaned in close. "To be honest, I still don't know my way around," she whispered as if it were a secret.

"I don't see how anyone does. Everything looks identical," Aviva said, noting the same stone wall in this room was the same as every other inch of the underground cave.

Idalia shrugged. "What can I do you for, little sister?" she asked, swinging an arm around Aviva's shoulders and walking toward another hallway. "Or did you just finally get bored of our room?"

Aviva was silent as they left the open area and traveled down another hallway that turned so many ways Aviva couldn't keep track. She wondered if Idalia even knew where they were going. "I've noticed something," Aviva finally said. "I don't know if it's a big problem or not. Might just take some time, but our people don't interact with one another."

Idalia nodded. "Yea, I noticed. Your Spring people are much more reserved than the people of Summer."

"Do you think it'll cause an issue?" Aviva paused. "If they don't get along, I mean."

Idalia pulled Aviva down another hallway. "I'm not sure. Doesn't hurt to fix it before it becomes a problem though. We need to unite our people. That's what will save us in the end. That's the only way to get rid of Eira, or so the advisors say."

"Unite them just to pit them against one another again if it comes down to just you and me?" Aviva asked, her voice low.

"We can't think about that," Idalia said, her voice tight. "Right now, we have to deal with Eira. And keep our people safe. That is all."

Aviva agreed with a nod of her head. Eira was the biggest of their worries right now. And as their advisors had said in countless meetings, Eira had far more people on her side than Idalia and Aviva had separately. They needed to come together. At least for a while. At least until the threat of Eira was dealt with.

"So how do we get them to come together?" Aviva mused.

"I have an idea, but I'm pretty sure you won't like it," she laughed.

A few hours later, Idalia pulled Aviva into the main meeting hall. A large room with high ceilings and lots of tables where most everyone sat to eat. It had completely transformed from the last time Aviva had seen it. The walls were decorated with random blankets, ribbons hung from the ceiling and blew lightly in the wind from a makeshift spinning fan. The tables were pushed to the wall leaving a large open floor. Food was set out on the tables on one wall.

Aviva grimaced.

"I told you you might not like it," Idalia said, bumping her shoulder against Aviva's.

"It's fine," Aviva said, looking around. A few people stood to the side, instruments in their hands. Ready and waiting. "I'm not sure if the people of Spring share my disdain for parties."

"I guess we'll find out," Idalia said, shrugging and walking into the center of the room. Several people in red greeted her, asking questions and floating away once she answered.

Footsteps approached, echoing off the stone. It sounded like thunder as more and more people spread the news of the party happening in the main hall. An onslaught of people draped in red rushed into the room. They were already dancing to the music that fluttered around. Slowly, the crowd of red mingled with shades of green.

Aviva watched as her people came in, most in small groups. They stayed by themselves on the outskirts of the red crowd.

Some even took seats at the tables lining the walls. They talked in whispers, no one able to hear them over the loud music.

"You might be right," Idalia said, standing next to Aviva once again. "Looks like your people aren't big on parties."

"Well, we can't all be like the people of Summer," Aviva said, glancing to the middle of the room where a large group of Summer people hopped around and swayed to the music. They laughed loudly, bumping and spinning into one another. All of Summer had come it seemed. And all of Summer was on the floor dancing away.

"This isn't going to do anything if they don't mingle," Idalia said, eyeing the seated people of Spring.

A girl walked past them, her hands in the air, getting ready to join the rest of her people. Idalia called out to her. She stopped and leaned in so Idalia could whisper in her ear. The girl nodded and danced through the room, headed to a small group of Spring people around her age. She extended her hand in offering and waited as the girls spoke quietly to one another. After a few beats, a girl in green took her hand and let the Summer girl lead her onto the floor.

A small smile played at the Spring girl's lips as the girl from Summer pulled her into the crowd. She stood uncomfortably for a few moments, and then as if she thought better of it, the Spring girl raised her hands and started jumping in time to the music. Her friends at the table quickly joined her.

The night raged on as more and more people joined in on the dancing and eating and enjoying one another's company. Aviva stood in the corner watching carefully as her people mingled with Idalia's. Finally, it seemed, they were getting along. Finally, they were united. At least for this one night. Aviva didn't know if it would roll over into the morning or the coming days of waiting for Eira's inevitable attack. All she knew was that her people were finally relaxing. Finally finding their place in the underground cave made to protect another princess of Season.

The torches twinkled as the fire slowly burned out, the night along with it.

Idalia twirled across the dance floor, leaving people smiling in her wake as she made her way to her sister. "Well, what do you think?" she asked when she reached Aviva's perch on the wall.

Aviva shrugged. "I guess they like to party," she said.

Idalia laughed. "Do you think it will bring them together? You think they'll fight for us?" she asked, bending her head down close to Aviva's in a conspiratorial way.

"For now," Aviva said.

Idalia straightened. "Well, that's all we need. For now," she said before twirling away and merging back into the crowd.

Aviva waited a few more minutes. After a while, her eyes grew heavy and her feet hurt from standing so long. She turned away from the party and found her way back through the various dark halls until she reached the familiar door of her and Idalia's room. She ignored the panicky feeling that had followed her the whole way. She closed the door behind her and fell on top of the bed. Within minutes, Aviva was sound asleep.

42

Eira was exhausted. She had spent days searching Summer and all its little towns. Her sisters weren't there. No one was.

"Let's go home, Willow," she said reluctantly to her horse who neighed softly and nestled her head against Eira's shoulder. Eira pulled herself up into the saddle and clicked her tongue. Willow walked them slowly through the town and back into the forest's edge.

The heat was a terrible thing that Eira couldn't get used to, even having grown up in Texas. Being in Winter all this time had done her a disservice. But, her powers kept them comfortable as they trotted toward her home. Hours passed and days waned as they traveled at a steady pace. The sound of a stream running through the forest made her pull Willow to a stop.

She dismounted and brought them through the brush until the sparkling stream was right in front of them. The clear water was inviting, so much so Eira partially undressed and stepped into the cool stream. The water was a welcome weight against her as it flowed all around. Energy filled her being as her element replenished her. She dunked her head under the water, closing her eyes and finally relaxing. Willow drank the clean water beside her as she sat on the pebbled bottom.

She didn't know how long they wasted by the stream. The minutes passed by in a hurry. But she didn't want to get out, not even when her skin wrinkled beyond recognition.

A cackling laugh froze her to her spot. Her heart hammered in her chest. She waited a few moments, and then not hearing anything else, pulled herself out of the stream. She paused, waiting for another sound. Voices floated toward her from downstream.

She quickly and quietly shook off the excess water and made her way into the dense part of the forest. Among the brush, she moved downstream.

A group of five men sat around a small fire. Their faces were covered in hoods. Red hoods. Summer people.

Eira watched as they fed sticks into the fire, the meat on the end sending a sweet smelling smoke into the air. They paid her no mind as she circled them withWillow a few paces behind her, staying hidden and quiet.

"Do you think we'll find her?" one of the hooded men asked the group.

Another one answered around a bite of food, "I don't see why she'd leave the comfort and security of her land, so I'm sure she's in Winter just as Lady Idalia believes."

Eira sucked in a breath. They were talking about her. And Idalia had sent them.

She waited for the day to disappear and slip into night. The group settled down onto their blankets and readied for sleep. Before the last one could lay his head down, Eira struck four of them through the heart with a dagger of ice. Blood poured into the earth.

The last hooded figure jumped up and sprinted away from

the fire. His panicked breathing led Eira through the darkening forest, Willow behind her. She mounted Willow at the same time the last scout untied his own horse from a tree trunk and fled.

Willow took chase.

Eira pulled the reins back, keeping Willow at a nice pace and far enough away from the fleeing scout. The scout never stopped, not once on their journey through the forest. So, Eira didn't either.

She slowed even more as the scout broke from the forest and ran toward a mountain range. She stayed hidden in the forest, close enough to see him riding across the rocky terrain but far enough away that the scout couldn't see her every time he whipped his head around to look into the darkness. He dismounted, slapped the horse on the butt, and ran toward a small opening in the mountain cave.

Eira watched him disappear into the mountainside.

A smile grew on her face.

She had found them.

She turned Willow and raced home to tell her people where to send their army and to prepare to end this once and for all.

Eira didn't stop on her way home. Not once. Willow didn't seem inclined to stop either as she kept barreling closer and closer to Winter.

Winter's closed gate creaked open on its hinges, allowing Eira and Willow inside. A crowd of people greeted her as she slid off her horse. Immediately Willow's reins were in someone else's hands, and she was being led to the stables.

Donovan hurried down the road toward her. "My queen," he said, bowing low as he approached. "How was your trip?"

Eira smiled and trekked to her house with Donovan following close behind. "Very informative," Eira said, walking up the steps. The manor's warmth greeted her as she stepped into the entrance hall. She made her way up to her bedroom. "Send Jedrek. I know where we have to go," Eira said before slipping into her bathroom and undressing.

"Oh, and bring some food," she shouted as she shut the door and stepped into a warm bath.

A knock sounded on the door a few minutes later. Reluctantly, Eira rinsed off and got out of the tub. She draped a robe around her shoulders and tied it closed in the front.

Jedrek stood by the door. A tray of food laid on her table. She sat and began munching on the food as Jedrek waited quietly. Donovan came in a few moments later. "So," Eira said between bites. "I did what you could not."

Jedrek nodded. "I hear you found your sisters."

"Yes," Eira said slowly. She let the sound of her chewing fill the room. "They are hiding in the mountainside. At least, that is where one of her scouts led me."

"You did not set eyes on your sisters?" Jedrek asked.

"No," Eira said, grinding her teeth. "The only people I saw the whole time were scouts. And once I killed his four companions, he ran off to a hidden cave in the mountain. So my guess," Eira said tightly, "is that is where everyone is hiding."

Eira plopped another bite of fruit into her mouth. "That is where we will send our army."

43

Idalia rolled over in bed, her arm covering up her face. She groaned and rubbed her eyes.

"You know," Aviva said from a chair across the room. Idalia sat up at the sound of her voice. "If you would quit staying up so late partying with everyone, you wouldn't be so grumpy in the morning."

Idalia chucked a small pillow across the room. Aviva easily dodged the throw. "I'm doing what I can to intertwine our people, Aviva. Someone's gotta do it."

Aviva laughed. "Yeah, it's a real hardship to dance and eat all night. I couldn't imagine."

"No, you can't since you hide away the whole time."

Aviva shrugged. "There are more pressing matters."

Idalia groaned again and rolled out of bed, instantly awake from the cold stone on her bare feet. She padded over to the small cutout bathroom. A chamber pot sat in one corner and a large water basin was in the other. A mirror hung over the basin so she could see just how terribly she looked. She changed out of her night clothes, readying for the day. The day that was the same over and over. There wasn't much to do in a secret underground mountain cave. Especially when everyone's goal was to keep you safe and alive.

Idalia shrugged off the unwelcome feeling and splashed her face with cool water. She left the bathroom to find Aviva in the same spot, a book in her hands.

"I'm going to the kitchens. You want anything?" Idalia asked as she headed out the door.

"No, I actually eat at a decent time since I wake up like a normal person."

"Yeah, yeah, yeah," Idalia said with a wave of her hand. She closed the bedroom door behind her and walked toward the kitchen. It took longer than it should have, getting lost around several turns, but Idalia kept going in what she hoped was the right direction.

The familiar wide open room of the main hall finally greeted her. Last night's decorations still hung on the walls. But several people were milling around putting everything back in place for today's meal times. Idalia had found that most of the people, Spring and Summer alike, loved to dine together. Every morning after a party, they would put the tables back out so they could all enjoy meals.

Idalia smiled as she walked through what was basically the cafeteria.

"Oh," she shouted as she was knocked back against a wall.

"Oh, my, I am so sorry," a man said, grasping her arms to steady her. "Lady Idalia, please forgive me," he said, once his eyes focused on her.

Idalia waved him away. "Of course," she said, rubbing the back of her head. "Why are you in such a rush?"

The man slid his red hood off his head. His eyes were wide but sunken as if he hadn't gotten a good night's sleep in a while. At least Idalia wasn't the only one.

"My lady," he said, his voice lowering as he noticed the small group of people in the main hall. "I was sent to scout for your sister," he whispered.

Idalia nodded. She faintly recalled her advisors asking to know Eira's whereabouts and suggesting a search party of sorts. "Where are the others?" she asked, looking behind him as if the other men would appear out of thin air.

He shook his head and closed his eyes. "I'm afraid," he said, choking on his words. "I'm afraid they are not coming back. They were killed in the night. Spears of ice."

"Spears of ice," Idalia said, her blood running cold. "Eira," she said.

44

News traveled fast of Eira's antics. The killing of four scouts set everyone on edge. The parties had stopped. The whispers spread, rampantly. Aviva ignored them all. Nothing good would come of the gossip. Nothing good would come of people believing Eira was unstoppable.

Aviva walked the halls, alone, basking in the silence she offered herself. She couldn't shake the itchy feeling crawling across her skin to get out, to get away. But there was nowhere to go. And she couldn't leave all of her people even if she had an escape plan. She couldn't leave them all to die at Eira's murderous hands. So, she walked. A lot.

The dark caves were less claustrophobic as the days went on. She grew used to them. But she didn't like them. She missed the light of day. She was glad she at least had the smell of the earth under her feet.

She took a sharp right and found herself face to face with the opening that would lead outside. She hadn't dared go outside since they'd been brought to the mountain. No one had. They were all content to live out their days in the darkness and shadows of the stone walls. But Aviva couldn't. She needed a break from the bleakness. Needed to see her green earth again. To feel its connection. To bathe in her element.

She looked behind and around her. No one would see her leave.

She took a deep breath. She felt the walls pressing in around her as she wiggled through the crevice. She held her breath, felt the beating of her heart grow louder and louder, harder against her chest. But she pushed it away. She could make the last few steps without succumbing to the fear. She could, she knew, because she'd done it before. Albeit with the help of her sister. But she was strong enough. At least that's what she kept telling herself. She was strong enough to take the final steps. So she did.

She blinked hard as daylight blinded her.

She bent down and placed her hand on the ground, feeling the grass come alive under her fingers. Energy surged into her body as she connected with her element again. She looked up at the sky, taking a deep, long breath.

Aviva stood, her legs sure as she walked across the ground, the grass sticking out from underneath the scattered rocks. The remnant of her injury was no longer present. A breeze ruffled her hair and clothes as she absentmindedly stretched out her body. She hadn't realized how cramped she had felt in the cave. How her body wasn't being used to its full capacity. How weak her powers had felt deep in the dark.

Aviva spent a long time exploring the outside of the mountain. She sat on the rocks, basking in the sun. She took her shoes off, feeling the grass between her toes. She threw pebbles as far as she could.

When the sun made its final descent, and the shadows started to surround her, she stood and ventured back to the mouth of the cave. She turned to look one last time at the ever expanding scenery around her.

Off in the distance, she spotted flickering lights. She squinted and peered into the growing darkness. Flames, that's what the lights were. Flames on the edge of the forest. Flames in the form of torches being held by people setting up tents.

Aviva left the mouth of the cave and wandered as close as she dared, close enough to get a good look. To see the people of Winter, in as few clothes as she'd ever seen them, rummaging around the forest's edge putting together a camp. And her sister, the sister with the most in common with her, sitting in the middle of them all, directing her people.

Eira was here.

Aviva ran back to the crevice in the mountainside and disappeared inside.

She broke through the other side and took off running. Her steps echoed off the walls, her feet pounding against the hard ground as she rounded corner after corner. She slid to a stop in front of her and Idalia's room. "Eira's here," she said as she threw the door open.

Stunned silence fell.

"What?" Idalia said, whipping around to face Aviva.

Aviva took a deep breath, trying hard to get her breathing under control. "Eira," she said, "is here. She's camped outside."

"How do you know?" Idalia asked, standing up and coming toward her.

"I was just outside," Aviva started.

Idalia's eyes widened. "Aviva," she said in a harsh tone.

Aviva rolled her eyes at the condescending timbre of her name on Idalia's tongue. "I was outside getting fresh air. Eira and a whole army is setting up camp on the forest's edge. She's here," Aviva emphasized.

Idalia ran a hand along her face, a shudder wracking through her body. "What are we gonna do?" she asked in a whisper.

"I don't know," Aviva said, "but we better do it fast."

45

The sound of tents rising into the night filled Eira with joy. A joy she hadn't felt in some time. She had done it. She had found her sisters. She had sent her armies. And she would destroy them.

Eira relaxed, laying back onto a bed made of many blankets and pillows. Two ladies stood near her waving large leaves in her direction despite the fact she could keep herself cool on her own if she desired. But she liked for her people to work, to do something for her. Even if it was less efficient.

Jedrek made quick work of putting up a tent only a few feet away from Eira's. Donovan sat by watching him work. It only made sense that Eira's two most important men would be close. And a good thing they were. "Jedrek, dear," Eira said in a sickly sweet voice. Jedrek paused in hammering the tent pegs into the hard ground. He turned on a heel and walked toward her. And then he stood silently, waiting.

"I would like to know a little more about what we're facing," Eira said, extending her hand toward the mountain that housed her sisters and their people.

He nodded curtly and strode away without a word. Eira clicked her tongue in annoyance.

"I know how much you like to play games with him," Donovan said, coming up to her side. "But I would let him be."

"Which is exactly why I'm in charge and you only advise," Eira said.

"That may be," he said, making himself comfortable on a pile of pillows next to her.

Eira looked over the growing camp. Even in the darkening night, she could see just how far and wide her army swept. She smiled at the thought of her sisters learning of her whereabouts. How frantic they would be when they realized they were trapped. That she was finally here to end them all.

"You sure do defend Jedrek a lot," Eira mused.

The pillows around her moved as he shrugged. "We must look after our people."

"Some more than others, it seems." Eira settled back and closed her eyes.

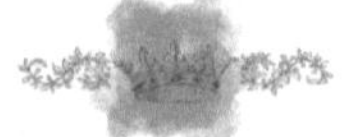

Some time later, Eira was awoken by footsteps. She peered into the darkness. The forest around her made everything pitch black except for the dying fires spread out around her camp.

"My queen," Jedrek said as he approached, followed by a few other men. They stood a few feet away as Jedrek came to Eira's side. "We have canvassed the mountain."

Eira nodded eagerly, a plan of attack already settling into her mind.

"Unfortunately, there is only one entrance. And from the looks of it, only one person will be able to fit through the crevice at a time. There seems to be no way to get our whole army in without allowing them the opportunity to pick us off one by one."

Eira blew hot breath out of her nose and straightened her spine. "So we came all this way for nothing?"

Jedrek shook his head. "I do not believe so. Of course, there is no way to know how many supplies they have inside, but eventually they will have to come out. We hold here until they do."

Eira nodded. "I will consider it," she said, dismissing him. Jedrek and the others disappeared into the night. "It's one thing after another," Eira said under her breath, her eyes rolling.

"Becoming queen of Season is no easy feat," Donovan agreed, closing his eyes and falling into a deep sleep.

"It would seem so," Eira mused to herself before she let herself get comfortable and fall back to sleep.

46

Idalia pulled Aviva after her, while Sara led the way. Sara opened the room they always used to meet with the advisors. And all of them were already there, whispering amongst themselves.

"Council," Idalia said in greeting. A hush fell over the room. "News of Eira's whereabouts is sure to surface soon," she started. The advisors turned wary eyes on her. "We need to come up with a plan so everyone doesn't freak out."

"Freak out?" one advisor said, his eyebrows raised in question.

"Uh," Idalia stammered. "Before we lose control."

"Ah, yes," the advisor said and buried his head back into his notebook.

"Is there a way we can all get out without coming face to face with Eira's army?" Aviva asked, taking a seat.

"No," a woman said, looking up toward Sara. "We made sure we were very secure when planning this mountainside escape. We didn't intend to have an army sitting outside."

"I'm sure no one intended it," Aviva said, her voice rising a bit.

Idalia placed a hand on Aviva's shoulder, sending a warming touch through her body. "The mountain was a great idea. Very strong. It will last for however long Eira decides to camp out. Will we though?"

Another advisor flipped through a small journal. "We have enough stock to last a few weeks. Maybe longer if we ration." The other advisors nodded in agreement.

Idalia finally sat in the last open chair and huffed a sigh. "There's got to be something we can do besides just sit here and wait for Eira to make a move." She rubbed at her cheek absentmindedly. "That's all we do is wait."

"And when the waiting is done," Aviva said, looking at her sister, "we won't even be ready to face her. She has an army. A fully operational and trained army." The emphasis on the word 'trained' hung in the air around them.

Idalia didn't have an army. Aviva didn't have one either. Not one that compared in any way to Eira's.

"We need an army," Aviva whispered, her eyes to the ceiling.

"Unfortunately, the people of Spring aren't the soldiering type. We don't typically fight," a small lady said from across the circle.

"Summer has a few soldiers, but not nearly enough to take on the Winter army," a Summer man agreed.

"But did Winter have an army, before Eira, I mean?" Idalia asked, standing and pacing around the room.

The advisors looked toward one another. "Not that we were aware of," one said.

"But they've always had to work the earth more, so they're inherently stronger," another said.

"Yes, and colder."

"Right, right," Idalia said, "we all have our strengths. We just need to learn what ours are and put them to good use."

Aviva nodded. "Do you know of anyone with any type of fighting experience?"

The advisors talked amongst themselves. Then, they listed out a few names.

"Great," Idalia said, "call them here. We need to start training."

47

The main hall was turned back into an open space with the tables up against the walls. Aviva, with Idalia at her side, stood at the front of the room. Sara and Mara were off to the side, a group of four men and two women lined up beside them.

A crowd of Summer and Spring people, young and old alike, lined the walls. They waited. Anticipation hung heavy in the air underscored by a nervous energy fluttering around. Aviva picked at her nails.

"As you all know," Idalia said, her voice loud and clear. "Eira has decided to camp outside. We don't know how long she will be there or what her intentions are. But with the guidance of our advisors," she said, nodding toward Aviva to include her, "we have decided the best use of our time is to begin training."

Idalia waited as the murmuring started. She let it slowly die down. "Eira has a large army. One that has been honed over the last few months under her direction. Now, we don't have that much time, nor do we possess the same skills as the people of Winter. But, I believe we can bring about our best abilities and stand a chance if it comes down to a fight."

Whispered conversations started again. They grew louder and louder as the seconds passed. As the people realized a battle was coming. As people finally understood just what kind of threat Eira posed to them all.

"Look," Aviva said, stepping forward. The crowd quieted. "I understand a lot of you haven't fought a day in your life. It's peaceful in Season. There's no need for controversy since the trials are supposed to give you the new queen or king. But, this time is different. Your wonderful King Quilo," Aviva said with a roll of her eyes as sarcasm leaked from her voice at the mention of her birth father, "decided to change everything and not even stick around to see how it affected Season. It won't be easy to change your mindset. But you will, to survive. You'll do anything to survive. Trust me on that."

Ted's face popped into her mind. Blood poured from his mouth. She trembled at the memory. But she was right, when the time came, these people would do whatever it took. It was either kill or be killed. And no one liked dying.

"Like Lady Aviva mentioned," Sara said, "you'll do whatever it takes. And the first thing is to train. These fine men and women have volunteered to assist us. We may not know much, but I know we can come together to form a united front against Eira."

More people nodded in the crowd. A sense of pride shuffled over them. A sense of determination. A sense of purpose.

"Let's begin," Idalia said, clapping her hands together once.

The six leaders went around the main hall, pulling people into groups. When there were six groups situated around the room, the leaders began going through simple stretches. Reluctantly, the people of Spring and Summer copied them. At first, they were small, awkward movements, but as the stretches deepened and the people focused more, there was a change.

Aviva sat back and watched.

"Let's hope this works," Idalia whispered.

Aviva nodded. "It's our only chance."

Their people took up several defensive stances under the leaders' instructions. A few of the younger children giggled as they moved their body this way and that way. But most everyone had a stern look on their face. Their eyebrows knitted together and their lips pressed tight in concentration as they tried to get the movements just right.

"It may be wise if you join as well," Sara said, stepping up beside Idalia and Aviva. "Your powers are exceptional, but I believe working alongside your people will instill a strong desire in them."

"Of course," Idalia said, walking to a group with mostly middle aged men and women.

Aviva joined a small group made of mostly children. They were more her size, anyways. Aviva got into line with them, eyes on the leader. She moved her body just as he did, leaning into a deep stretch. A kid beside her lost his balance and stumbled into Aviva.

He nervously laughed and righted himself. Aviva stuck out her hand, still halfway bent in the stretch. "I'm Aviva, what's your name?"

"I know who you are," he said quietly. "Everyone knows who you are." His small hiccup of a laugh echoed in their corner of the room.

Aviva smiled and turned her eyes back on the leader.

"John," the boy whispered. "My name's John."

"Nice to meet you, John," Aviva whispered back.

Aviva jogged down the hallway, the children in her group following close behind her. Her breathing was steady as they ran and ran. People dodged them as they had been doing for days now. The children behind her laughed as they made their way through the mountain in continuous circles.

They stopped jogging in the main hall. "Good run," Aviva said to the kids before they ran off to play.

Idalia found Aviva stretching on the floor a few minutes later. "Enjoy your run?" she asked.

Aviva looked up at her sister. "I'm pretty sure we'll be the fittest group of us all," she said with a laugh. Idalia plopped down next to her.

"I don't know about that," she said, sticking her arm out and showing off her biceps. "Pretty sure we have more muscles."

"Yeah, that's what all those push-ups will do for you," Aviva said, stretching out her other leg.

"Hey, you need to strengthen your leg," she said, nodding toward the scar on Aviva's leg, "and I need my arm to be in tip-top shape."

"We all have our strengths and weaknesses," Aviva said, copying the same slogan they've been saying for the last week. And it had been true, too. A lot of their people had weaknesses, but a lot had hidden strengths that would come in handy if Eira decided to ever stop squatting outside the mountain.

"Has anyone been out to see if Eira is still there?" Aviva said quietly.

Idalia shook her head. "I don't think anyone wants to risk it just yet."

"Probably a good idea," she said. Silence covered them for a while.

"All this exercising we've been doing," Idalia said, pushing herself to a stand, "has got me starving. You want something from the kitchen?"

"No, thanks," Aviva said, letting her walk a few paces away.

Idalia screeched as she toppled to the floor, barely catching herself before her face slammed into the stone. Everyone in the room paused.

Idalia turned and looked sharply at Aviva. "Really?" she said, reaching down to her legs and unwrapping the vines that stuck them together.

Aviva laughed. "All this exercising has me wanting to exercise my element," she shrugged.

"I wouldn't do that, if I were you," Idalia said, her eyes squinting as she looked at the vines playing in Aviva's hands.

Aviva stood up slowly. "Good thing you're not me," she said, shooting out her hands. Vines flew through the air and Aviva took off running. She didn't even turn around to see Idalia burst into flame, the vines disintegrating around her.

"Oh, I'm gonna get you for that," Idalia called after Aviva.

"Not if you can't catch me," Aviva said as she disappeared around a corner.

Idalia's laugh echoed off the walls as she chased after her. Aviva paid no mind to everyone scooting away from them as they ran.

Idalia shot her hand out, a fireball blasting through the hall. Aviva threw up a wall of dirt as she skidded into another hallway. She stumbled backwards, falling to the ground at the force of another body. "Oh, get up, get up," John said, scrambling toward her. "She's coming," he squealed as he pulled Aviva to a stand.

Aviva laughed as John ran toward Idalia, giving her time to

get away. And she did, she took off running, leaving Idalia in her dust.

She didn't stop running, putting distance between her and Idalia until she heard a scream stop short. She skidded to a stop, doubled back, rounded the corner, and saw John crouched down with his arms tight around his body. He had his back to Idalia who was a few feet away. A fireball raced toward John in what felt like slow motion.

Aviva shouted, her words bouncing all around them but the roar in her ears made it impossible to discern the words.

Without a thought, Aviva rushed to John and pulled him into herself. She put her back to the oncoming fire. The hallway rippled with heat. She stomped her foot on the ground. Behind her, the cave walls caved in, shielding them from the fire.

"Are you okay?" Aviva asked John when the roaring in her ears stopped and the rocks settled.

John looked up at her, his lips trembling with his reply, "Yes."

"It's all right," she whispered, pulling him closer and hugging him as hard as she could. Finally, his trembling stopped.

Idalia's muffled voice worked its way through the small openings in the rocks. "Aviva? Are you okay?" Aviva could hear the panic in her voice, the worry. She took a deep breath and stomped her foot again. The rocks rained down around them.

"I'm so sorry," Idalia said, slowly approaching. "I couldn't stop it once it left my hand."

Aviva nodded. "I know."

Idalia kneeled down to John's level. "I'm so sorry, John. That must've been scary."

John nodded, not looking at Idalia. A small tremble still present on his lips. He looked at Aviva once more before unlocking himself from her grasp and running off.

Aviva stood up, shaking off the dirt that had collected on her shoulders. "We can't be the one to put our people in danger," she said, her voice hardened.

"I know," Idalia said, her head hanging in shame. "I didn't mean to."

Aviva nodded and turned away from her. "We need to find a better place to practice. Because we do need to practice, but there's no point if we kill all our people in the process."

"I'll ask Sara."

Aviva nodded and left Idalia standing in the middle of the broken hallway.

48

Idalia stood alone, leaning against the wall. She watched Aviva train with her people using her hands and feet to fight—fighting with everything except her powers.

She hadn't touched them since the incident with John, at least not to Idalia's knowledge. The sinking feeling in the pit of Idalia's stomach deepened. She was the cause. The cause of all of it. She would be the reason her people weren't ready to face Eira. The reason Aviva wasn't ready.

Idalia pushed off the wall and left. She felt Aviva's hard stare as she walked away. But she didn't turn back, not that Aviva would speak to her even if she did turn around.

Instead, she went to find Sara.

She found her a few minutes later sitting in the middle of a group of older individuals from both Spring and Summer. They talked quietly amongst themselves, hidden away in the corner of the poorly lit room.

Idalia waited a few moments before interrupting. As soon as she approached, Sara stood and excused herself. The others were back to murmuring before they had gotten a few steps away.

"Had a secret meeting, huh?" Idalia asked as they meandered down a hallway.

"Not secret," Sara said. "We had things to discuss."

"Privately," Idalia said. Sara nodded her head in agreement.

They walked quietly through the halls. Idalia wasn't sure who was leading the way, just that they were moving. And to be perfectly honest, she was a little lost.

"I take it you sought me out for a reason?"

"Oh, yes," Idalia said. "I need to talk to you."

Sara glanced at her. "About?"

Idalia smiled nervously. She tried pushing the feeling away, but for some reason the thought of asking Sara for even more than what she had already been given felt selfish. And she knew, without a doubt, Sara would give her what she asked for. As she always had.

"Aviva and I," Idalia started. "We need to train. With our powers."

Sara nodded again.

"We need more room. Without the others." Idalia pulled up short, placing a hand on Sara's forearm. "We need to go outside."

Sara's eyes widened. Her mouth tightened into a straight line. "Absolutely not," she said with no room to argue.

"No?" Idalia asked, confusion muddling the syllable. "We need to train. Without the chance of hurting the people who are supposed to fight for us. Who will likely die for us," Idalia said in a harsh whisper. "That's not up for discussion."

Sara took a breath. "I agree you need to train. I agree you need to keep everyone here safe. But you will not, under any circumstance, step foot outside of the mountain."

Idalia's eyebrows shot up, and she took a step back. "Are you my mother?"

Sara laughed. "If I was your mother, you'd already be dead, Lady Idalia," she said with a small incline of her head and a slight curtsy.

"That is very true," Idalia said, "but the fact remains. We need an arena to use our powers. Otherwise, we'll be no match for Eira."

Sara nodded and began walking again. "As it happens, the secret meeting we were having was considering just that."

"Oh really?"

"Really," Sara said. "Follow me."

And so Idalia did. They walked through the mountain, farther than Idalia had ever gone. So far it would've been pitch black if not for the small flame she called to her palm.

"After the incident," Sara started cautiously, "with John, we knew it was no longer safe for you and Lady Aviva to train with the others."

Idalia made a small sound of agreement. She pushed the image of Aviva holding John's little body behind the wall of earth away. She didn't need a reminder of how terribly close she had come to hurting a child. Let alone a child who would fight to keep her sister safe from Eira.

They walked even farther into the mountain. "I've been working on a space that would keep everyone safe."

Sara stopped walking. Idalia pulled up beside her and peered into the darkness. The flame on her palm grew.

Shadows scattered around the now visible room. Pillars of earth dotted the room randomly, holding the ceiling and the whole mountain above them. They were deep underground.

"This is perfect," Idalia breathed.

Sara nodded her head once, quickly, "I thought so."

The room was far larger than any other one Idalia had seen. It was tucked away from everyone. It was safe.

Idalia swung her arm out. The flame in her hand shot through the room and splattered against a wall. The answering darkness made Idalia sigh with relief.

"Just checking to see if it was fireproof," Idalia said with a shrug of her shoulders.

Sara shook her head, but Idalia saw the small smile that crept onto her lips.

"I've gotta show Aviva."

"Of course," Sara said, turning on her heel and leading Idalia back to the main workings of the cave.

49

Eira walked the perimeter of the camp. She peered through the cover of trees to look at the mountain. She had sent scouts many times, and every time she got the same response. Only one entrance. Her sisters were contained inside. It'd be best to wait them out.

But she was tired of waiting. Always waiting. She needed action. Needed to feel productive, like she was working toward her goal of becoming queen instead of just sitting on her butt.

The weeks had been long, and with it, Eira grew more and more restless. Her people distanced themselves with each passing day. They didn't want to be near her. She could hardly blame them. Bubbles of anger rose in her stomach. The need to be active set her body on fire. If only she had her sister's power, she could burn the world around her. But instead, she'd have to freeze it.

She walked to the very edge of the camp. A distinct shift in the earth, how flat the grass laid on her side, showed just how long they had been here. Long enough for the ground to grow weary under their feet.

She longed for the comforts of her manor in Winter. The comfort of the chill wind back in her town, but she would stay here, on the edge of Summer until her sisters faced her once and for all.

She placed her hand against a tree trunk. Ice instantly covered its bark, from the roots all the way to the leaves. The leaves snapped off the branches, icicles sprinkling down around her. The tightening in her chest eased just a bit as the ice sucked the life out of the tree. Just as she would do to her sisters. She would do whatever it took for Season to be hers alone. For Season to finally be her home.

Eira whirled around at the sound of footsteps. Donovan stepped gingerly in her path. He bowed his head slightly. "My queen," he said, and then he waited.

"Yes?" she asked, the urge to roll her eyes at his interruption strong.

"Your food awaits you at your tent."

"I would barely call what we've been living on food," she said, letting her eyes do what they wanted.

"You are always welcome to return to Winter. You would be far more comfortable there," Donovan said as if he had read her longing thoughts.

"I'm aware," Eira said, finally dropping her hand from the trunk. "But this isn't about comfort. I will stay here until I have no choice but to go, and given that my sisters don't seem inclined to ever leave the mountain, I'll be here a while."

"As you wish." He turned and walked away.

The sticky silence surrounded her. Eira rubbed her hands together. Ice crumbled between her palms. She formed a long spear, reared back, and let it fly through the air.

The spear landed with a satisfying thud against the rocks in front of the entrance to the cave. Not close enough to do any damage, but close enough to send a message. She was here, and she wasn't going anywhere.

She let go of all her power, pushing it toward the mountain cave. Her element poured from her, shooting across the land in a single sheet of thick ice. Finally, she could breathe again. She wasn't drowning in her power. She wiped her ice cold hands against her pants and turned away, the remnants of her message at her back. Already, the ice seeped into her veins, her element coming back even stronger.

50

Aviva followed Idalia into the darkness.

"Sara said they've been looking for a place for a while," Idalia said as she made the final turn into the deepest cavern.

Aviva kept her distance, a few steps behind her older sister. Idalia stopped walking. A flame grew brighter in her palm. Aviva could feel the heat of it on her face. For a second, Aviva could only see a similar flame hurtling through the air toward a boy. She shook her head, clearing her thoughts. Idalia had apologized. It had been an accident. John was okay.

"What do you think?" Idalia asked when Aviva didn't say anything.

Aviva finally took in the room. There was plenty of space. It was dark, but it was better than the hallways flooded with their people. "I think we may need some more of your fire," she said, attempting a smirk.

Idalia laughed. "Sara's already on it."

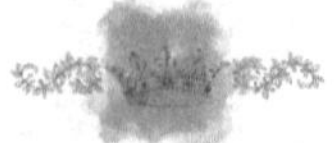

Aviva met Idalia in their secret training arena each day after training with the others. Each day, they ran around the room, dodging the pillars and their elements. They spent hours upon hours preparing. Getting stronger. Honing their skills.

Aviva wiped her brow with the edge of her shirt. "Break?" she asked between huffs of breath.

Idalia took a swig of water and nodded. "Yeah, but only for a little bit."

They headed out of the room together. Idalia passed Aviva the jug of water which she greedily drank. After a pause, she said, "You know we won't be ready to fight Eira if we exhaust ourselves every day prior."

"We won't win the fight against Eira if we don't prepare," Idalia snapped. She took a deep breath. "We don't know when Eira might attack. Or even when the next trial is going to start. Better safe than sorry," she shrugged.

"I know," Aviva said. Her voice dipped as they rounded a corner and people came into view. "What if it's all for nothing anyways?"

"What is?"

"All this training. All this preparation. What if Eira wins despite it all?"

Idalia was silent for a moment.

Aviva waited for Idalia to speak, watching the people around her running around, tending to things, getting ready for the inevitable fight they would all face.

"If Eira wins, at least these people will know we did all we could. At least we didn't just give up and leave them all to die."

"Eira will kill them," Aviva whispered.

Idalia nodded. "That's why we have to be ready. One of us has to beat her," she said, her voice strong with determination.

"It's not gonna be me," Aviva said with absolute certainty.

Idalia opened her mouth to disagree with Aviva. She didn't know who would end up winning this thing. She hoped they would figure out a way around the trials. But she did know that she'd do anything to keep her little sister safe.

A man rushed by, knocking into her shoulder. "I'm so sorry," he called behind him as he ran toward the entrance of the cave. Idalia glanced at Aviva, a question plain on her face.

Aviva shrugged just a bit, and they both picked up speed to follow the man.

As they reached the entrance, more people gathered. Sara was among them, talking quietly to a few nervous looking scouts.

"What's going on?" Idalia asked, planting herself in the middle of Sara's conversation.

Sara pursed her lips like she didn't want to speak, but when Idalia crossed her arms and tapped her foot on the ground, the advisor spilled what she knew. "Eira. She sent a message."

Idalia's stomach dropped. She could hear the sharp intake of breath from Aviva beside her.

"What kind of message?" Aviva asked when Idalia didn't speak.

"She blocked our view. We can't see her army anymore."

"How?" Idalia asked.

The nervous scouts looked at Sara before looking toward her, then one said, "Ice, lots of ice."

"Let me see," Idalia said, stepping toward the tunnel that led outside.

Sara moved toward her. "You can't go outside." She reached out a hand to stop her.

Flame bloomed on Idalia's forearm. Sara quickly pulled her arm back. "Watch me," she said, stepping around Sara and heading into the tunnel.

"Eira could be out there," Sara said.

"Good thing I'm in the mood to burn something," she said, her voice stern. She let her flame burn a little brighter before disappearing into the darkness.

Her flame lit the whole tunnel, as bright as day. It took a few moments to cross through before the light from outside blinded her.

Idalia released her flame, stepping onto grass. Her feet sunk into the soft ground, a feeling they hadn't felt in weeks. Months. She didn't know how long. She shielded their eyes from the burning sun, blinking furiously until her eyes adjusted to the onslaught. The warm air breezed over her skin, setting it on fire. She felt alive, finally out in the open air.

Aviva stepped through the tunnel next to her, placing a hand on her forearm. "What in the world," she said, her jaw falling open at the sight.

A thick sheet of ice spread in front of the cave obscuring the view of Eira's army, if she was even still in the same spot. It was so thick Idalia couldn't see through it. And it wrapped around the mountain, so far that it was all she could see. And in the wall of ice were several spears sticking out. They lined up, forming words.

"She must think she's hilarious," Idalia said, no hint of laughter in her body. It took her a minute to figure out the words.

"Tag, you're it," Aviva read. "I mean, it is kind of funny."

Idalia cut her a look. One that said their older sister's games weren't the least bit humorous.

Idalia walked closer to the wall. "We need to get rid of it." She placed her hand on the wall. Cold seeped into her palm.

Focusing, she brought all the heat she could muster into her hand. The ice around her palm began melting, waters dripping down to the ground. She kept pressing harder and harder until more and more of the ice melted.

"Idalia," Aviva warned.

Idalia ignored her, continuing to melt the ice. She placed her other hand on the wall. Slowly but surely the wall came down. She splashed through the puddle at her feet to get to another section. And another. Until there was only one side left.

Aviva followed close behind her. As did a few men and Sara.

By the time Idalia was done melting the massive wall, she was slumped over, breathing hard. Sweat dripped down her face. She could barely move. Her muscles ached with each ragged breath and awkward step.

Aviva wrapped an arm around her and together they hobbled back to the cave.

Idalia wasn't even strong enough to call a small flame to light the way through the tunnel.

51

Idalia rolled over in bed and groaned. Her body ached. Her head pounded. She was starving and utterly exhausted.

"How do you feel?" Aviva asked from her spot in the chair across the room.

"Like crap," Idalia admitted. She swung her legs over the edge of the bed and made to stand up.

Aviva tsked. "That'll happen when you deplete all of your power to melt an ice wall."

Idalia stood up straight. Her head swam. She braced herself against the wall, the cool rock under her fingers grounding her. "Someone had to do it."

Aviva nodded. "But not alone."

Idalia took a test step, and when her head stopped spinning, she crossed the room to the small feast laid out on a table. "Who else has control over fire?"

"There is a thing called man made flame. Torches. Lanterns. All things that could've been used."

Idalia rolled her eyes and dug into the food. Aviva let her eat in silence.

The door swung open, the hinges creaking at the force. Sara stomped inside. "What were you thinking?"

Idalia shrugged. "We needed visibility."

"You need strength," Sara said sternly.

"Sara, I'm gonna need you to stop with the motherly love," she said. Sara opened her mouth to respond, but Idalia quickly continued, "And yes, I know, our mother didn't love us." She shoveled more food into her mouth. Sara stared daggers at her. "Is Eira's army still there?"

"Yes," Sara said shortly.

"Then mission accomplished," Idalia said. She took a long drink of water. "We can't fight an enemy we can't see. Didn't they cover that in your training to be the right-hand man of the princess?"

Sara fell into a chair, a loud breath escaping. "Unfortunately, there are many things they forgot to mention in that training."

"Take that up with your teachers then, not me," Idalia said, a smirk playing on her face.

"I would," Sara said softly, "if they weren't all dead."

The silence in the room blanketed them. It was heavy. Idalia went back to eating. Aviva picked at her fingernails. Sara finally stood up. "Don't do something that reckless again," she said. When Idalia side-eyed her, she added, "Please."

"I'll consider it," Idalia said around a mouthful.

Sara nodded and left to do more right-hand man things.

"She's so uptight," Idalia said when she was no longer in earshot.

"Well, she is solely responsible for one of the Four who has a twenty-five percent chance of dying by the end of these trials," Aviva said with a shrug. "I think anyone in their right mind would be a little uptight at those odds."

"Slightly better odds now," Idalia whispered.

"I really don't know if Orla got the easy end of this. To die before we barely started," Aviva said, her eyes to the ceiling of the cave. "We still have three more trials to go."

"And we'll make it through it. For Orla."

"For Orla," Aviva agreed.

Aviva watched Idalia walk down the hallways. She kept only a step away all the way from their room to the main hall. "You know I don't need a babysitter, right?" Idalia asked, stopping and turning toward her.

Aviva nodded. "Sure do, but I'm also not gonna let you faceplant in front of everyone." She grabbed Idalia's elbow and led her to an open bench.

"I'm fine," Idalia said, rolling her eyes.

Aviva waved her off. She walked away to get them some food and was back before Idalia could fully settle onto the bench. Aviva wasn't going to leave her unattended for long. She couldn't take her chances. She needed Idalia. And she needed her to be healthy and strong and able to fight Eira. She needed to not be alone in whatever was coming for them next.

No one bothered them while they ate their lunch. Aviva put up their trays when they were done and helped Idalia to her feet. They made their way out of the cafeteria slowly. "You really need to rest," Aviva said, pulling Idalia back to their room.

"I'm fine," Idalia repeated. "Really."

Aviva kept her hand around Idalia's arm, not daring to let

her go stumbling down the hallway by herself. "If you're so fine, let me see some of that fire."

Idalia clenched her fist together, but nothing happened. She chuckled nervously.

"My point," Aviva said. They made it to their room, and she all but pushed Idalia down on the bed. "Rest," she said, turning away to sit in the chair beside the bed.

"You also are not my mother," Idalia said, but climbed into bed.

Aviva shrugged. "Yeah, well, you need one."

Idalia laughed and closed her eyes.

Aviva waited until her sister's breathing slowed and she was asleep. Then, she settled back into the chair. Her eyes drifted closed. She was so tired. After weeks of training, weeks of worrying about Eira and when she'd attack, she just wanted to sleep. She wanted to forget about everything, just for a moment. But she couldn't. She had to keep her people safe. She had to keep Idalia safe. She had to stay alive. She had to fight.

But she was so tired of always fighting. Every day of her life felt like a fight. She couldn't remember a time where she wasn't fighting for something. Fighting for freedom from Ted and Kathy. Fighting for freedom from Eira. Fighting just to live. When was the fight going to be over? When could she let go? When would she be able to breathe?

A tingling took her by surprise. Her eyes shot open.

She felt the familiar pull of the Tree of Season and the paralysis of its calling. The Trial of Spring was beginning.

52

Eira seethed. Her wall of ice was gone, but at least her army had moved closer. There was no way anyone would be able to leave the mountain without Eira knowing about it. No way they would be able to run. All they could do was hide away in the mountain like the scared little children they were.

Jedrek marched up to her. She didn't bother turning. She couldn't bear to tear her eyes away from the cave. She hoped she'd spot a little black headed girl or a slightly taller redhead. She wanted so badly to see her sisters. To watch them try to escape before she set her army on them. Before she ended them as quickly as she did Orla.

"My queen, is there anything more you'd like done?"

"No." Eira shook her head. He had done everything she had asked. He had moved the army closer, set up a perimeter, started digging through the mountainside, and handed out the capes Eira had ordered. He had done everything, and yet, it never was enough.

He turned away.

"Wait," she said, slowly turning around. He pivoted back to face her. A familiar tingling started in her toes and spread through her legs. "It is time. I want you to attack."

"Attack? There is no way to get more than one in at a time. We have not made a dent in the mountainside."

Eira's feet were numb. She could barely feel herself standing, and any second she would disappear. "It is time. The Trial of Spring is beginning. My sisters will be distracted. Go, now."

Jedrek stared at her. She lifted a hand to point at him, but it was slowly disappearing before their eyes. "Now," she yelled.

He turned and ran.

Just before Eira blinked out completely, she watched her army march. Every able bodied man and woman gathered at the entrance to the mountain. And one by one, they dipped into the darkness. Disappearing into the cave just as Eira slipped through the portal beneath her.

Golden light blinded her as the portal opened before the Tree of Season. She dug her feet into the soft ground and called her element to her hands.

She clutched two daggers of ice in her fingers. She waited for her vision to clear so she could rely on more than the muffled sounds that reached her ears.

A sound to her right had her whipping around, thrusting the dagger out in front of her.

Her eyes focused. The dagger was at Aviva's throat. Her hand twitched, itching to slice into her youngest sister's neck. It'd be so easy to end her, so very easy to rid herself of one of her problems. But for some reason, one she couldn't comprehend, she paused. She couldn't make the cut. Not while she stared into Aviva's wide eyes.

She screamed as something barreled into her, pushing her into the tree so hard she dropped her daggers. She righted herself and faced Idalia, Aviva at her side. They looked at her, their fists clenched together, their feet set into the earth. They hated her. And they were ready to fight.

She brought new daggers to life in her hands and let a crazed grin spread across her lips. "Funny seeing y'all here," she said with a little laugh.

"We're not here to play your stupid games, Eira," Idalia said through gritted teeth.

"Actually, that's exactly why you're here. It's why we're all here. To play a little game of life or death." She took a step toward them. They backed away. "I do wonder though," she said, rubbing her chin, the tip of her dagger gliding across her skin, as if she was really considering what she was about to say, "How do you think your people are faring against the army I sent to the cave once the trial started?"

Idalia and Aviva exchanged a glance. Eira took another step forward.

"Do you think any of them will live while you're here fighting me? I don't." She didn't give them a second to answer. Instead, she rushed toward them, her daggers drawn and ready to meet their target.

She sliced into the air with one dagger before her feet were pulled out from under her and she was thrust back toward the tree. The tree was hot under her body as it spun her around before shooting her out across Season.

She rolled against the earth and stood. Her sisters were gone. The forest sprawled out around her. She clutched her daggers tighter and went to hunt.

53

Idalia landed with a thud. She should be used to being catapulted from the tree, but for some reason, it always surprised her. She pulled herself to a stand and looked around. She had only been in Spring a few times, and each time, noting the landscape was the least of her worries. She was lost with no idea where to head.

She walked. On and on. It was early afternoon, so at least she didn't need her flames to light the way. A small victory since her fire was absent. She was exhausted, each step laborious, but she kept pushing. She had to find Aviva. And she needed to stay far away from Eira, at least until she could get some power back. She wouldn't be able to defend herself, and the thought scared her. More than the thought of what the trial may bring. She was scared to face Eira with no powers— scared to walk through the forest with only her less than superb hand-to-hand combat skills for protection.

She would surely die here if Eira found her.

She would die, just as her people were probably dying at the hands of Eira's army. *If Eira's even telling the truth,* she thought. She could've been lying. She'd lied about plenty. But a gut feeling had Idalia speeding through the forest to find Aviva.

She needed to find Aviva and get out of Spring.

Tears fell down Aviva's cheeks. She wiped away the snot dripping from her nose. She hated what Spring had become. What Eira had done to it, destroying villages and cutting down trees. She couldn't believe Eira had ordered Spring's demolition.

Even though Eira had killed Orla and destroyed her home, Aviva still held out an inkling of hope Eira would change. That she would come around, be on their side. But she wouldn't. Eira was too power hungry. Too used to having to take everything. That's what growing up in the system had done to her, and Aviva promised herself she wouldn't let her circumstances change her. Not the way it changed Eira.

No, she would help people instead of hurt them. She would shelter people instead of destroying their homes. She would be good, the opposite of Eira.

Her necklace warmed on her skin. A tug on her gut sent her in a new direction through the forest. Deeper and deeper, the trees so close together they brushed her sides. But she followed the feeling, hoping it would lead her to Idalia.

Aviva stepped into a clearing and her stomach dropped. A few paces away, Idalia kneeled down to the earth. Aviva slowly approached her. Each step felt impossible. Her hands were sweating and her pulse picked up. Everything in her was telling her to turn, run, and never look back. But she walked until she was just behind Idalia.

Her foot crumpled a leaf, the sound deafening in her ears. Idalia didn't even turn.

Aviva sank down beside her.

Idalia's hands were buried in the earth. "I still can't believe it," she whispered.

Aviva nodded and wiped the tears from her face. She could barely see what was beyond her. The land spread out infinitely, it seemed. But there was only so much farther they could go before the ledge dropped off. The ledge where Orla had died. The ledge where they had all jumped to get away from Eira.

"I can feel it," Aviva said, bringing her hands into the earth like Idalia. "I can feel the sadness." And she could. The dirt around her, in this clearing, was not bountiful or hopeful. It did not fill her with power. Instead, it seemed to drain the life from her. It held onto Orla's death.

"How did we let Orla die?"

Aviva shook her head. She reached for Idalia's hand. "We didn't. It wasn't our fault."

Idalia sprang up from the ground, wiping her hands on her pants and the tears from her eyes. "Not everything can be blamed on other people. Sometimes you have to blame yourself."

Aviva watched Idalia walk away from her. Idalia was right. Not everything could be put on someone else, but this could. It wasn't their fault that Orla was dead. It wasn't their fault that Eira was trying to kill them. It wasn't their fault that in fewer than six months, both of them would be dead unless they defeated Eira and found some way to stop the finale from happening.

Aviva ran to catch up to Idalia. "Where are you going?"

"Away from here."

Aviva clutched her necklace. "Wanna get out of here?"

Idalia raised her eyebrows.

"It worked to get us out of the Trial of Winter, remember?" Aviva said, unhooking the necklace and putting it in her palm. It was still warm to the touch.

Idalia nodded and did the same. Without Orla, it was easier to figure out how to hold on to one another and their necklaces. The thought squeezed Aviva's stomach. "Back to Summer?" she asked.

"Yes, we need to help our people."

Aviva closed her eyes and thought of Summer. Of the cave that had been protecting her for weeks. The people who were surely being murdered by Eira's army. Hopefully, the training they had been doing would pay off. Hopefully, they were still alive.

Her necklace warmed. The heat seared her palm and she dropped her necklace onto the ground. She opened her eyes. Spring was still around them, the ledge was behind her back, the forest spreading on each side. It didn't work.

"I guess we have to wait."

Idalia nodded. "Until the trial is over. We have to wait for whatever storm is coming."

Aviva took a deep breath. It could never be that easy for her. For them. They couldn't just skip out. She wished she could fast forward to the end of all these trials. But she couldn't. She had to keep surviving.

"There's a town not too far from here. That way," Aviva said, pointing to the left where the trees grew thick again. "It's probably no longer standing, but maybe we can find shelter there."

Idalia nodded and let Aviva lead them to the town.

Idalia nibbled at the charred and questionable meat Aviva had found in the destruction of the little town. It was better than nothing. But it was hardly food.

Aviva lay next to her, but Idalia couldn't bring her eyes to a close. She couldn't rest. She hated being here, in Spring, while her people were hurting. While Eira's army was attacking them. They were probably trying to find her. Sara didn't even know the trial had started. Idalia had just disappeared, leaving them helpless.

She clenched her fist together and took a big breath. A small, flickering flame ran the length of her fist, tickling her knuckles. It wasn't enough.

She needed her strength. She needed her flames.

She sighed, unclenched her hand and leaned her head back against the half eroded wall of what used to be a building. She closed her eyes and waited until sleep took her away.

Eira hunted for days. She found nothing. She found no one.

Her sisters had managed to evade her. She couldn't find one trace of them and with her army in Summer, she had no help. She filled her palms with her element, drinking the water to quench her thirst. She raided towns for food, but found little. Only now did she regret having her army destroy everything.

She was starving, her stomach caving in on itself. But she pushed onwards, still searching, still looking for her sisters. She was so close to winning this thing. To becoming queen. To never being without a home again. No one would be able to take Season away from her once she was queen. She had made sure of that. And she would continue to do whatever it took to ensure her crown.

She walked into yet another town, quickly searching the remains. No sisters.

A sharp jolt of the earth sent her falling to her knees. She came down hard on her wrist. She tried standing, but the ground kept moving underneath her. She couldn't get up.

The half destroyed structures around her shook violently, falling in on themselves. She had to get out of there, and fast before the whole town came pummeling down, but where would she go? And how was she supposed to even move with the ground unsteady beneath her?

She wrapped her hands over her head as the building fell above her. A partial roof tumbled toward her too fast for her to get away. She swam in darkness.

Aviva found Idalia at the edge of the town. "What are you doing?"

"Waiting. Why's it taking so long for the trial? It's been days. We need to get back."

Aviva sat beside her. "I don't know. Maybe it's because we're not all together?"

"I'm not going searching for Eira. She can come find us."

Aviva nodded. She wasn't going to go looking for Eira either. She was perfectly content staying far away from her. She only wished she knew what was happening at the cave. She only hoped they'd make it back soon.

Vibrations swept through her body. If she hadn't already been sitting, she would've been knocked to her feet. A tree a few paces away cracked under the rumbling earth. The tree crashed to the ground, the sound deafening.

"What's happening?" Idalia asked, her voice shaky as waves after waves rolled toward them.

The town collapsed behind them, a great sweep of debris flying through the air. "The trial," she answered finally.

She stayed low to the ground, letting the rolling of the earth pass by. Making it pass them by. Her hands dug into her element, calming the waves, letting the land flatten back out. She stayed like that, lying on the ground, her hands splayed out under her, until the earth came to a stop.

"What was that?" Idalia whispered into the silence that followed.

Aviva sat up slowly, making sure it was over. It was. "An earthquake. Gotta say, I much prefer this trial than the others so far."

Idalia agreed. "Let's get out of here."

Idalia pulled her to her feet, and together, they portaled out of Spring.

54

Idalia stepped through the portal. Her feet crunched against the leaves. Trees surrounded her on each side. She was deep in the forest.

"Are we in Summer?" Aviva asked from beside her.

Idalia nodded slowly. She said in a quiet voice, "Yes, but we're in the forest near where Eira's army was stationed."

Aviva clamped her mouth shut.

Idalia stepped forward. She walked until the trees thinned. In the distance, she could see the mountain range and the cave that opened onto their underground fortress. But between the forest where she stood and the mountain where her people were trapped, Eira's army camped.

"We have to get around somehow," Idalia said, making sure to stay within the trees. She followed the tree line down until she was much too close to the army for comfort. Aviva said nothing beside her. Idalia pulled up short. She pointed toward the mouth of the cave.

Aviva gasped beside her.

The mouth of the cave was blocked off by Eira's men. They

stood all around, their weapons drawn and ready. Most of the camp was empty, with only the few soldiers guarding the cave. They were inside. They had to be. They wouldn't have left without Eira's command, and there was no way Eira would give that command with them still alive.

"How are we going to get in?" Aviva whispered harshly.

Idalia shook her head. She couldn't speak. All she could see was Brey's severed head, Orla's still body. All the death around her. And here she was, about to witness a ton more of it. It was a massacre. There was no way her people got out. No way Aviva's people escaped. They were fighting for their lives. All while she had been stuck in Spring doing absolutely nothing.

"You think you could make a new entrance without the whole cave collapsing?" Idalia asked, her head spinning with plans. They couldn't go through the front. Not with all of Eira's men there. And there wasn't another way to get in. They would have to make one, or they would have to fight through the army. Idalia didn't think they'd be able to get through the whole army to get to their people.

"I can try."

"Good enough," Idalia said, leading Aviva around the mountain in the middle of the range, sure to stay out of the soldiers' sight.

She stopped at the back of the mountain. "This should be about where our training room was, don't you think?"

Aviva didn't answer her. Instead, she placed her hands on the mountain. Idalia waited, watching as Aviva had what felt like a conversation with the rock. After a few moments, the rocks opened up with a rumble. A similar tunnel to the one in the front dug into the mountain. They had a way in.

"Let's go," Aviva said, her breath fast.

Idalia ducked into the tunnel, bringing a small fire to her hands to light the way just enough to see but not enough to let anyone know they were there. She jumped down into the room below, her feet echoing against the ground. They were in the training room, just like she thought.

It was silent. No one was in the room, and she couldn't hear anyone in the nearby hallways.

She walked slowly through the area, her head on a swivel. Her flames were ready to go. She felt powerful again. Finally, her element was back in full charge. Her fire would have to be enough to protect them all.

A footstep sounded in front of her and she dropped down, kicking out a leg. The body tumbled to the ground. She was on them before they could say a word, a burning palm hovering over their mouth. They writhed under her.

Their eyes met.

"Sara," Idalia whispered, getting up quickly and pulling her up beside her.

Sara was covered in blood. Her hair disheveled, her clothes torn. Bruises formed on her arms and face. She swung her arms out and around Idalia, taking her up in a hug. "Thank goodness," Sara said against her shoulder. "I've been searching everywhere. I thought Eira had taken you."

Idalia pushed her out at arms' length. "We were in the Trial of Spring. For days."

Sara wiped her tear stained face. She nodded. "I should've guessed."

"What's happening here? Where's Eira?" Aviva asked.

Sara sniffed. "No one has seen Eira. Only her army. We've been trying to hold them off. But..." she paused.

Idalia placed a hand on her shoulder. A warmth played in her palm.

"We're not holding up well. They've gotten through. They're everywhere," she whispered.

"Where are our people?" Idalia asked. Apart from their

words and shaky breaths, she couldn't hear anything else. She should be able to hear the fight. Her people. Something.

"Hiding," Sara said. "Or dead."

Idalia gulped. "We have to do something."

"No," Sara said, pushing Idalia back the way she'd come. "You have to get out of here. Both of you. Save yourselves."

"We're not going to leave y'all here to die," Idalia said, swatting at her hand.

"Leaving is not an option. We brought everyone here for protection. Now we have to protect them." Aviva stood with her arms across her chest.

Sara shook her head. "If you die, then all of this has been for nothing."

"If Eira becomes queen, then all of this has been for nothing," Idalia said, squaring her shoulders and walking away from Sara. She disappeared into the hallways.

Footsteps reverberated behind her. She turned to see Aviva running to catch up and Sara a few steps behind her.

She made her way through the hallways, slowly clearing each room as she went. They were deep into the cave, and so far, she hadn't found her people or Eira's army. But the more she walked, the more sounds she could hear. She heard the scratch of spears along the rock walls, the clangs of swords against another bit of steel. The sounds of battle.

Her stomach squeezed tight. Bile rose in her throat, threatening to come up. She wasn't ready for war. How could she be? She was just a college girl who happened to be the daughter of a king in a faraway fantasy land. None of this was real. She still couldn't believe that any of this was reality.

She prepared herself for what she would see as she rounded the last corner before entering the main hall. But nothing could prepare her.

Blood was everywhere in slippery puddles on the floor, in

splatters on the walls. Bodies piled on top of each other as more and more were cut down. Shades of red, green, and blue mixed together until she could hardly see the colors separately. Flashes of torn clothes, sparks of flying weapons. Everything moved at warp speed. She could barely track anyone. And if she kept her eyes on someone too long, they fell with a sword in the gut in the next second.

Her body was frozen with one foot in front of the other, her balance unsteady. She wanted to bolt. She wanted to turn, run down the halls, climb through the new tunnel Aviva had made, and disappear into the forest. Or better yet, go back to Texas.

In Texas she wouldn't have to deal with any of this. She wouldn't have to see people she had come to know, people she had promised to protect, die. She wouldn't have to kill her sisters or be killed. She wouldn't have to worry about any of this.

But she couldn't run. She couldn't turn back.

Her body ignited into flames as she ran into the room. She went straight for a man in blue. He had a sword hovering over his head, inches from connecting with a small girl's neck.

Idalia pushed the girl behind her and tumbled into the man, wrapping him in fire.

He screamed. And screamed. And crumpled in her arms.

She let him drop to the floor before going to the next soldier in blue. One by one, she saved her people, and burned her enemies.

"Get over here," she heard Aviva call from behind her. She turned her head to look, a rock wall had jutted into the middle of the room, blocking Eira's army. Only a small opening remained accessible.

A man with a dangling arm hurried to the opening. And a man in blue pulled a dagger from beneath his cloak. Idalia ran for him.

She tackled him to the ground just as the dagger released from his grasp. He melted beneath her.

"Idalia!"

Her name ringed in her ear as she pushed herself to her feet, huffing. Every muscle burned, barely keeping her from collapsing. She slowly backed up to the opening Aviva held for her.

Her flames were bright, lighting the entire room and the soldiers' faces. All of them, set in hard lines. Their weapons were ready, swords swiping the air, daggers spinning in their fingers. But they didn't move toward her. They watched as she slid through the wall of rock before Aviva closed the hole, making it impossible for them to get through.

Her fire extinguished, and she put her hands on her knees, breathing hard.

The room spun. And she fell.

55

"Idalia," Aviva yelled, running for her. She skidded to a stop beside her sister and gently scooped Idalia's head into her lap. She patted Idalia's cheeks gently.

Idalia's eyes fluttered open. "I'm okay," she said, her voice rough.

Aviva looked Idalia over. Her skin was red. The heat from her flame was still prevalent, but it didn't disguise the soldiers' blood, flesh, and clothes stuck to her. The smell of burnt skin filled Aviva's nose and the small room she'd made to save them.

Blood pooled at Idalia's side. Aviva lifted her soaked shirt to see a deep slice in her side. "Idalia," she said, her throat closing. Tears threatened to fall from her eyes.

Sara rushed to her and pushed her hands into Idalia's side.

"Ow," Idalia said, her eyes fluttering again. "I'm fine."

"You're not fine," Aviva said, shaking her head even though her sister couldn't see with her eyes closed.

Idalia opened her eyes, looking up at Aviva. "I'm fine," she said again, pushing herself up into a sitting position.

Aviva held onto her shoulders to steady her.

"It's just a graze." Idalia stood.

Aviva stood up next to her and watched her closely. Maybe she was fine. She wasn't wobbly, not much. "Okay, but you need pressure," Aviva said.

Sara ripped a strip off the bottom of her tunic and helped Idalia tie it around her waist.

"Now," Idalia said, reaching a hand out to Aviva's shoulder. "What do we do now?"

Aviva breathed deeply. She hadn't really thought about her next step. Or what walling them off from the rest of the cave would mean. She had only thought about getting all of their people to this side and getting Idalia out alive.

"You leave," Sara said.

Idalia shook her head. "Answer's still no."

Sara rolled her eyes.

"We still have the tunnel I made. We could leave," she said.

"And go where?" Idalia asked.

Aviva shrugged. She didn't know anywhere that would be safe. Not for all of them.

She walked through the room and the hallways that spread from it. It was crowded with scared and battered people in red and green. They huddled together, hugging one another, standing against the walls, waiting. They looked at her and Idalia expectantly. Expecting them to know what to do.

But there were too many of them to move without detection. Small children who wouldn't know how to be quiet, elderly who wouldn't be able to move fast enough, men and women wounded from the fight. They couldn't move them, but they couldn't leave them either.

Sara leaned close to Idalia and Aviva. "Our food and water supply is on that side of the wall," she whispered, pointing to the solid rock wall.

"So we have to leave?" Idalia asked.

"Or we have to get food and water in here." Aviva turned her back on the people, their unwavering stares making her nervous. She wasn't old enough to be responsible for all of these people. She wasn't old enough to make life and death decisions. She didn't want to do this.

She rubbed her hands against her face, blowing out a hard breath.

"Can the army get through this?" Idalia asked, placing her hand on Aviva's wall.

She shook her head. "No way. Not unless they have a jackhammer."

"A jackhammer?" Sara asked.

"Exactly," Aviva said. "It stays put."

"Okay, so the only way out is through the new tunnel, which Eira's army doesn't know about," Idalia said.

"Yet," Aviva breathed. "They don't know about it yet. But they're going to figure out that we got in somehow. They're going to find it and it'll be the same slaughter we just went through again." She couldn't imagine what their people thought when the army got in. When they had to fight. When their friends bled. She didn't want to imagine it.

Idalia nodded. "So we need to close it off."

"And trap everyone in here?" Sara whispered harshly. "With no food and water?"

"We send a few people out to gather food and water and bring it back. That's all we can do," Idalia said.

Aviva shook her head. "That's not good enough."

"What else can we do?"

"Go home," Sara said. The finality in her voice made Aviva take a step back.

"We cannot leave you all here to die," Idalia said, her voice just as final.

Aviva watched as the group of people closest to them started whispering and turning to the person next to them to whisper some more. A soft hum filled the area. A man stood up near the entrance of a hallway.

"Go home," he said. "We will take care of ourselves here. But you need to live. You have to live."

A woman stood on the opposite side of the room. "We need you alive. One of you must be queen."

"Go home," a small child said, holding on to the pant leg of an older boy.

Aviva looked at Idalia. "I can't go to Texas. You know that."

"I'm not going without you," Idalia said.

She looked out at the people again. More and more of them had stood up. More and more were whispering, practically pleading for them to go home. To keep themselves safe. To take care of themselves. "Fine," she whispered.

Her stomach dropped as she pulled out her necklace. She didn't want to leave them. She didn't want to go to Texas. She didn't know what to do, but neither option appealed to her.

Idalia faced her with her hand out. She clasped it. Her hand warmed as their necklaces opened a portal.

She looked back at the people one more time before Idalia pulled her through.

56

Eira opened her eyes, but all she saw was black. She couldn't breathe. Something, or someone, was on top of her, pinning her against the ground. She couldn't move. Her heart raced and her body shook.

Get it together, she thought, rolling her eyes. Even if someone was holding her down, she was strong enough to get them off. She was strong enough to do anything.

She took a deep breath, her chest burning, and pushed against whatever was on top of her. She groaned against the weight of it. But finally, after several pushes, it slid off her and she could breathe easily again. She rolled to her side, her face in the grass and breathed deeply. She didn't know how long she stayed there, on her side, breathing in the fresh aroma of the Spring grass, but the world around her quickly turned a deeper shade of blue. Sparkling stars lit up the sky.

She stood shakily, rubbing her head. It hurt. Already a huge knot was forming at the base of her skull.

She looked to her side. The building had fallen into a massive pile, the roof crumpled near where she had laid.

I could've died. She shook the thought away, letting the worrisome feelings dissipate from her body. She turned her back on the building, on the town. She walked a few paces away. Her legs worked, so did her arms. She was fine. Everything was fine except for the raging headache.

She grabbed for her necklace, but clutched at nothing. "Crap," she said, her voice croaky and loud in the silent town. She ran back to the wreckage, digging around. "Where are you?" she asked no one. She huffed, throwing pieces of the building aside, scratching at the grass, searching and searching.

She found it attached to the edge of the roof, broken. She pulled it from the roof, placed it in her palms, and hoped. Hoped it would still work even if it was broken.

But it didn't. A portal didn't open. It didn't get warm. Nothing.

She threw the necklace to the ground. Her foot came down on it again and again until only tiny pieces remained scattered in the earth. "Useless," she yelled at it.

Tears sprang to her eyes, but she angrily wiped them away. "So freaking useless," she whispered, turning away from the mess. Without the necklace to portal her, she would have to walk to Summer.

So she did. She walked and walked for hours. Until the darkening sky turned pitch black and then bright again. She walked, only stopping for sips of water and a few berries she found on her way. She walked all the way to Summer.

When she got there, Eira paused. A few of her men stood outside the cave, blocking people from exiting. Her camp was practically empty, only a few small fires were left burning. They all had to be inside the mountain. Which means that they had invaded the cave. They were winning.

Eira trudged through the rock ridden field, watching her step, until she was right outside the mouth of the cave.

A young soldier turned to face her, drawing his sword and leveling it at her neck. The bite of the metal kissed her throat.

Her heart skipped a beat and her breath stopped, but she looked him dead in the eyes. "And what do you think you're doing?" she asked, crossing her arms.

The older soldier beside him swiped the sword from his comrade's hands. It clattered to the ground. "That is our queen, soldier," he whispered sharply.

The guy's face turned bright red, and he dropped to his knees. He bowed his head. "I apologize, my queen. Punish me as you see fit."

"It's fine," Eira said, waving him off. He breathed a sigh of relief and pushed himself to a stand.

"I'm sure I don't look quite like myself after the trial." She looked down at herself. Her clothes were ratty and torn. Dirt stuck to every crevice of her. Her skin was pale and she was thin. It had been a hard few days reminiscent of her old life in Texas. She hated the feeling of being vulnerable. Hated how the dirt made her feel. Hated remembering a time where she felt weak. But now was not the time to reconcile on that. No, now was the time to make sure her army had done what she told them to and put an end to all of this mess so she would never feel like this again.

"You look as exquisite as ever," the young soldier said.

Eira rolled her eyes. "Where is Donovan or Jedrek?"

"Inside."

"Then take me inside."

He nodded. "Right this way." He moved toward the opening.

She followed him through the darkness. The rocks on each

side squeezed her tight, but she managed to make it through the tunnel and to a big open room.

A rancid smell filled her nose. Her stomach threatened to come up. She put a hand to her mouth and swallowed. Bloodied bodies, discarded weapons, and burned flesh were scattered around the room. A few of the bodies wore blue, but many, many more wore green and red.

The soldier led her through the room. He stopped only when Jedrek and Donovan came into view. They stood just before a wall.

"You shouldn't be here," Donovan said to her.

"And why not?"

He placed a hand on her arm to lead her away. She shook free.

"In war, the queen should be hidden," Jedrek said. "We wouldn't want anything to happen to you."

"Yes, well, in this war the queen would like to know if her enemies are dead."

Jedrek looked back at the wall. "We are unsure."

"Unsure?"

Donovan nodded his head. "Your sisters returned mid fight. Lady Idalia tore through our men while Lady Aviva constructed this wall." He knocked on the rock for good measure.

"You have men posted outside. How did they get in?"

"We are unsure," Jedrek said again.

Anger rose in Eira's belly. Her face turned red. "Are you sure of anything at all, Jedrek?" Her voice echoed around the room.

Donovan took her arm again and spun her toward him. "We do not know how they got in. There was only one way to enter before we invaded. It is possible that Aviva constructed a new way in."

"Then find it," she said through gritted teeth.

"We are searching. But what we do know now, is that their people are on the other side of the wall. They are trapped. Their food and water is here. They will be trying to escape."

Eira nodded.

Her head pounded. She didn't know if it was from fury or from the blow to the back of her head. She rubbed her eyes and sighed.

"You need rest. A bath. Good food," Donovan said in a quiet, calm voice like he was talking to a child. But Eira didn't need anyone to cater to her. She didn't need anyone, period.

"I can take care of myself."

"Yes, you can. You've shown that numerous times already. You've survived three trials now. If we do not find and end your sisters, you only have two more to go before you are crowned queen. Let us do the hard work so you may rest." Donovan peered into her eyes, his face soft.

Eira rolled her eyes. "Fine," she said.

"Good, good," he said, leading her out of the cave. He gathered a few men as he went.

When they stepped outside, he helped her onto the back of a horse. "Go to Winter. We will join you shortly."

Eira nodded. She hated being told what to do, but unfortunately, Donovan was right. She needed to bathe. She needed new clothes. She needed food. And she needed to sleep. Especially if she was going to be strong enough to take on Idalia and Aviva the next time she saw them.

She would see them soon. And she would kill them just as quick.

57

Idalia slid her key into her door. She jiggled it, but it wouldn't slide all the way in. "Crap," she muttered under her breath.

She could feel Aviva's breath on her shoulder as she peered around her. "What?"

"I can't get in. They must've changed the locks."

"Why would they do that?"

Idalia shrugged and went back down the stairs. She walked to the parking lot, found her car, and slid in. Aviva opened the passenger side door and got in with her. "You know what day it is?" she asked as she turned the ignition, found her phone, and plugged it up.

Aviva shook her head.

They sat quietly for a few minutes waiting. Idalia felt odd.

It felt strange to sit in her car, to hold her phone in her hand, to have the air conditioner blowing on her. All the things that used to be normal were no longer ordinary. She had grown used to being in Season. To not have the technology, the ease she had in Texas.

Her phone finally blinked to life. The screen displayed the date. *June 7, 2023.* No wonder her key hadn't worked. "It's past move-out day. They locked me out."

"What are you going to do?" Aviva asked, her voice soft.

"Go to my parent's house."

Aviva nodded. She made to get out of the car.

Idalia leaned over, her arm across Aviva's lap, and closed the door. "Where are you going?" she asked.

Aviva shrugged. "I'll figure it out."

Idalia shook her head. "I think not. You're staying with me." She straightened up and put the car in reverse to back out of her parking spot. "We're in this together, Aviva."

Out of the corner of her eye, Idalia saw Aviva's slight nod of the head.

Idalia knocked on the door. "Hi, Papa," she said when her father opened the door with a smile on his face. She wrapped her arms around his neck and hugged him. She had missed him. Missed his hugs and soft laughter. She had missed home.

"Where have you been? We were expecting you days ago," he said against her hair.

She nodded. "I know. I had a few things to take care of before coming home."

He held her out at arm's length and sniffed the air. "What

happened to you? It looks like you're in need of a shower," he said. "Come in, come in," he said, stepping aside and letting them into the house.

"We've been camping," Idalia lied. "Where's Mom?" she asked when they settled into the living room.

Her father shrugged. "Running around. You know how she likes to shop," he said with a laugh. "So who is this?" he asked with a wave of his hand toward Aviva.

"Oh," Idalia said, looking toward Aviva. She raised an eyebrow toward Aviva. "So, funny story. This is Aviva. She's my biological sister."

There was a beat of silence. Then, her father pulled Aviva in for a hug. "So nice to meet you," he said, a bright smile on his face.

"You too," Aviva said, awkwardly hugging him back.

Idalia scratched her head. "I was thinking she could stay here with me during summer break? If that's okay with you and Mom," she said.

"I'll talk to your mother when she gets home, but I'm sure it won't be a problem," he said to her.

"Thanks, Papa," she said before dismissing herself from the living room. She headed to the guest room with Aviva a few steps behind.

She rifled through the closet and threw some clean clothes at Aviva. "You can take a shower in there," she said pointing to the adjoining bathroom. "I'll go to the other bathroom."

Aviva nodded, stepped inside the bathroom, and closed the door. Idalia heard the lock click before she went searching through the closet for clothes for herself. She padded down the hallway to the other bathroom and took a long, hot shower. Her skin was sparkling when she got out. Her hair was back to a bright red-orange instead of clouded with mud. Her fingernails were no longer rimmed with dirt. The cut to her side throbbed but felt better now that it wasn't going to be infected by her dirty clothes. She felt brand new.

And yet, stepping out onto the tiled floor, it felt incomprehensibly wrong to be in Texas.

58

Aviva leaned against Idalia's bed. She still wasn't used to being here, surrounded by Idalia's family. She wasn't used to being back in Texas. It had been weeks, and yet, she still couldn't shake the feeling that she didn't belong. Not to Idalia's family and not to this world.

A soft knock on the door sounded. "Come in," Idalia called, not getting up from her place next to Aviva.

"Hi," Idalia's mom said, sticking her head inside the room.

"What's up, Mom?" Idalia asked, pausing the movie playing on the TV.

That's all they had been doing for weeks. Watching TV. Staying in Idalia's room. Aviva was utterly bored, but she was also scared to get out. Scared to walk around the streets, to be seen by anyone besides Idalia's parents. No one had come looking for her. She wasn't sure if anyone was searching for her, but just in case, she stayed holed up and Idalia stayed with her.

"Well, y'all have been in this room since you've been home

for the summer. Don't you think it's time to get out some?" Idalia's mom said as she walked into the room and sat on the bed.

"I don't know, Mom," Idalia said, looking over at Aviva.

Aviva didn't know what Idalia wanted. She had never asked her to stay with her. Never asked anything from her, not really. She would've gone back to Season if it hadn't been for Idalia. She would've gone back, hid out, and tried to stay alive until the next trial. And then the Finale. She would've tried to stay alive until she had no other choice. Because she wasn't going to hurt her sisters, either one. She couldn't. And so, she stayed with Idalia, here in Texas. At least here Idalia was safe.

Aviva shrugged.

"Come on," Idalia's mom said, pulling Idalia's hand. "At least come to the living room for a while. Come hang out. We miss you," she said, leading Idalia out of the room.

Aviva got off the bed and followed them.

"Happy birthday!" a group of people screamed when Idalia stepped into the living room. Idalia smiled brightly, laughter escaping her mouth. She hugged her mom.

Aviva shrunk back against the wall.

There were too many people. Family and friends of Idalia. People Aviva didn't know. She didn't like being around people she didn't know. Didn't like when unknown eyes saw her. She liked being invisible. She liked to be hidden away.

Fireworks crackled in the sky, the light filling the night sky. Aviva stood against the wall, her hands in her pockets as she watched over the party.

It was late. And it didn't seem like the party was ever going to end. But there was food, a lot of it. So she ate, sat in silence, and waited for an appropriate time to dismiss herself.

She turned her back to the party to slip inside, but was pulled back by a hand on her arm. She fought the urge to call the earth to her. She didn't need her powers here. She didn't. She was fine. She was safe. Ish.

She turned to see Idalia smiling at her. "Where are you going?" Idalia asked, dropping her hand from her arm.

"It's late. I'm gonna get to sleep," she said.

"You're not enjoying yourself."

Aviva shrugged. "Never been big on parties."

Idalia's face dropped. The smile wiped away and the light in her eyes dimmed. Aviva felt bad. She wasn't trying to ruin her birthday, a birthday she hadn't even known about. Just like her birthday during the Trial of Spring. They still knew so little of each other. But what was the point in putting in effort to get to know each other, really know each other, when one or both of them would be dead by the end of the year.

"Kinda hard to get into it with the Trial of Summer and the Finale right around the corner," Idalia whispered. "But I'll pretend for my parents. It may be the last memory they have of me," she said, searching them out in the crowd.

Idalia left Aviva alone to go to her parents, to hug them, to feel their love. A twang in Aviva's stomach had her going inside and hiding away in Idalia's room.

She hated being jealous. Especially when it came to having a family. She should have people she loved. Parents who loved her. But she had no one. And no one would miss her when she was gone. When Season took her one way or another. No one would look for her, no one would search for her. Being back in Texas only proved it more. Aviva was alone in this world. Even killing her foster dad didn't make her valuable enough to have cops search for her.

She was almost too good at being invisible.

59

In the Land of Season

It had been a long, boring summer for Eira. For weeks, all she did was sit around her manor and wait for the messenger to ride back and forth from Winter to Summer with news. Over and over again. Weeks and weeks wasted.

There was no news. Her sisters had vanished. Their people were holed up in the cave. They still couldn't get through the wall. No one knew how they were surviving with no food, no water, no way out. But they were. And Eira's army was all but wasted sitting there just waiting for them to escape.

But she couldn't pull back now. She wouldn't. She would leave her army at the mountain cave until her sisters were dead. Until she sat on the throne and ruled over Season. Until she was sure no one would take away her home.

And she would enjoy her home while her army camped in

the forest near the mountain range. She would enjoy being the next queen of Season.

Eira stood from the steaming tub and dried herself with a towel. She had found that sitting in her tub for hours while her servants brought her hot water, food, and drinks helped pass the time. Slowly, but surely. But everything else dragged by. She had no one to entertain her. She had no friends, not that she had ever had many friends. She almost missed her sisters.

Almost missed the beginning of all of this when they had accepted her. Before Quinn had given her the keys to the kingdom. She almost missed the possibility of having a family.

She shook her head at the nonsense. *Useless thoughts.*

She went to her room and dressed quickly. Not that she had anywhere to go.

Eira huffed and found herself outside, on her porch, overlooking Winter. She'd been here a dozen times before. She'd looked out at her people, the ones who were unable to fight and had stayed behind, and wished that any of them would approach her—as a companion, not as a ruler. But it didn't matter. No, she was their ruler and there would always be a distinct line between them. A distinction she had longed for. Once.

Now, so close to being their queen, her heart had melted. Just a bit.

She gripped the railing, her knuckles turning white with the force. "This is ridiculous," she whispered to herself. "This is everything you have always wanted. So close."

She stayed there until her legs were numb and the feeling of wanting more disappeared. She had a home. She had people who obeyed her. People who feared her. What more could she want? What more could Season give to her?

Nothing. This was it.

60

Aviva looked at the map Idalia had drawn. Two of them. Identical. It was a nice rendition of Season. As nice as she could have drawn with her limited knowledge.

"Here," Idalia said, pointing to the section of Summer. "This is where we'll meet when the trial starts."

Aviva peered closer to the map. Idalia's finger hovered above a tear shaped object surrounded by boxes. "And that is what exactly?"

"The tower, duh," Idalia said.

"Oh, yeah, looks exactly like the tower," Aviva said, a laugh escaping. Planning for the trial wasn't a laughing matter. None of this was, but it felt good. The need to lessen the burden on her shoulders was heavy. She was tired of feeling tight, squeezed for life. Tired of feeling scared. Anxious. Nervous. Tired of feeling.

Idalia shrugged. "I'm not an artist. But anyways, we meet here and wait out the trial. We didn't even run into Eira during the Trial of Spring. Maybe this time we'll be as lucky."

"Right because luck has always been on our side."

Idalia rolled up the map and handed it to her. "Just keep this on you. Find one of the markers and then find the tower. That's where I'll be heading whenever this thing starts."

Aviva nodded. She tucked the map into her boot. She'd keep it there until Season took them back. She'd keep it close. It was as good a plan as they were going to get. At least it was something. At least she'd know where to go to find Idalia.

"What about the cave?"

"You mean the cave infested with Eira's army. I think it's probably best to stay far away from the cave for now," Idalia said, rolling up the other map.

"You really think Eira is still there?" It had been two and a half months. Would Eira really wait them out that long? Was she really willing to do whatever it took to kill them? Aviva hated that she knew the answers were yes.

Idalia nodded. "Definitely."

Aviva knew she was right. Even if she didn't want to believe it. Eira would do anything to find a home, especially one away from Texas. She didn't have to run from cops in Season. She didn't have to worry about finding a place to sleep or anything to eat. She was taken care of there. She wouldn't give that up. Aviva was close to wanting the same things. But she couldn't kill her sisters in the process. She couldn't hurt someone just to get the things she wanted.

Maybe she was weak. Or maybe her inability to hurt someone who wasn't hurting her was a strength. She didn't know. All she knew was that the Trial of Summer was coming. Eira was coming. The Finale was coming. The end of all of this was coming.

Would she be alive to see it?

61

Idalia got out another clean piece of paper from her desk and scribbled a note on it. Tears welled in her eyes, but she rubbed at them. She needed to do this. She would leave her parents with something. She couldn't leave them wondering what happened to her like Orla's parents probably still were. Her parents were not going to have to search for her.

She folded the note, wrote her parents' name on the backside, and went into the kitchen. She didn't want them to find the note immediately, so she slid it under a jar on the counter. There was no point in them reading her goodbye if she wasn't gone yet.

She went back to her room. Aviva was asleep on her bed. A surge of emotion flooded Idalia. She didn't understand how in less than a year, Aviva had become one of the most important people in her life. She didn't remember them being together as kids, before their biological parents sent them away to Texas. She had no memory of it, but her body seemed to.

She wanted nothing more than to protect her. She was the

big sister. It was her duty to protect her. To save her. And that's what she would do.

She climbed into the bed and laid down. Her eyes drifted closed.

It had been months of good food, good rest, good healing. Her element was primed and ready for the trial. She felt full. Her fire was rumbling in her belly. Her whole body tingled with energy. She felt more powerful than ever before.

The trial was coming. But she was ready.

Her eyes snapped open. She could hear her parents rummaging around in the living room and Aviva's deep breathing next to her.

And ever so subtly, she could hear the tearing of the world.

A portal opened in the room. It pulled at her. She shook Aviva awake.

"What?" Aviva asked groggily.

She slid off the bed and stepped toward the portal. "It's starting," she whispered. "The Trial of Summer is starting."

Aviva jumped up beside her.

Idalia stuck out her hand. Aviva clasped it. "We got this," she said, stepping toward the portal and pulling Aviva with her.

Together, they stepped through the portal to Season.

62

In the Land of Season

E ira plummeted through the sky. Her sisters hadn't even said anything to her at the tree, let alone looked at her. She couldn't really blame them. But a little friendly banter was always nice.

She skidded to a stop and looked around her. She wasn't too familiar with Summer. She had ridden in a carriage the whole trek from Winter. She didn't know where to go, but she knew she wanted to find her sisters. She wouldn't be left alone like in the Trial of Spring. She needed to find them, fight them, and win.

And this nightmare of conflicting feelings would cease. The crown would be hers. She was going to rule. Season would be her home. But she'd have no family.

"Shut up," Eira murmured to her own mind.

She turned in a circle, taking in her surroundings. The land was pretty flat and bare. There weren't any trees that she could see. There would be trees near the cave. She had hidden in a forest that lined the plane while her army searched the mountain for points of entry. Where was it?

So she started walking until she came upon a small splatter of trees.

It was hot. Hotter than she ever remembered Texas to be.

She called water to her palms and drank slowly. Then, she splashed the sweat away from her brow. She kept walking.

She followed the tree line until she saw buildings. A town.

"Welcome to Summer," she said with a sweep of her arm. She laughed. The sound was weird in the humid air.

In the distance, she saw a tall building. She shielded her eyes from the sun, looking at the cloudless sky. The building shook. Waves ran through it. Then, the building vanished.

Eira blinked, but it didn't come back. The heat was driving her crazy.

She ducked inside a nearby small building. It was vacated, the furniture dusty. But she welcomed the darkness. Her skin was taught against her. Heat radiated from her. She created a bubble of water and stepped through it. The water clung to her, cooling her. She took a long breath. Much better.

Eira dusted off the couch and laid down. She would rest for a moment. And then she would continue her search. She should be close. At least closer to her sisters.

She hoped, anyway.

Aviva leaned down and cupped her hands in the stream. She took a long drink. A sigh escaped her dried lips. She cupped another handful of water and splashed her face, arms, and neck. It didn't make much of a dent in Summer's heat.

Aviva pulled the map from her boot. She rolled it out onto the ground and found where the stream was in Summer. Not too far away was the town and the tower in the middle.

She could make it. She had to. And when she got there, she would find food and more water.

She took another drink before rolling the map back up and heading north toward the tower.

Miles later, the town came into view. She made her way to the middle where the tower stood. She still couldn't believe how structurally sound Summer was. The stone tower stood out. It was strong, infallible. Just like Summer's people hoped their princess would be.

She pushed open the door, and the cool air hit her in the face. She blinked several times before her eyes adjusted to the darker light inside the tower.

"Idalia?" she called, her voice croaking. She needed more water.

She rummaged through the tower, not sure exactly where she was going. And there was no one around to guide her. Finally, she found the kitchens. A huge basin hung on the wall. She turned the knob and water flowed through the pipe. She stuck her mouth under it, gobbling up the cool water. It dribbled from her mouth.

"Someone's thirsty."

Aviva jumped, her head hitting the faucet. She stood up, rubbing the sore spot. "Ow," she said.

Idalia laughed.

"Not nice," Aviva said as she turned the faucet off. "When did you get here?"

"Not long ago," Idalia said. "I'm also in need of water."

Idalia turned the faucet and water ran into the basin. She drank it quickly, wiping her mouth when she was done.

"Did you see Eira?" Aviva asked. She hadn't seen anyone on her trek to the tower. But she wasn't really looking. She was focused on finding water.

Idalia shook her head.

"Me either."

Idalia turned away from the faucet and went to the cabinets. Aviva watched her rummage through them, pulling out several things. A mini buffet of food laid on the table before them.

Aviva's stomach growled. She took a bite of bread, savoring the taste even though it was a bit stale. It would do. It had to for the couple of days they would be stuck in Season before the trial really began. Before Season put them through some type of fiery natural disaster.

A few days later after dark had fallen, Idalia climbed out of the bed she had claimed. Aviva turned toward her.

"Where are you going?"

Idalia avoided her eyes. "I'm going to look for Eira. You stay here."

Aviva shot up from the bed. "No way."

"You're safe here. Stay," she said, opening the door and walking out of the room. Aviva's footsteps followed her. All the way through the tower to the entrance.

"What are you going to do when you find her, huh?"

"What do you think, Aviva? I'm going to stop her from hunting us. I'm going to stop her from ruining Season." She squeezed her hand into a fist. Hard.

Aviva grabbed for her arm, but she dodged it. "So you're going to kill her?"

Idalia laughed a humorless laugh. "Isn't that the point of this whole thing?" She waved her hand around. The point of Season was to have them kill one another. They only existed to fight, to survive. Or die trying.

"You won't be the same after killing someone," Aviva whispered. "It changes you."

"Yeah, well, Eira deserves it."

"No one deserves to die," Aviva said on a breath.

Idalia rubbed her eyes. She strained to understand Aviva, she really did, but she couldn't. Eira was the worst of them. They couldn't let her win. They couldn't let her rule over Season. They couldn't keep dying by her hand. Idalia took a huge breath. "I'm not going to watch another sister be killed by Eira."

Idalia turned around and walked out of the tower.

"Orla wouldn't want this," she heard on the wind.

"Orla doesn't have a choice. She's dead," Idalia said, not even bothering to turn around to look at Aviva again. "Just stay here. Stay safe."

She didn't wait for a response, didn't even know if Aviva would give her one. But she didn't hear any footsteps, so she kept walking away.

She had no idea where Eira could be. Or where the Tree of Season had sent her. But she would find her. She would hunt her down. She would put an end to Eira and keep Aviva safe. She had to. It was the only way. Aviva needed to be kept safe. She deserved to be protected. She wasn't going to lose another sister.

Eira was close, surely. Aviva hadn't been far behind her on the way to the tower. And Eira would most likely try to find them. At least Idalia hoped.

Her hand went to her neck. The Tree of Season that hung there warmed under her touch. She was in her section. It was her element that would be tested. She was strong and powerful. She could find Eira, stop her from hurting Aviva and from destroying everything.

The necklace grew hotter. She felt a tug at her back and one to her right. Aviva was behind her, so Eira had to be to the right. She walked, letting the necklace guide her until it was burning her skin.

She ended up right outside of a building near the border of Summer. Not too far from the tower.

She waited outside, hidden in the shadows. She didn't see anyone or hear anything. But her necklace was red hot on her skin, so Eira had to be in there. But what was she going to do? Was she going to just jump in there, flames blazing, and take her out? Should she wait outside instead? Could she actually do this?

Idalia rubbed her eyes. This was insane. She was hunting down her older sister. To kill her. What. Was. Happening.

What was wrong with her?

Who had she become?

She couldn't do this.

Idalia turned away from the building. Her foot snapped a twig under her. The sound was a cannon in the silent night.

Water surrounded her. "Nice of you to find me," Eira said from the doorway to the building. "Save me the trouble."

Idalia didn't say anything. She didn't know what to say. She didn't know what to do either. She was frozen in her spot. Unable to decide if she should run back to the safety of the tower or fight this battle. Because it would be fought. Eventually. And it would be her or it would be Aviva.

She couldn't let it be Aviva.

Flames erupted over her skin, dancing the length of her arms and legs.

"Ooo," Eira smiled. "Someone's ready for a rematch."

Spears of ice shot toward her. Flames turned them to mist before they reached her. The water surrounding her rained down, extinguishing her flames. She shook her hands clean and brought the fire back. A woody scent rose into the air. The ashen smell of it was thick. She clapped her hands together and the flames shot from her hands, ran across the ground and surrounded Eira.

She squeezed the ring of fire closer and closer to Eira as she stalked toward her. "This is no rematch," she said as she got closer.

Eira smirked. "Then what is it, little sister?"

"The end of you."

Eira stepped backwards, into the flame. The hissing of burnt hair sizzled into the air. The sulfur smell turned Idalia's stomach. But she kept marching forward.

Eira stumbled and fell. Idalia pounced on her, covering her body with her own. She held down her arms. Eira kicked, but Idalia didn't budge. She pressed her sister into the dirt, which scorched and hissed under her power.

A knee rammed into her lower stomach, and she let go to clutch at the pain. Eira rolled away and sprinted for the building. As Idalia caught her breath, she debated. Should she follow Eira and finish this fight? Or return to the tower? Flame danced among the trees, skirting through the underbrush and pirouetting along low lying branches. Sparks flicked into the treetops, diving from pine to oak until the forest around Summer glowed red orange. The smoke burned her eyes. She coughed and coughed as the fire sashayed ever closer, leaving black footprints of singed earth as it moved. Idalia ran to the building. "Eira, get out," she yelled, hoping Eira could hear her over the pop of sap and crackle of falling wood. "Get out now!"

She threw the door open.

Eira stood in the doorway, hand slashing down. The glint of a dagger, flames dancing on the steel, in Eira's hand blinded Idalia. She tackled Eira to the floor, her hand going for the dagger. Trying to take it from her hand, dislodge it from her grasp. Anything before it met its mark.

Idalia gasped. Her body froze. She tried taking a breath but couldn't.

She fell off Eira, blinking up at the ceiling. Over and over. A blackness crept into the edges of her vision.

The walls around her erupted in flames. The building was going to collapse.

Idalia gasped another hard breath. Her chest moved. Her hands and feet tingled. Her eyes watered. She sat herself up slowly, leaning onto her elbows and looked around.

Eira lay on the ground next to her. The dagger she had been holding was plunged into her chest, blood covering her clothes. She clutched at the hilt. Her eyes were closed but her mouth was moving. She was laughing.

"Eira," Idalia said, rolling to her side and shaking her shoulder.

Eira's laugh grew louder. She coughed and gurgled, blood trickling from her lips. She looked up at Idalia. She smiled, teeth slicked with blood. "You've done it now."

"Eira," Idalia repeated. She pressed against Eira's chest, hands slippery with blood.

"You're gonna have to kill Aviva now."

"No," Idalia said, her teeth gritting.

"Or she'll kill you," she laughed.

Idalia shook her head and pressed on her sister's chest

harder, but the blood pooled underneath her, staining her clothes and spreading across the floor.

"Doesn't matter to me since I'm dead now." Eira's eyes fluttered close. She took short, raspy breaths.

"Eira, no. I didn't mean to." Tears fell down her cheeks, mixing with the blood. "Eira, please."

Eira's chest didn't move again. Her eyes didn't open again. Not even when Idalia smacked her cheeks. Not even when Idalia yelled her name. Again and again. She rocked back on her heels, took her hands away from Eira's chest, and stood on shaky legs.

Smoke filled the room, making her cough. She covered her mouth. Blood smeared on her face. She wanted to gag. She needed to rid herself of the feeling of death on her hands. She needed to get out of here before it burned down.

She turned toward the door and kicked it down. It crumpled beneath her and the flames. She shielded her eyes from the bright line of fire around the building.

And then she ran. She ran as far and as fast as she could before falling to Aviva's feet at the entrance of the tower.

63

"What happened?" Aviva asked, rushing to Idalia. She dropped to her knees next to her. She wanted to place her hands on Idalia, to comfort her, but she was covered in blood. She didn't know if it was her own or someone else's.

"Eira," Idalia said shakily.

"Are you hurt?"

Idalia shook her head. Tears fell from her eyes.

"I was going to leave. I was gonna turn around and come back here," Idalia cried.

"What happened?" Aviva repeated, placing a hand on her shoulder. Idalia wouldn't look at her.

"A wildfire. Eira attacked me with a dagger. I don't know what happened. I don't know how." Idalia trembled under her hand. "She's dead."

Aviva's stomach dropped. Eira was dead.

Was it true? Was she really dead? Had Idalia really killed her?

If it was true, then there was no one standing in their way. No one was going to be hunting them down. All they had to do was face the finale. And that would be it. They were almost done. Free.

"Come on," Aviva said, pulling up Idalia and leading her to a bathing room. She helped wash Eira's blood from her face and hands. The water turned a sickly red.

Aviva tried not to remember her first kill. She didn't want to see Ted's face and his lifeless eyes. But the image stuck in her mind. She was sure Idalia was living the same nightmare. Killing someone, even in self defense, was life changing. Brain altering. She hated how she wished she hadn't killed Ted even though it was her only chance to survive.

She'd existed on scraps—of affection, of food, of dreams so far out of reach they were more like nightmares. Why cling to either world when neither wanted her in it?

Aviva looked down at Idalia. She was shaking, but she was clean. She didn't say anything as she led her to the room and helped her under the covers of the bed. She watched over her until Idalia finally fell asleep. And then Aviva followed her into slumber all the while thinking of how much they had gone through just to live.

Aviva groaned. The chair she had fallen asleep in wasn't comfortable. Her back hurt. Her stomach growled. She stretched her arms out, sighing.

She looked to the bed. Idalia was gone.

"Idalia?" Aviva called. No answer.

She listened, as hard as she could. A soft brushing sound

met her ears. She followed it into the bathing room to see Idalia kneeling beside the tub. Her hands were bloody. She had scraped them raw with washing.

Aviva tore the soap from her sister's hands and held them tightly in her own. "What are you doing?"

"I can't get it off."

"Get what off? Your hands are clean."

Idalia shook her head. "They don't feel clean."

"Idalia," Aviva whispered. "You're bleeding."

Small droplets of blood dripped into the tub. *Plop. Plop. Plop.*

Aviva dipped her hands into the water once more and then used a nearby towel to dry them. Idalia winced. Aviva rummaged through the drawers but didn't find anything to bandage the wounds. She went to the room, found a shirt, and tore off the hem. She wrapped Idalia's hands the best she could.

"Let's go," she said when she was done.

"Go where?"

Aviva pulled her to her feet and out of the room. "To the cave. If Eira is dead then the war she started is over. So let's save our people."

Idalia nodded and followed her through the tower.

Hot air hit her in the face. Beads of sweat prickled on her brow. She wiped it with her sleeve but instantly more sweat appeared. It was so hot. The earth vibrated under her. She turned toward its source.

Two horses peeked their heads out from behind a nearby building.

"Milo," Aviva said, running toward her horse. She rubbed his nose and then hopped onto his back. Idalia found her place on Lady's. "Let's go set our people free," she said with a nudge to Milo's belly. He started toward the mountain with Lady following at his side.

It didn't take too long to make it to the cave on horseback.

They moved from beyond the edge of the forest. Aviva pulled Milo's reins and he stopped. It was very different from the first time Aviva had seen the mountain. When they had been escaping Eira and heading toward safety with all of the people from Spring and Summer. The field had been cleared. Wild horses had roamed the area.

Now, empty campsites splotched the grass. Fires that had burned out left blackened branches. The smell of old, rotted meat hung in the air. But at least, the people weren't there. At least they wouldn't be ambushed on the way to the cave.

Aviva gave the reins some slack, and Milo cantered as close to the cave as he could get before she had to dismount. She stayed low to the ground, stepping across the rocks and staying hidden as best she could, with Idalia on her heels.

A soldier stood at the mouth of the cave, his sword ready at his side. His eyes slid over Aviva. Before he could move or shout, Aviva called the earth to her and filled his mouth with dirt. The ground crawled over him, packing him into his spot with only his head remaining visible.

"Stop resisting," she said, standing fully upright. "We are not here to hurt you." She let the earth fall from his mouth, and the soldier took a deep breath.

He shook his head, dirt dribbling out of his mouth. "Then why have you returned?" He coughed.

"Eira is dead."

Shock registered on his face, but he said nothing.

"Call off your army and go home to Winter," she said, her voice strong as she strutted up to the soldier. He towered over her, but her voice held all the command of a queen.

"And why would we do that?" he asked gruffly.

"Your queen is dead, which means one of us," she said, pointing toward herself and Idalia who had stayed back a few paces, "will be the queen of Season. You must obey your queen, yes?"

The soldier looked between them. Then, he bowed his head.

"Gather your people, and never harm another Spring or Summer person again."

The soldier nodded. Aviva let the earth fall from around him. He disappeared inside the cave.

Aviva trekked back to where Idalia waited. They walked quietly to where their horses were nibbling at the grass of the plane. She mounted Milo again and waited. The soldier could be telling the others they were here, could be setting up an ambush. Could come out swinging. So she waited, ready to defend herself and her sister if need be.

But instead, one by one, soldiers in blue exited the cave, bowed to them and returned to their camp to pack up their stuff.

The very last soldier and an older man exited the cave. They bowed but did not go to their camp. The older man looked up at Aviva. "Where is she?"

"In a building next to the tower," Idalia said, her voice a harsh whisper in the wind.

"Thank you," he said. "We will bring her to Winter, if it is acceptable with you."

"Donovan," the soldier hissed.

Aviva looked at Idalia, letting her decide, but she was no longer looking at the men. She stared off to the side away from Eira's people.

Aviva nodded. "That's fine," she said.

Donovan bowed slightly and made to walk away. He passed by Milo. "Good luck to our next queen," he said.

The words sent shivers down Aviva's spine. One of them would be the queen. Either Idalia would kill her, or she would have to kill Idalia. When would the killing stop? When would the deaths cease? She was going to be sick.

Eira's army packed up and vanished. They were gone. Eira was gone. All that was left was Idalia.

64

Idalia clicked her tongue. Lady moved into a walk. She led her to the backside of the mountain where the tunnel Aviva had made was still open.

She dismounted and quickly made her way through the tunnel to the training room. Her landing echoed around her. Her eyes took a second to adjust to the darkness. "Hello?" she called into the dark room. There was no answer.

Aviva dropped down beside her. "Where do you think they went?"

Idalia shook her head. She didn't know. She didn't know anything anymore. How could she have let everything get so confusing? How could she have done what she did? She left these people here. She killed Eira. Every decision she'd made was wrong.

"The army is gone," Idalia said, her words reverberating around the room. She walked further into the mountain.

She lit a flame in her palm. Shadows climbed the walls, but there were no people. Not in this room, anyways.

She walked farther and farther into the mountain. She

searched every room, looked in every hallway. She only stopped when she reached the stone wall that divided what used to be the main hall. She placed her hand on the stone. It was cold under her fingers.

"There's no one here," she said to no one in particular.

"They got away," Aviva said, coming to her side. "There's no one here, but there are also no bodies. Not inside or outside. They got away."

Idalia made her way back outside into the Summer air. She searched the nearby area but found nothing. It was like they had disappeared into thin air. Idalia mounted Lady and nudged her.

"Where are you going?" Aviva shouted after her.

"To find answers."

Idalia rode through Summer, Aviva silent next to her. They stopped at a stream for water. Stopped during the night for sleep. But got back on their horses and rode some more the next day. And the next. Until Conformity Castle was before them.

It had felt like ages since she last saw the castle. When was the last time? She couldn't answer that, but it didn't matter anyways. All that mattered was finding a way to stop the Finale from happening. She needed to know how to save Aviva. Because she couldn't get more blood on her hands. She couldn't be queen.

She slid off Lady and walked up the steps of the castle. Aviva stuck beside her. The sound of servants working filled her ears as she stepped inside.

So many people were there. So many she hadn't seen before, didn't recognize. Where had all these people come from? What were they doing here?

She reached out to a girl passing by. The girl's face lit up with a smile. She bowed her head. "Lady Idalia. Lady Aviva. I'm so glad you have come home. We'll set your rooms up if you are here to stay."

"Where are King Quilo's things?"

"King Quilo?" she asked, surprised.

"For what?" Aviva asked.

Idalia ignored Aviva. Her grip on the girl tightened slightly. "His things?"

"Right this way," she said, setting down the basket of laundry she had been holding. She led them up the stairs to the highest floor. She opened the last door for them. The room was full of papers, books, boxes. "Queen Quinn had us move all of his stuff here after his death," she said, a sad tone tugging at her words.

"Thank you." Idalia walked into the room.

The servant girl left. Idalia didn't know where to start. There were so many things here, in no particular order, and not organized at all. But if anyone had the answers she was need-ing, it would be her biological father. Right?

"What are we looking for exactly?" Aviva asked.

Idalia ran a hand along the table, skimming over the papers scattered there. "Anything that will tell us how to stop the Finale." She took a big breath. "I don't care what Eira said, I'm not fighting you, Aviva. So we need to end this. Somehow."

"I'm not fighting you either," Aviva whispered.

Idalia didn't respond. Instead, she flung back the heavy curtains to let in even more daylight. She started in one corner of the room and slowly went through each scrap of paper. Each book. Each box.

Idalia could see her father, a man she didn't actually remember, sitting at a desk writing these things. His hand-writing was fluid. It was nice. Not rushed. Nothing like her chicken scratch. Did she get anything from him? Did she look like either of her parents at all? She didn't know.

She rifled through a dusty box. Her hands were grimy and she wiped them on her pants. Inside the box was rolled up and tied letters on the same parchment Brey had used.

She took one out, unrolled it, and tossed it aside. She took another one out. Eira's name was written delicately at the top. Her stomach turned at the sight. She looked away for a second.

She could feel the slippery blood beneath her fingers. She needed to clean her hands again.

Idalia took a deep breath, closing her eyes. She took another and another until the feeling on her hands lessened. The sickness rolling in her belly dissipated. She couldn't smell the smoke and death in her nose any longer.

She opened her eyes, put Eira's note aside, and found more letters. One was addressed to Orla. One to Aviva. And one to her.

"Here," she said, holding out Aviva's letter. Aviva crossed the room to grab it from her.

"What's this?"

Idalia shrugged, pulling hers open. "I don't know. But there's one for each of us."

Aviva stepped away and began reading her letter. Idalia flattened hers out on the table next to her, holding it in place.

Idalia,

My darling second-born. My firestarter. You must be so lost here. I am sorry. Please forgive me for the measures I had to take to keep you and your sisters safe.

If you are reading this, if you have found my things, then all that I did was not in vain.

You have survived. It is all I want. You and your sisters deserve to be safe. To endure what I endured is a great disservice to my children. I wanted you to get a chance to bond with your siblings. A chance I did not get.

No, ever since I was a wee child, I knew it was my destiny to kill my brothers. It is the way of Season.

But Season needs to change. I hoped marrying and conceiving children with your mother, a human, would alter things. Your mother bore four children, four daughters, and I knew it had not worked. So I sent you all away, to your mother's land. She assured you would be taken care of. That the humans there would shape and mold you into a fine lady. I hope she was right.

I do not know if the trials are upon you. I do not know if Season has reclaimed you all. I fear for you. I fear for all of my children.

I am sorry that I am not there to give you answers. But you will have Queen Quinn and Brey to guide you. Let them guide you to answers. Let them guide you to change.

I love you.

Eternally,
King Quilo

"Human?" Idalia whispered, mouthing the words as she read.

"What is that supposed to mean?" Aviva asked, coming to her side and looking around her shoulder at her letter.

Idalia shrugged. "I don't know."

Idalia put her letter down and searched the rest of the box, but she didn't find any other answers. She moved to a bookshelf full of hardbound leather books. She pulled one off the shelf and rifled through the pages. Every page was full of her father's handwriting. "It's a journal," Idalia said.

"So is this one." Aviva held up another hardbound leather book.

They read silently.

Idalia put the journal down and looked through a different box. A small picture of Quinn was nestled between two sheets of parchment. She was in plain clothes with a blue background. A school picture. She had gone to a high school just like them.

She found more pictures of Quinn. Different ages, different clothes. Idalia recognized some of the buildings in the pictures, the college spread out behind Quinn in one as she sat on the lawn. Quinn had been in Texas.

"This is so weird," Idalia said, handing Aviva the pictures.

"So Quinn was just like us?"

"I guess so, except she didn't have to kill her siblings, if she even had any. Our father was the one who had to go through the trials."

"If he wasn't human, what was he?"

"What are we?" Idalia asked.

Idalia couldn't shake the feeling spreading through her body. A slow numbing covered her. She didn't know what she was. Everything she thought she knew was wrong. Everything she thought she had figured out was wrong. Was she ever right about anything?

She spent all day and night reading through Quilo's things. Even when Aviva left to find food, she stayed and read. Her eyes blurred. The letters melded together. Her head hurt trying to read in the low light of the flames now lit around the room.

Aviva swung the door open and carried in a tray of food and a pitcher of water. Idalia's stomach grumbled, and she made room at the table for the tray. Aviva sat across from her.

Idalia leaned back in her chair, a cracker with cheese in one hand and a letter in the other.

"Listen to this," she said. "In the event of my death, a new ordinance shall be in place. All mention of our fae heritage must be hidden from the Four. It is in their best interest they remain ignorant of their birthright."

"Fae?" Aviva asked.

Idalia put down the letter and picked up a picture. She stared at a small child with wild, wavy red hair. Bright brown eyes stared back at her.

"Is that you?"

"I think so," Idalia whispered. She traced her finger over the picture, over the delicate features of her childish face. Over the slightly pointed ears.

She looked back at the letter and read farther down the page. "The Four will be sent to Texas, their mother's homeland. Their ears are to be clipped so they may be human-passing. All servants must hide their own heritage in the event of their return to Season."

"This is too much," Aviva said.

Idalia let go of the letter. It fluttered to the tabletop. She rubbed her eyes. "Why don't we pick this back up tomorrow?

Maybe then we'll find something that can actually help us with the Finale instead of turning everything on its head once again."

Aviva agreed.

Idalia stuffed her face with the food and water. After her stomach was full, she left the room, closing the door to her father's knowledge.

65

A viva held up a journal. The handwriting was different from her father's. It was one she recognized immediately. "This is Brey's," she said.

She skimmed the words, flipping pages as she read over Brey's words.

"What does it say?" Idalia asked from her chair on the opposite side of the room.

Aviva flipped to another page. "Here it talks about the Finale," she said, holding her breath. Hoping that Brey had managed to find something helpful before Eira had killed him.

"Well?"

Aviva held up a finger, reading to the bottom of the page. "There's nothing we can do." Her stomach sank, and she dropped onto a stool. "There's no stopping the Finale. At least Brey didn't find a way."

"There must be something we can do," Idalia assured her while going through more and more books.

Aviva shook her head. "How are we going to stop something that Season demands? How are we going to end a tradition that's been happening for way longer than us?"

She flipped back to the beginning of the journal and reread the words. "The Finale is a culmination of all of the trials. It will test the Four's powers. It will test their strength."

"We know that," Idalia said.

"We don't know anything," Aviva said, throwing the journal down. "We were set up to fail."

Aviva stood and left the room. Idalia called after her, but she ignored her. She was tired of the suffocating feeling that room gave her. She needed air, sun, earth beneath her. She fell to the grass outside of the castle, letting it ground her. Letting it fill her with a different feeling. She could breathe easier with her element around her.

The grass was prickly underneath her palm as she ran her hand through it. She breathed deeply.

Footsteps sounded behind her and she turned. The grass grew all around her, and roots snaked through the ground knocking the intruder to the ground.

"Ow," Idalia said, rubbing her butt.

"Sorry," Aviva said, hopping up from the ground. "I didn't mean to do that."

"Yea, yea." Idalia rolled her eyes.

Aviva helped her to a stand. Her hands warmed in Idalia's. Her skin sizzled. "Idalia, stop," she said, trying to let go. Panic filled her. She tried pulling her hands free, but she couldn't. She yanked and yanked. But her hands kept burning.

"I'm trying!" Idalia finally pulled her hands free and looked at her palms. They were red.

Aviva turned her hands over, angry blisters sprung up on her skin. She gritted her teeth against the pain. "Let me guess. You didn't mean to?"

Idalia shook her head, wide eyed.

"Brey's journal said the Finale could happen at any point after the last trial. And that any of the Four left would lose control of their powers until they faced each other."

"I'm not fighting you," Idalia whispered.

"I'm not fighting you," Aviva agreed. She held her hands against her chest lightly. She needed something to take the burn away. She needed a doctor.

"Go to Gro," Idalia said with a nudge. "She'll fix those right up for you."

Aviva nodded and left Idalia to find the healer.

She knocked on a wooden door in the back of the castle. "Yes?" a gruff voice called from inside. Aviva pushed the door open and stepped inside.

Gro turned from a table full of vials of liquids. She took one look at Aviva's hands before motioning for her to sit down. Gro got a large wooden bowl and filled it with water. She added a vial to the water, the liquid splashing around. She turned and instructed Aviva to dip her hands in.

Aviva let her fingertips rest on the surface of the water. It stung. She pulled her hands out. "What is this?"

Gro tsked and grabbed Aviva's hands, putting them fully into the bowl. Aviva screamed. Her hands burned, even more than when Idalia's flames had kissed them. Gro kept her hands in the mixture despite Aviva fighting against her.

The bowl turned a milky white. The burn lessened and lessened.

Gro removed her hands, letting Aviva pull her hands from the bowl. Her palms were no longer blistered or red. They were smooth and pale.

Aviva rubbed her hands together, in awe. "How did you do that?"

Gro didn't answer. She just turned her back to Aviva,

clanging around on the table. So Aviva slid off the chair and headed for the door.

"Here," Gro said just as she opened the door. She tossed a vial into the air.

Aviva clumsily caught it. "What's this for?"

"Just in case you run into flames again."

Aviva nodded, put the vial in her pants and walked back up to her room. She needed a break before going back to reading through all of Brey and Quilo's things. She didn't like reading, especially when it wasn't helping them find a way around the Finale.

She didn't want to hurt Idalia. And she didn't know how to stop the Finale or change Season like her father had wished.

She needed a break. Just a small one.

She slid into bed, pulling the covers over her and quickly fell asleep. When she woke up later, the light from outside was much darker. She rubbed her eyes, ridding herself of the sleepiness gnawing at her bones. She left her room and went to find Idalia.

Aviva was sure she'd still be reading. She didn't like to give up or admit defeat. It was one thing she loved about her sister. But it also was one thing she knew Idalia needed to change. No one could keep pushing as hard as her forever. She'd eventually break. They both would.

She opened the door to Quilo's library of things. The room was more organized. The boxes they had looked through were stacked on one side and the ones they still hadn't managed to get to were on the other. But Idalia wasn't in the room. She wasn't in the chair, leaning back, reading yet another piece of parchment like she'd been for two days straight.

She turned away from the room, heading back out to the hallway when a paper fluttering on the tabletop caught her attention. She fetched it, holding it out in front of her.

Aviva,

It's about time someone left you a letter saying goodbye.

I'm going back to Texas. You will stay in Season. And hopefully we won't end up hurting one another. Hopefully the distance will be enough for the Finale to stop. But knowing our luck, Season will take us one way or another. Just know that I love you, my little sister. I never want to hurt you. I want to protect you. I'm sorry I wasn't around sooner to save you from your foster parents. I failed as a big sister.

But I won't fail you now. I will save you. I have to.

Hopefully we won't see each other again. If I have a say, I will never return to Season and you'll be able to call it your home. You will live.

I love you. Goodbye.

Idalia

Aviva crumpled the paper up. She threw it to the ground and stomped out of the room. She wanted to go after Idalia, to tell her it wasn't her responsibility to protect her and that she could protect herself. She'd been doing it all her life. But Idalia was right. They had to try something. And obviously being in the same place wasn't going to stop the Finale. It was only going to lead to them hurting one another.

But she hated the loneliness that crept in, settling on her bones as she walked back to her room.

She hated being alone. She should be used to it. But after a year of being someone's little sister, she had grown accustomed to having someone with her.

She crawled back into her bed. It was nighttime, but no matter how hard she tried, she couldn't go back to sleep. Instead, she made a list of all the things she needed to do in Season. Starting with finding the people of Summer and Spring.

66

In the Land of Texas

Idalia stepped through the portal into the front yard of her parent's house. Her car was still parked out front, and so was her parents'. They were home. *Oh, this is great,* she thought to herself as she walked up the driveway and knocked on the door.

"Idalia?" her mother said when she opened the door.

"Hi, Mom."

"It's been a week. Where have you been?"

Idalia stepped under her arm to get inside. "I just took a little trip with Aviva before school started again."

"So you said in the vague letter you left," she said, following Idalia into the living room.

"How was your trip?" her father called, not taking his eyes off the TV.

Idalia shrugged. "We didn't really have a plan. We just went with the flow and where the bus took us. It was good," she lied. She hated how easy it had become to lie to her parents. Hated that her guts twisted with each word, but the less they knew, the better. Right?

She took a seat next to her father. He wrapped an arm around her. "Are you ready for classes to start?"

Idalia nodded. She would've been ready. If she had remembered to sign up for classes or pay for her dorm. But she hadn't done any of that. And she couldn't tell her parents. The last time she told them she wanted to take a break from school, they had made her go anyway.

"When do you go back?"

Idalia looked around the room. The clock hanging on one wall blinked the date. "Tomorrow, classes start in a few days," she said.

Her mother sat on her other side. "I thought you were cutting it a little close after being gone so long."

Idalia squeezed out a smile. She didn't know what else to say, so she didn't say anything. She just leaned back and watched the TV with her parents.

Idalia slid into a cubicle. She clicked the computer on and waited for it to boot up. The library was quiet around her. Not a lot of students milled around since classes had only just started a few days ago. She clicked the internet open and started her research.

Fae. What was fae? And why did her father think it would be best to hide the fact that they weren't fully human? None of it made sense.

But at least she knew why they had powers now. She didn't belong in the human world, she didn't belong in Texas, so it was a good thing Season was going to end up killing her. Unless she found a way around the Finale. Or she managed to stay away from Aviva. Maybe then they'd both survive. But she couldn't get over the fact that she no longer felt like she belonged in this world.

She clicked through article after article. Some were just fan sites. Some were theories about certain fictional books about fae. And some were mythological definitions of the fair folk.

Mythology. Like the class she took from Professor Hendrix. He would know about the fae. But did she really want to invite him back into her life? She'd rather stay far, far away. So she continued to search but nothing stuck out to her. None of the articles or websites told her exactly what she was. No one had any idea what being half human and half fae meant. She definitely didn't.

But that wasn't the most important thing Idalia should be worrying about. *No, I should be worrying about how to survive this mess.*

Idalia sighed and clicked the computer off. There was nothing here. The real research she needed to be doing was back in Season. She needed real accounts. She needed to know why Quilo had married Quinn instead of some other fae, why he had hidden their true identities, why Brey went along with it all, and why Brey never once mentioned it when he was alive. Why didn't he at least hint toward it? Something. Anything to help them know themselves.

Idalia traced her finger along her ear. The slight, almost unnoticeable point of it had her skin crawling. How had she never thought her ears were strangely shaped at the top? How had she been so stupid?

She left the cubicle to exit the library but stopped just inside the entrance door.

She had nowhere to go. Her parents thought she was back at school so she couldn't go home. She hadn't registered for a dorm so she couldn't go there. She had nowhere to stay.

She was homeless.

A familiar face passed by her. "Hey," an old friend said, skidding to a stop beside her. "I haven't seen you around lately." She wrapped her arms around Idalia's shoulders.

"Hi, Katie," Idalia said, awkwardly hugging her back. She couldn't remember the last time she spoke to Katie. It seemed so long ago. And to think they had been best friends. Her, Katie, and Brittany. They had been inseparable until Season tore Idalia away.

"Where'd you move?" she asked.

Idalia raised an eyebrow in confusion. "What are you talking about?"

"You moved out of your dorm. Did you go to a different one?"

"Oh, no. I forgot to reapply. How'd you know I moved out?"

Katie laughed. "Because I moved into it. You know I always liked yours better than mine."

"Right. Well, I should get going," Idalia said, stepping away.

Katie reached out her hand and wrapped it around Idalia's bicep. "You said you forgot to reapply. You don't have a dorm?"

Idalia shook her head. "No, I completely spaced."

"You can crash at mine if you want. Until you find a new place or whatever."

Idalia's eyes widened. "For real?"

Katie smiled. "Of course. I've missed you!"

"You're a lifesaver, Katie."

Katie put her arm around Idalia's shoulders and they exited the library together. "I'm here to serve," she said, laughing.

Idalia let Katie guide her through the college campus back to her old dorm, thankful someone had come to her rescue.

67

In the Land of Season

A knock on the bedroom door startled Aviva awake. Within seconds, her room was covered in vines, a wall she couldn't see through encircled the bed, protecting her.

"Princess Aviva?" a soft voice said from the other side of the wall.

Aviva took a deep, calming breath. She was fine. She was in Conformity Castle. She was not in danger.

The vines slithered away. "Sorry, Lace," she said looking up at the small lady. Her blonde hair was pulled into a tight bun on her head.

Lace gave a soft smile. "It is quite all right, Princess Aviva. I understand how difficult adjusting must be."

Aviva nodded. Lace didn't know the half of it. She'd had to adjust several times over. Adjust to new foster homes again and again. Had to adjust again when finding out she wasn't even from her world. Adjust to her biological parents being dead. Her sisters being dead. Learning she wasn't even a human being. She was bone tired of adjusting.

Lace set down a tray of food on the nearby table. "What are you wanting to do today, Princess Aviva? You have the whole castle to yourself. I'm sure we could find something to entertain you."

"I don't need to be entertained."

"Of course," Lace said with a small nod. She turned to head back out the door.

"Wait," Aviva said. Lace stopped in her tracks. "I want to find my people. And my sister's. They were at the cave in Summer but they're no longer there. Do you know where they could have gone?"

Lace shook her head. "I'm sorry, but I do not." She paused, her eyebrow rising on her forehead as she thought about something. "There's not many places they could have gone, though. Your sister, Lady Eira, destroyed all of Spring. They wouldn't go to Winter. If you've already searched Summer, then you may want to look in Autumn. Though I'm not sure they'd be much help after Lady Orla was killed."

Aviva nodded like she understood anything Lace was saying, but her mind was muggy in the morning. She hadn't gotten much sleep. And no matter how hard she thought about it, she couldn't figure out where her people would go. She didn't even know if her and Idalia's people would've stayed together.

"Let me ask the other ladies. Maybe they've heard something," Lace said, curtsying and hurrying out of the room.

Aviva fell back onto the bed. Her eyes fluttered shut. She could go back to sleep. She probably should. But with the

Finale looming over her and her people missing, she was restless.

She scooted to the edge of the bed, picked up the tray of food and ate quickly. Then, she dressed for an adventure. She would wait on Lace to return and then she would head out in whatever direction the workers in the castle suggested.

The floor under her wavered and a portal ripped the boards apart. She jumped away from the hole.

Idalia hurtled through the air, surrounded in fire. Aviva put her hands up, covering her face. The room erupted in vines again. Some burned to the ground as Idalia flew through them.

"What are you doing here?" Aviva shouted. She tried looking through the vines, but they were thick. A fireball shot through the wall in front of her. She jumped back, cowering in the corner. A tree branch twisted into the room, busting the window into a million shards as it swiped against the floor.

Idalia cried out. The sound of her hitting the floor clanged around the room.

Aviva wanted to pull the earth back. To get rid of the vines and the tree, but she couldn't. They wouldn't pull back. They weren't listening to her.

Another fireball shot into the room. She ducked just as it landed above her head. The wall behind her lit on fire. She hopped away, but the room filled with smoke. Her vines were kindling to Idalia's flames. She was going to burn the castle down.

"Idalia, stop," she yelled.

Idalia grunted. "I'm trying, but I can't."

Their powers were not their own. They were no longer in control. Season would take one of them if it had to. Season would make them fight.

Aviva ran to the shattered window and jumped.

Idalia's screams followed her.

Her stomach caught in her throat. She hurtled to the ground, faster and faster. Wind whipped around her as she fell. This was going to hurt. Aviva closed her eyes as the ground sped closer.

She landed with a thud, breath surging from her lungs, side aching. She looked up into the perfect sky, dazzling blue and sunny.

She rolled off the makeshift net her element had made before she collided with the earth. She stood on shaky legs.

"Are you okay?" Idalia yelled, hanging out of the window.

Aviva nodded. "Yeah. Yeah, I think so," she said.

"I'm so sorry."

Aviva clutched her side. She would have a bruise, no doubt. But it was better than being burned alive. Better than dying. "It's not your fault." Aviva took a big breath, her chest expanding. A sharp pain shot through her midsection. "What are we going to do?"

"I don't know, but I'm leaving," Idalia said.

Before Aviva could say anything, another portal opened and Idalia disappeared. Aviva crumpled to the ground. She took long, deep breaths. Each one sent a wave of pain through her. *What are we going to do?* she asked herself over and over.

Finally, her breaths came easier, and she pushed herself back up to a stand.

She walked slowly through the yard and up to her room. It was a mess. The walls were covered in blackened vines. Everything had been thrown around when the portals opened. It smelled of smoke.

Lace stood in the doorway, her jaw to the floor.

"I spoke to Candace and Pete," Lace said when she recovered from the shock of the room. She began picking up the broken pieces of furniture. Aviva moved to help her but Lace waved her off. "Harriet, Lady Eira's maidservant, never returned from Winter. Candace said she didn't know where the Summer people went after the mountain, but Pete did say that she got word from her cousin's nephew that a handful of new inhabitants visited Autumn."

"So they're in Autumn?" Aviva questioned, standing by the door out of Lace's way.

Lace shrugged and pulled vines off the wall. "That would be my best hypothesis. Though why they would go to Autumn I have no clue."

"Thank you," Aviva said, turning her back to the messy room.

"Where are you going?" Lace asked, standing up from setting a chair on its legs.

"To Autumn. I told you I was going to find my people."

Lace nodded and went back to cleaning. "Go safely. Return soon, Lady Aviva, so that I may know you are alive."

"I don't know how much longer I'll be alive, but I'll try my best to return," Aviva said.

"Try your best to live," Lace whispered as Aviva left.

Milo galloped to Autumn. Aviva remembered the first time she had made the trip on horseback. She had all of her sisters with her then. And they had a guide. Things were so much different then. Aviva slipped off Milo at the edge of Autumn. She walked into the town.

The streets were busy, full of people, bustling from one chore to the next. It was much different than the first time Aviva had seen it.

She found her way to the center, to the cathedral.

A wind blew her hair all around her face. The sharp

cinnamon scent smelled just like Orla. A tear rose to Aviva's eye. She sniffled and wiped her face. Orla was here. She could feel her. She wanted to melt in the scent, to let it consume her. She wanted to feel the wind again and again just like she had felt Orla's caring touches. She missed her sister. Terribly.

A boy ran past her and rushed into the cathedral, throwing the doors open. The building was jammed full of people just like the streets. And they weren't all wearing shades of yellow.

Aviva rushed to the door and walked inside. The room went silent. Every eye in the building turned toward her. The hair on the back of her neck stood up. Shivers ran down her spine. She hated being looked at. Hated it more than anything.

"Lady Aviva," the whispers started until the whole room erupted in a chorus of her name.

"Thank the heavens," a lady in red said, running toward her. She flung her arms out, enveloping her in a hug.

Aviva wanted to crawl out of her skin. She pushed the lady back, held her at arm's length.

A smile broke out on her face, "Sara." A hiccup of a laugh escaped her lips as she pulled Sara back into a hug.

More people she recognized from the mountain moved forward, toward her. There weren't a ton of them, but they were here. They were safe. They looked cared for.

"Lady Idalia?" Sara asked, her voice quiet.

"She's in Texas," Aviva assured her.

Sara let out a breath. "Thank the heavens," she said. "I'm so glad you are both safe."

"Yes, for now."

A man in yellow made his way through the crowd to stand before Aviva. "It is an honor, Lady Aviva." He bowed slightly to her.

"Thank you for taking in my people. And the people of

Summer," Aviva said, taking his offered hand in a weirdly informal handshake.

The man inclined his head. "It was the least we could do for the future queen of Season."

Of course. Of course they would take their people. Either Idalia or herself would be queen. All of these people would be one of theirs. All of these people would bow to one of them. It wasn't kindness that made them offer a hand to her people. It was a way to get on her good side should she win this race to be queen.

Aviva recalled a section in Brey's diary where he explained how the people of Season rarely interacted with each other. Each section had always been separated by more than just boundary lines. Even after one of the Four became the king or queen of Season, the people remained in their own section with the exception of those that served in Conformity Castle. Though the people of the winning section did have an easier life for the ruler's duration since Season transformed into the winner's element.

"And would you also take in the people of Winter?"

The man shook his head. "We would make no such deal with the people of Winter. It is because of their princess that ours is dead."

"Well, luckily for you and everyone here, that threat has been dealt with."

"Lady Eira is dead?" Sara asked.

Aviva nodded.

"Lady Eira is dead," Sara said again, her voice louder. It carried around the room. Everyone looked at one another, questions on their faces.

Then, the room erupted into cheers. "Lady Eira is dead! We are safe again."

Aviva's stomach turned at the sight. Of all these people

cheering for the death of her sister. She understood that Eira was their enemy, that she had instructed the death of many of their people, but she was still her sister.

"Is this how you'll cheer when I'm dead? Or when Idalia is? Is this how you cheered when news of Orla's death came?" Aviva shouted. Her fists balled in anger. The trees outside swayed back and forth, scraping against the building. The rocks rumbled under their feet. Roots crawled up the side of the building, intertwining together on the ceiling.

A nearby tree branch punctured a window, tiny sparkling shards of glass shattered across the building. The people screamed.

"When will enough be enough?"

Aviva couldn't control it. She couldn't control the earth as it ripped into two. Still the people screamed as they ran toward the back of the building away from the canyon forming beneath them.

She fell to her knees, putting her head in her hands. She cried out in frustration. What was happening to her?

"Lady Aviva," Sara said, kneeling next to her. She wrapped her arm over her shoulders. "It's okay," she whispered.

"None of this is okay," Aviva said through gritted teeth.

Sara closed her mouth and gave a curt nod.

Aviva breathed in and out. Steadily. With the beat of her heart. With the beat of the earth around her. She felt the earth moving, could sense its unease. But it wasn't the earth's unease, it was her own. And she could control it. She had to. Or she'd be the next dead princess these people cheered for.

Slowly, she stood up. She squeezed her hands together, imagining the earth knitting itself back together into one flat bottom. The ground moved beneath her. The canyon disappeared. The cathedral floor repaired around her. The people took a tentative step forward.

"I'm sorry," Aviva said to all of them.

"We are sorry," the man in yellow said, taking a step toward her, placing a hand on her shoulder. "The hardship of being a princess of Season is not one I would wish on my greatest adversary."

68

Idalia turned on her side, her hip digging into the hard couch. She was grateful for Katie, but the couch sucked. She needed to figure something else out. But she had no job and no money. She couldn't go back to her parents. Or she could, but she would hate having to leave them again when Season took her back. She wanted to put space between them, let them get used to her goodbye. Because eventually it would be goodbye for good.

She sat up, putting her elbows on her knees and her head in her hands. She hated just sitting around. But she'd gone to the library several days in a row. She had stuffed her brain full of every and anything fae. She had searched and searched for anything about Season but couldn't find anything. This world didn't know about Season and what was known about the fae seemed like fictional crap. She couldn't trust any of the sources.

She wished she had her father's journals. Or Brey's. She wished she had authentic accounts of Season. But instead, she was left with nothing to help her figure out who she was now–*what* she was.

As if finding out she wasn't from this world and that she could conjure up fire with a simple thought was enough, she also had to be something else entirely. Though, the more she thought about it, the more it made sense. Did she know of any humans that had powers? No. Not one.

Quinn didn't even have any. At least she hadn't ever shown if she did. And she definitely would've made it known. Quilo must have been the one with the ability to conjure his season. Only the Four had access to the elemental magic. Why was that?

Idalia rubbed her eyes. Her hands warmed. She saw red behind her closed eyes.

She jumped up from the couch, just as it burst into flames. Her body was ablaze. She was burning up. She tried to rein the fire in, to stuff it back into her body, but it danced around her, hopping from her body to the couch, to the rug, to the papers on the desk beside her.

She stomped on the rug, but her foot was covered in flames and the fire only grew.

Water rained down from the ceiling. The fire alarm went crazy.

A portal ripped open in the room. Through it she could see Season. She could smell the fresh grass, she could see the horses roaming around the castle.

She backed up against the opposite wall, as far away from the portal as she could get. She wouldn't go back. She had to stay here. She had to stay away from Aviva. She had to protect her. She had to get her powers under control.

Fire grew around her, running up the walls. Black smoke filled the room.

Stop. Stop. Stop.

Idalia dropped to her knees. The portal pulled her across the floor. She clutched at the burning floorboards. She didn't want to go to Season. She couldn't go to Season.

"No! No, no, no," she cried as the portal wrapped around her leg, as she disappeared from Texas, leaving nothing but flames behind.

In the Land of Season

Idalia stayed in a ball, refusing to move or to get any closer to Aviva than she already was. The stench of burning grass met her nose, and she wanted to run away from it but she stayed put. Her flames burned and burned.

The world around her turned dark. She could see nothing but the red of her flames. The ground around her had blackened.

She stretched out her fiery limbs, starfishing on the ashen earth. She looked up at the night sky. Only the twinkling of stars lit it. It was beautiful, a deep dark purple stretching as far as she could see. But she couldn't stay here in this beautiful place that called to her.

She had to go.

She grabbed the necklace around her neck. "Take me to Texas," she said, harshly. The words burned her throat. She desperately needed a drink of water. Something to staunch the flames.

The necklace glowed, mixing with the red of her fire. But a portal didn't open.

"Take me to Texas," she said again, her teeth gritted as she clenched her fist tighter around the necklace.

She waited. But still nothing happened.

She stood, turned her back on Conformity Castle, and walked away. She wasn't going to Aviva. Season couldn't make her. Season would not control her.

She walked until she found a pond, her footsteps burning into the ground. She slid into the water. She submerged herself into the cool liquid. She held her breath as long as she could, letting the water take away her fire. Letting the water calm her. Her throat burned, needing air. But she pushed herself farther under the surface. She would stay here. She would keep Aviva safe from her flames. She would let Aviva win.

Her feet kicked against the bottom of the pond and catapulted her above the water. Her lungs filled with air.

She hated how weak she was and how she couldn't make it easier for Aviva. She wasn't the answer to their problems. She was part of a problem she couldn't solve.

Idalia sat on the edge of the pond, her feet dangling in the water, and breathed until it became easy.

What was she going to do? Season was forcing her here, but she couldn't go to Conformity Castle. Not while Aviva was there. She could go to Summer. No one would be there. Her people had vanished. Everyone would be safe from her there, locked away in her stone tower.

Idalia nodded her head. To Summer. That's where she'd go. She set out, her feet no longer leaving a burning path behind her.

69

Aviva had asked her people to join her at Conformity Castle. But they had denied her. They had already made a plan with the people of Summer and Autumn. They would each help one another rebuild their towns. They would help Season become what it once was. Before the Four destroyed it all.

So Aviva rode back to Conformity Castle alone.

She took several days, enjoying the earth around her. Letting Milo pick which path they took. She didn't really have a need to rush back to the castle except to prove to Lace that she was still alive. But that could wait a few days.

Aviva stopped by a pond to get a drink. She cupped her hands into the water and brought it to her lips. It was cool on her tongue. She sat by the pond for a while, letting Milo graze around her. She leaned back with her eyes closed and nestled against the ground. Her hands stretched out around her, taking in the scratchy texture of the grass.

She turned her head to the side and opened her eyes. Next

to her, a large patch of earth was black. It crumpled under her fingertips.

A step away was another, smaller patch of black, and another. They were shaped like footsteps, leading to the pond. Aviva pushed herself up on her elbows. "Strange," Aviva muttered.

She stood and went to Milo. She wanted to follow the black footsteps, but another set of footsteps called to her, leading her away from the pond and deeper into the forest.

"Go away."

Aviva stopped walking. She could feel the earth readying under her, the roots rumbling, the grass lengthening. She could feel the control slipping from her. "Idalia?" Aviva called into the thick woods, searching for her sister.

"Go away, Aviva."

Aviva's stomach sank at the words, at being sent away. She had always been disregarded, told not to take up too much space. But this was different. This was to save them both, so she turned away, heading back in the direction of the pond, but her feet stopped working. Her legs wouldn't push her forward. She was stuck.

"I literally can't," she said, trying to pull her feet from the sinking ground.

"And I can't portal back to Texas," Idalia said, stepping out from behind a tree.

Aviva pulled and pulled, but Season had a hold on her. She couldn't get free. Milo whinnied beside her, unsettled. He pushed his head against her back, but she didn't budge. "I don't think this whole staying away thing is working."

"Obviously not."

"Season wants us to fight," Aviva said, meeting Idalia's eyes. Idalia nodded. But she stayed by the tree. And her flames were nowhere to be seen. Thankfully.

"What are we supposed to do now?" Aviva whispered.

"I don't know."

Aviva hung her head. She needed to get out of here. Needed to be far away from Idalia. But she couldn't move.

The ground around Aviva's foot fell away, dissolving as a portal opened under her. "Idalia," she said. Worry filled her. She didn't want to go through the portal. She didn't want to go wherever Season was going to send her next. She didn't want any of this.

Idalia hopped back as a portal opened near her. She took off running in the opposite direction, leaving Aviva as the world sucked her under.

She slipped out of the portal, and the Tree of Season loomed over her. Its golden array blinded her. She rolled to her side and stood. The broken walls of the arena surrounded her and the tree. She ran toward the arched entrance, but no matter how long she ran, she never got any closer. It stretched out ahead, always out of reach.

Another portal opened a few feet away from her, and Idalia fell out of it.

Aviva turned toward her. "We're stuck," she said.

Idalia shook her head and ran to the entrance, but she never made it.

The stone walls thickened, the cracks repairing and strengthening. The walls pushed from the ground, growing taller so they had no chance of escape. A glistening dome appeared over them. Aviva could see through it to the auditorium seats that rose from the earth and encircled the arena. Sparks fluttered around, portals tearing into the world. People in all shades of red, yellow, green, and blue filtered into the seats. They looked down at them like specimens. They were going to watch one of them die.

"It's the Finale," Aviva breathed, her heart caught in her

throat as her insides twisted. There was no escaping it. Nowhere to go. Nowhere to run but into the fight ahead.

70

Aviva didn't move. She was petrified to step toward Idalia, her body frozen in fear. She didn't want to see what Season was going to make them do to one another. Her limbs were heavy, a weight pushing her into the ground. She could do nothing but stand there.

"Why is everyone here?" Idalia asked, looking out at the crowd.

Aviva shrugged. Dread filled her. "To witness the victory of the Four." She shivered. The hair on the back of her neck rose, her hands and feet tingled. Her stomach squeezed. Breathing was becoming harder.

"They didn't watch any of the trials except for the Trial of Autumn."

"I guess we're not the only ones brought here by Season," Aviva said through a tight throat.

Idalia turned away from the crowd to look at her. "I'm not going to fight you, Aviva. I'm serious. I'm not doing this."

"I don't want to do this either," Aviva said. Tears threatened her eyes. She couldn't hurt Idalia. She couldn't kill someone again. She wanted to leave.

The Tree of Season lit up, a bright white light blinked once.

The wind around them picked up. Aviva's hair whipped across her face. Her cheeks stung from the onslaught. Leaves were caught in the wind, twirling into several tornadoes. One raced right for her.

"Don't follow me," Idalia said before turning to the left and running away. A tornado chased after her.

Aviva's body filled with adrenaline, her heart beat faster, her lungs filled with air. She darted right, heading straight for a tornado. Her legs screamed against the wind as she pushed herself to keep going forward against the wind. She ground her teeth as she fought through the wind, spinning around the mini tornadoes.

A big gust of air knocked her to the ground. Then lifted her briefly from the earth. She raised her hands, roots snaking around her body and pulling her back to the ground safely. The tornado raced over her. She could only hear the rumbling of the air as she covered her head and waited it out under her mountain of roots.

A few seconds passed.

The sound around her died.

She let the roots go, and she stood up. She turned in circles. She was close to the outer wall, but she could still see the Tree of Season. She couldn't see Idalia though. She must've made it farther to the other side. Or she was hiding. Where Aviva didn't know. It wasn't like there was anywhere to hide in the open field. But at least the tornadoes were gone.

The Tree of Season lit up, a bright white light blinking twice.

The ground froze under her. She slipped, hitting the ground hard.

Snow fell around her. She shivered. She wanted to find Idalia, wanted her fire to keep her warm. But she couldn't go near her. She had to stay away. She had to fend for herself.

Her lips quivered as she walked toward the wall, careful of her steps over the ice.

The snow fell harder around her. Soon, her legs were covered and her steps were very slow. She lifted her leg, shaking the snow off before plunging it down into the heap of snow again. She did the same with her other leg. Again and again. Each step slower and slower as the snow piled up. Until it was up to her waist. Then her chest. Then her shoulders. And over her head.

She pushed her arms and legs, trying to swim through the snow. Trying to get above it. Trying to breathe.

The snow packed around her, a heavy weight pressing on all sides. She couldn't breathe. She couldn't see. She couldn't move as the cold seeped into her bones.

A solid surface moved under her, lifting her up, pushing her through the snow. Until she was above it. Until she could breathe again. She doubled over, her tree roots protecting her from going back under the snow. Her chest heaved as air filled her lungs. Her throat burned and her eyes brimmed with tears.

The Tree of Season lit up, a bright white light blinking three times.

The snow melted away, soaking back into the earth. The ground was a mud pit.

Aviva looked up into the sky, the dome sparkling above her. A rumbling filled the air. She jumped as a bolt of lightning crackled nearby. She smelled the stench of burnt grass as the lightning struck it. The earth under her protested, rolling around her. She fell to her side, letting the quakes wrack through her. Over and over. She rode it out with nowhere to hide or escape.

Tears streamed down her face. She couldn't keep this up. She couldn't keep going. This was too much. It was all too much.

Idalia's screams echoed around her.

She rolled over, on her hands and knees. She pushed herself up, the world shaking around her less and less as the seconds passed by. She took a careful step forward, toward Idalia's voice.

The earth stopped rolling. She took off running.

The Tree of Season lit up, a bright white light blinking four times.

Aviva ran as fast as she could, jumping over fallen branches, rocks, muddy spots. She ran so fast, smoke filled the air. No, it wasn't her creating the smoke. It was the line of fire shooting across the grass, chasing after her.

The fire blazed across the field, gaining speed, strength, height. It was going to get her. Heat radiated off the wall of flames.

A few yards away, Idalia struggled to get up. Aviva sprinted, her breath coming fast, her heart beating faster. She skidded on her knees when she reached Idalia. Her foot was stuck in a crack in the earth. Aviva placed her hands on both sides of Idalia's foot, concentrating her powers on the crack. It widened just enough that she could pull her sister's foot free.

Aviva helped Idalia stand.

Idalia pushed her away, hard.

"What are you doing?" Aviva asked, her words catching in her throat. More tears threatened to fall. Her eyes burned from the smoke gathering around them. Her whole body tightened from the heat.

"Go," Idalia shouted, pointing up.

Aviva looked to where she pointed. The Tree of Season loomed over them. And fire was beginning to circle it.

Aviva scrambled up the tree, using her element to create footholds as she climbed higher and higher, away from the flames. "What are you doing?" she called down to Idalia who stood at the base of the tree. "Come on."

"I can walk through fire," she said.

Aviva turned back and hauled herself up another branch. And another. And another. Until she was at the very top of the tree.

She could see the whole field from her view. Everything was on fire except for the Tree of Season. Everything was ruined.

The Tree of Season lit up, a bright white light holding steady for five seconds.

The flames seeped into Idalia's body, turning it a bright red. It didn't bother her. It strengthened her. But then, the flames disappeared. And she felt cold.

The grass turned a brilliant green again, a new life after all of the destruction the trials had caused. Aviva climbed down the Tree of Season, landing softly onto the ground. "Is it over?" she whispered, as if speaking too loud would awaken whatever beast Season was.

Idalia shook her head. "No way. We're both still here."

A tingling sensation took over her body, the familiar warmth of fire took over. She burst into flames, so close to Aviva she could hear the sizzling of her hair.

A wall of earth smacked into Idalia, pushing her back. The earth crumpled at her feet. Her flames disappeared. A fireball erupted in her hand. "Duck," she yelled as the fireball went spiraling across the field toward Aviva.

She wasn't in control. Season was. And Season was going to make her kill her sister.

She squeezed her hands together, taking deep breaths. Trying desperately to not send another fireball toward her little sister. She wanted to save her, not kill her. She wanted Aviva to live.

Another wall of earth smacked into her, knocking the breath from her, sending her sprawling on the ground. She got to her feet quickly, staring across the field. Her little sister. Her little sister stood beside the Tree of Season, her hands ready for an attack.

The earth rumbled under Idalia. She looked down. In between her legs, the ground split apart. Her legs widened as the crack grew. She hopped to one side, rolling away from the crevice forming.

A line of fire shot straight toward Aviva. It disintegrated in the trunk of the Tree of Season.

"Just kill me," Aviva cried, tears pouring down her face. "Please."

The earth rolled under Idalia's feet, knocking her to the ground. She took a deep breath, her body hurt. She was tired. But it didn't matter. She would take this as long as she could. She would do whatever it took to keep Aviva alive. Even if that meant letting Season kill her. Her little sister would win.

She pushed herself to her knees and looked at Aviva through the blanket of her red hair. "No," she said, breathlessly. "I'm not going to kill you."

Idalia stood on shaky legs, barely able to balance herself. Flames shot from her body, running the length of the space between them, leaving charred grass in its wake. "No!" Idalia shouted, trying to pull back her element.

A wall of earth stopped the flames before it could reach Aviva. Idalia sighed in relief.

The earth crumbled around Aviva. "I can't live in a world without you," Aviva said, her voice carrying across the field. "I can't be here alone. If I lose you, if I kill you, I won't have anyone!"

Idalia shook her head again. "I can't." Another root snaking up from the ground sent Idalia sprawling on the grass again, landing on her arm. She groaned, but picked herself up. "I love you too much, Aviva. We either both win this or we both lose."

She could withstand this. She would take the earth pounding her again and again. She would die. So long as she didn't have to hurt Aviva.

Another fireball erupted from Idalia. It shot into the air and landed right in front of Aviva. The ground erupted in flames, encircling her. "Put it out!" Idalia called, taking a step toward Aviva. She didn't want to get too close. Didn't want to know what would happen if they got any closer together. But she needed to put her flames out. She needed to stop herself. She needed to control herself.

"There's only one queen," Aviva whispered. She raised her hands into the air, the earth following her hand movement.

Idalia took a deep breath as the flames around Aviva went out. She closed her eyes, exhaling. *I can do this. I can withstand this.*

Idalia opened her eyes. The earth around Aviva came down hard. And Aviva went with it, disappearing into the earth. "No!" Idalia screamed. She ran toward the mound of earth pushing her legs as fast as they could go. She slid to the ground, her knees tearing on the grass. She clawed the earth until her fingertips bled.

"Aviva, no," she whimpered. Tears mixed with the earth.

The ground around her sunk. She skidded backwards, pushing her feet against the grass to get away from the sinking earth.

The dirt settled. Idalia crawled back to where Aviva had disappeared. A patch of green, fresh grass sprouted from the spot. She dug it out, but she couldn't get through the soil. She couldn't find Aviva. She couldn't pull her free.

She banged her fists into the ground and sobbed.

Roots snaked up from the ground. A small trunk rose into the air. Branches shot from the trunk, green leaves sprouted. It grew and grew over Idalia, shading her from the beating sun.

She laid under the new tree, her tears soaking into the soil.

Thunder rumbled around her. She looked up, through the thick branches of the tree to see the people of Season standing on their feet, applauding.

71

The dome disappeared above the arena. The stone walls slid down to their normal height. The auditorium seating melted back into the ground. The crowd of people walked around the stone walls to the arched entrance. And all Idalia could do was look up at the tree Aviva had grown with her sacrifice and cry.

"Lady Idalia," a voice said through the noise of the arena settling and the people of Season muttering their excitement over the new queen.

Idalia didn't turn to face the voice. She stared at the trunk of the tree where she could almost make out a face in the bark.

A hand came down on her shoulder and she jumped away, scuttling toward the trunk.

"I'm sorry," the voice said. Sara's face came into view. "I'm so sorry," she whispered.

Idalia said nothing. She couldn't speak. Her throat was sore from screaming. Her heart beat furiously in her chest, making it hard to breathe. Her head pounded. Everything hurt, but nothing hurt worse than watching her little sister dig herself a grave.

Sara bent down and wrapped an arm under Idalia's. She hefted her up. But Idalia didn't want to stand. She didn't want to do anything. She wanted her sister back. She wanted all of her sisters back.

"Come on," Sara said, leading her away from the tree.

They walked through the field and under the archway. The people of Season stood in two lines, creating a walkway for Idalia and Sara to pass through.

"Congratulations," a woman said when Idalia passed.

"Hail to the new Queen of Season," a man yelled, kneeling down.

Idalia wanted to throw up. She didn't want this. She didn't want to be here. She didn't want to be queen. She didn't want any of it.

The people reached out to brush her arms, her legs, her hair, anything they could get their hands on as if she was some prized possession. And maybe that's all she was. Maybe that's all she'd ever been. She was doted on by her adoptive parents, a blessing to them. And she was made just to fight to the death for Season. She was to be used. Over and over. Until there was nothing left.

She felt like nothing.

Sara led her inside Conformity Castle, up to her rooms where Candace waited. The little lady had a huge smile on her face, her eyes bright with adoration. "My queen," she said, bowing down to Idalia.

Idalia pitched forward, her stomach emptying all over the floorboards.

"Well, that's quite all right," Candace said, the smile not even faltering. "I will clean this right up. Go wash yourself."

Sara opened the bathroom door where steam rose from the

full tub. Her other ladies were already there, prepared to help her with hair and makeup just like they had for her father's funeral. But this wasn't for a funeral. Not really. This was to celebrate deaths, not to say goodbye to the dead.

Idalia was numb. She barely noticed as they scrubbed her down, rinsed her off with lukewarm water, pulled her into a chair, yanked her hair as they braided it back so her face was in full view, slapped makeup on her eyelids and cheeks. She let them lead her into the bedroom where they clothed her in a dress, buckling the straps over her shoulders, tightening the strings at her waist. She didn't even bother looking in the mirror they placed before her.

Even with all of these people around her, she felt alone. A piece of her had been buried along with Aviva. Several pieces of her were missing.

A while later, Sara led her through the castle, back down to the foyer. The doors were closed, the outside world hidden from view. And all she wanted to do was go back up the stairs, crawl into her bed, and never come out again.

She didn't want this. She didn't deserve to be here. She should've sacrificed herself. She should've been strong enough to save Aviva.

Sara brought a young boy up to Idalia. He reminded her of Brey, with the same floppy brown hair. But at least his head was intact. At least he had warmth in his eyes, a warmth Brey was missing the last time Idalia had seen him with his head in a box. Idalia met his gaze but said nothing. She didn't even know if her voice would work. Not that any words came to her mind.

"This is Goren," Sara said, pushing him forward a step.

Goren wasn't very old. Probably way younger than her.

"I will be your Hand," he said, with a sweet voice that

hadn't hit puberty yet. The mild squeakiness pierced Idalia's ears.

"Since Brey is dead," Idalia said, her voice cracking. She looked away from him. She stared at the doors in front of her. Her mouth was set in a firm line, her eyes barely opened wide enough to see. Her face was blank. Her eyelids fluttered shut for a moment, before lazily opening again. She might as well have been dead. She felt nothing. She was so void.

Goren nodded. "I studied under him and many others."

Idalia didn't care. She couldn't. She didn't know how to care about anything when everything had been ripped away from her. Season had taken everything and only offered her a boy as a replacement. It wasn't good enough. Nothing would be good enough.

Goren stepped into place beside her. He held his arm out, waiting for Idalia to take it, but she didn't. He grabbed her hand and placed it on his arm. He stood tall next to her, his shoulders pushed back and his face held high. She towered over him.

Sara opened the door. Twinkling lights blinded Idalia momentarily. Goren pulled her forward.

They walked outside, into the darkening night. Lamps floated all around them. Small flames burned in pots positioned along a walkway. Goren led her to a small stage, near where her father's body had burned on a pyre so long ago.

A year had passed since she'd last stood in this spot. A year of trials. A year of death.

She wanted to throw up again. But she closed her mouth tightly and looked out into the crowd forming around the mini stage. The people melded all together, their colors barely perceptible in the glistening of the flames, lamps, and night.

Goren dropped his arm and stepped up. "Welcome, people

of Season. The Finale has been completed. A new queen has risen."

The crowd screamed with joy. Idalia screamed inside. She was trapped here, in her body. Her skin didn't feel like her own. This world didn't feel right.

Goren turned to the side where a small girl ran up to the stage. She offered him a red pillow. On top rested a gold crown. The crown sparkled with yellow, blue, green, and red jewels. The color of each season, element, girl.

Goren took the crown carefully and turned toward Idalia. He walked up to her side and held the crown as high as he could into the air. Idalia bent so he could place it on her head.

"All hail the queen of Season," Goren called, stepping out of the way so that the crowd could see her rise with the crown on her head.

Tears pooled in her eyes, falling down her cheeks. She looked out into the crowd. They smiled back at her. They clapped for her. They congratulated her.

And all for nothing.

She was a killer. She had killed her sisters. All of them. She had only wanted to save them but she had failed. She always failed.

One by one, the people of Season knelt down, bowing their heads. Goren knelt down beside her, looking up at her with bright eyes. Hopeful eyes. Trusting eyes.

She would fail them all.

The fires around her shot into the air. She could feel her power rumble, wanting to be let out. But she reined it in. She didn't let her flames out, she kept them burning her from the inside out.

The leaves of the nearby trees dropped to the ground. A blast of heat washed over her. Her forehead beaded in sweat.

The grass lost a shade of green. The people dropped their coats onto the ground.

"Welcome to a new reign," Goren said. "The reign of Summer. The reign of Idalia."

Idalia let it all out. All her power, her frustration, her sadness. Her body turned into one fireball, standing on the stage for all to see. She burned and burned as they watched. As they cheered. As they rejoiced at their new queen. Idalia burned and burned. Her clothes fell to ash around her. The crown melted into a pool on her head. Every remnant of her old self seared until she was left with nothing.

She turned and walked off the stage.

Idalia walked outside of the castle, finally alone after days and days of meetings, fittings, and celebrations. She hated it all. Especially the parties. She didn't feel like commemorating this time. She felt like dying. She wanted to be with her sisters. She wanted to see them again. She wanted to hear their voices again. But she couldn't. She had to stay here, in Season, because without her all of the people her and Aviva had fought to protect would die. And that would be another thing on her long list of failures. So she had to do this. She had to be a good queen.

She found the last spot she saw Aviva alive fairly easily since the huge tree, almost identical to the Tree of Season, had taken over. The tree sprawled out around her. She could almost feel the life coming from it.

She placed a bowl down on the ground near the tree. She walked a few feet to the right and knelt down. With her hands, she tore into the ground. The dirt turned her skin black, her fingernails full of the earth. When it was deep enough, she grabbed her bowl and sprinkled seeds into the dirt and covered it back up. She went to the other side, kneeling down, digging a hole, and planting the seeds.

She stood, wiping her hands against her clothes. The dirt stuck. Just like it had when she had tried to free Aviva. She clenched her hands, hating the way they felt. She needed to clean them. She needed the dirtiness to disappear.

She went to Aviva's tree and sat at the trunk, her back resting against the warm bark. "Hi," she muttered, closing her eyes.

"I miss you," she said. A tear welled in her eye, falling down her cheek. She tried to stop the rest of them from following, but she couldn't. Soon her face was covered in tears. "Why'd you do it, Aviva?" She put her head in her hands, the dirt getting into her hair.

The smell of fresh grass, of Spring, fluttered around her. She wiped her nose. "I love you," she said, her voice breaking. "I love you, and I miss you. And I didn't want you to be alone. So you can have your own mini forest. You, Orla, and even Eira."

The smell of Autumn and Winter mixed around her. As if they were here with her. As if the trees she had planted for them held their essence just like Aviva's did. As if this truly was a forest of her sisters.

She leaned her head against Aviva's trunk, looking up through the leaves to the bright sun posted over Conformity Castle and all of Season now that Summer had taken over. "I'll do this," she whispered. She stood on shaky legs. " I'll be the queen of Season. And I'll do it for y'all. I'll do it for every Four before us who died for nothing. I'll put a stop to this. I'll stop the trials." She nodded her head. She would, she would do anything it took to make sure no one had to go through this. That no one else was subjected to this type of loss. That no one else had to die just to keep Season alive.

She put her hand on Aviva's trunk. It warmed under her.

"Thank you," she said, bringing her lips to the trunk, and kissing her sister goodbye.

Idalia walked away from her sisters. She walked away knowing they would be the last to die. They would be the reason Season changed. Got better. Healed.

Idalia would be the last Queen of Season who got her throne on the backs of her sisters.

EPILOGUE

9 Years Later

"I can't do this," Idalia said, gritting her teeth and holding her breath. Pain rolled through her body. Over and over, every minute it intensified. Every minute she was closer to breaking apart.

Candace wiped the sweat from her brow with a wet towel. "Yes, you can."

Idalia shook her head back and forth. She fought against Candace's grip on her arms. "I can't, I can't," she cried, tears rolling down her face. Another wave of pain squeezed her body so tight she held her breath again.

"You've done this thrice before. It is no different now," Gro said from her position in front of her.

"It is different!" Idalia closed her eyes. "I don't want this. I don't want another."

Candace patted her head and hummed a tune Idalia

couldn't place. Not that it distracted her much from the pain she should be used to by now. She'd gone through it three times in the last seven years. Childbirth should be easy for her. Instead, she felt like she was ripping in two.

Gro snorted. "It's a little late for that."

Idalia opened her eyes and stared daggers at her. But Gro wasn't easily scared. Especially while Idalia laid bare before her, sweat filling her every crevice, her body plumper than it had ever been.

"Shall I fetch the king?" Candace asked.

"Definitely not," Idalia said, her voice firm, her grip tightening on Candace. A scream ripped from her throat as her body convulsed in another rolling wave. Her stomach tightened so hard she could feel nothing else. Her eyes rolled back, her head falling into Candace's lap.

"You have to push," Gro instructed.

Idalia shook her head. "No, no I don't." She took a big breath, letting another wave of pain roll off her. "I cannot have this baby. I cannot have four. I haven't figured out how to stop the trials yet!"

Candace petted her head again. "You will."

Idalia tried stopping the contractions, but it was no use. Her fourth baby was coming. And soon. She pushed Candace and Gro aside and stood on weak legs. She turned to lean over the bed, bearing down. Gro repositioned under her, ready to catch.

Idalia pushed, gritting her teeth and screaming.

A moment of silence, and then a precious cry filled the room. Idalia breathed a sigh of relief. She turned around slowly, Candace at her side, to see Gro holding a wrapped baby girl in her arms. Candace helped her onto the bed. Gro offered the baby to her.

"Welcome, little princess," Idalia said with a kiss to her

head, holding the baby tight against her chest. She couldn't quit looking at her. Even after three, the new baby smell was intoxicating. The rush of emotions that filled her almost let her forget that now that she had four, she had failed again. She had not protected her children. Just as she hadn't protected her sisters. Her children would be back in the trials after she died. Her children would become murderers because of her.

"Two boys and two girls," Gro whispered. "Unprecedented."

Candace left Idalia's side to follow Gro out into the hallway. "Little Aris and Aviana are already showing control over an element. That is unheard of. The Four's powers are usually held until the Releasing Ceremony."

Gro nodded. "Prince Atlas will surely come into his element shortly."

Idalia held onto her new baby, staring at her. She did not notice them leaving. And she did not notice when the king returned to their bedchambers.

"Idalia," the king said, his deep voice sending shivers down her spine. Even now. Even seven years after they first met.

She looked up at him, then back to the baby. She tightened the wrap around her and held her out for him. He gladly took her, cradling her in his arms. "Ada," Idalia said when he looked at her questioningly.

He nodded. "Princess Ada, how lovely to meet you." He kissed the top of her head.

"Which one do you think will win?" Idalia asked, leaning her head back, eyes closed, tears streaming down her cheeks.

The Tree of Season watched Idalia and her children grow. The queen tried to teach them how to survive the trials that would inevitably kill all but one of them. The king searched for answers to stopping the trials. The children grew and grew, learning their powers and growing stronger and stronger with each passing day.

The Tree of Season quivered with the energy from the nearby trees. The trees the queen had planted. And the tree the lost princess had created with her sacrifice. The power of the sacrifice soaked into the tree's roots, bringing more and more light to its bark. So bright, anyone who passed by was blinded. So bright the children playing on the nearby field couldn't bear to look at it.

And when the queen took her last breath many, many years later, the tree took nothing. It did not call her children. It did not conduct the trials. It did nothing but take more and more power from the sacrifice. The sacrifice that saved them all.

ACKNOWLEDGMENTS

This book has been a long time coming. It all started with an idea. And in the beginning, this idea was going to be four separate books (one for each main character). But as I wrote, and got more into the story, things changed (as they often do). Instead of four books, it became two.

This second book here has never been published in any format before (unlike book one). I have had a few family members waiting years to read this ending, and it is finally here.

So, to everyone who has waited and pushed me to finish this series, thank you.

To my granny and my stepmom, thank you for always asking when the end was coming. I know this isn't your typical read (far from it), so thank you for reading my story anyway. Thank you for being one of my first supporters.

To Victoria Smart, I will probably always have to add you to the acknowledgements since you are my number one motivator/supporter/friend. I feel like I get on your nerves with the many texts about my books and the millions of ideas for my next series. But you never act annoyed. So thank you again, and always, for being my bestie.

To Selkkie Designs, my cover designer, I love this cover. It fits so nicely with book one. Your designs are so vibrant and on genre. I love it. Thank you.

To my editor, Becky Wallace, thank you for editing this

book in such a short timeframe. You did a wonderful job. It definitely would not be in as good a shape without your work.

Lastly, thank you to my Kickstarter backers who are some of the first supporters of book two. I was shocked that my Kickstarter even funded. So I hope this series is all you wanted and more!

Note from the Author

Thank you so much for your time, reader! I hope you have enjoyed this story. If so, be on the lookout for more of my books. I'm planning on writing at least one more series that connects with this duology. I'm also writing a novella that will follow the new Queen of Season.

I just wanted to ask you one favor, if you don't mind. As an indie author, reviews are very important. Marketing is hard. So if you could leave a review for this book on Amazon or Good Reads, I'd be so very thankful. If you could tell your friends or family about this book, I'd be overjoyed.

I want this book and the rest of the books I want to write to get the fans they deserve.

Thank you. Thank you. Thank you.

Keep reading!

H.E. Shows

COMING SOON!

Two years ago, Idalia Gallagher became Queen of Season. Now, she must find her king.

In the aftermath of the five deadly trials that left Idalia alone in Season without her three sisters, she is tasked with finding a king. She is uninterested in finding someone to produce heirs with. So her Hand selects four suitors, one from each section.

Stamen from Spring, Cadmar from Winter, Volaris from Autumn, and Fervis from Summer come to Conformity Castle for a battle for her hand in marriage. She must choose one. But when one of them tries to kill her, her focus turns to finding her assassin instead of finding a king.

Can she find who wants her dead? Can she find someone who will keep her alive?

DO YOU WANT TO BE THE FIRST TO KNOW OF FUTURE BOOKS?

SUBSCRIBE TO H.E. SHOWS' NEWSLETTER

Signup for book news, inside looks, character art, ARC sign ups, and special offers!

Email

You can unsubscribe anytime. For more details, review our Privacy Policy.

Opt in to receive news and updates.

SUBSCRIBE

I HOPE TO SEE YOU THERE!

ABOUT THE AUTHOR

H.E. Shows (Shows like cows, not TV shows) has always dreamed of being a best-selling fantasy author. Actually, her ultimate dream is to star in a TV or movie based on one of her novels. (Gotta have big dreams, kiddos!) She has been reading and writing for as long as she can remember. She earned a bachelor's degree in Creative Writing and English from SNHU. Then, she went on to teach English for a year and a half at the high school level and two years at the middle school level. Although she enjoyed teaching (for the most part), she has decided to stay-at-home with her newest child. This will hopefully give her the time she wants to focus on becoming the author she's always wanted to be.

H.E. Shows currently lives in the Dallas area with her three wonderful children who take up a majority of the free time she believed she would be getting without a traditional job. You can follow H.E. Shows on Facebook, TikTok, Instagram, Goodreads, and Amazon or at her website heshowsauthor.com.